James May

101 MINTO CRES
Glenrothes

GULLIVER'S TRAVELS

GULLIVER'S TRAVELS

by

JONATHAN SWIFT

THE CHILDREN'S PRESS
LONDON AND GLASGOW

This Impression 1971

ISBN 0 00 166143 0

PRINTED IN GREAT BRITAIN

Contents

*Travels into Several Remote Nations of
the World*

A LETTER

from Capt. Gulliver, to his
Cousin Sympson

I HOPE *you will be ready to own publickly, whenever you shall be called to it, that by your great and frequent Urgency you prevailed on me to publish a very loose and uncorrect Account of my Travels; with Direction to hire some young Gentleman of either University to put them in Order, and correct the Style, as my Cousin* Dampier *did by my Advice, in his Book called,* A Voyage round the World. *But I do not remember I gave you Power to consent, that any thing should be omitted, and much less that any thing should be inserted: Therefore, as to the latter, I do here renounce every thing of that Kind; particularly a Paragraph about her Majesty the late Queen* Anne, *of most pious and glorious Memory; although I did reverence and esteem her more than any of human Species. But you, or your Interpolator, ought to have considered, that as it was not my Inclination, so was it not decent to praise any Animal of our Composition before my Master* Houyhnhnm: *And besides, the Fact was altogether false; for to my Knowledge, being in* England *during some Part of her Majesty's Reign, she did govern by a chief Minister; nay, even by two successively; the first whereof was the Lord of* Godolphin, *and the second the Lord of* Oxford; *so that you have made me say the thing that was not. Likewise, in the Account of the Academy of Projectors, and several Passages of my Discourse to my Master* Houyhnhnm, *you have either omitted some material Circumstances, or minced or changed them in such a Manner, that I do hardly know mine own Work. When I formerly hinted to you something of this in a Letter, you were pleased to answer, that you were afraid of giving Offence; that People in Power were very watchful over the Press; and apt not only to interpret, but to punish every thing which looked like an* Inuendo *(as I think you called it.) But pray, how could that which I spoke so many Years ago, and at above five Thousand Leagues distance, in another*

Reign, be applyed to any of the Yahoos, *who now are said to govern the Herd ; especially, at a time when I little thought on or feared the Unhappiness of living under them. Have not I the most Reason to complain, when I see these very* Yahoos *carried by* Houyhnhnms *in a Vehicle, as if these were Brutes, and those the rational Creatures ? And, indeed, to avoid so monstrous and detestable a Sight, was one principal Motive of my Retirement hither.*

THUS much I thought proper to tell you in Relation to your self, and to the Trust I reposed in you.

I DO in the next Place complain of my own great Want of Judgment, in being prevailed upon by the Intreaties and false Reasonings of you and some others, very much against mine own Opinion, to suffer my Travels to be published. Pray bring to your Mind how often I desired you to consider, when you insisted on the Motive of publick Good; *that the* Yahoos *were a Species of Animals utterly incapable of Amendment by Precepts or Examples: And so it hath proved; for instead of seeing a full Stop put to all Abuses and Corruptions, at least in this little Island, as I had Reason to expect: Behold, after above six Months Warning, I cannot learn that my Book hath produced one single Effect according to mine Intentions: I desired you would let me know by a Letter, when Party and Faction were extinguished; Judges learned and upright; Pleaders honest and modest, with some Tincture of common Sense ; and* Smithfield *blazing with Pyramids of Law-Books; the young Nobility's Education entirely changed; the Physicians banished ; the Female* Yahoos *abounding in Virtue, Honour, Truth and good Sense; Courts and Levees of great Ministers thoroughly weeded and swept; Wit, Merit and Learning rewarded; all Disgracers of the Press in Prose and Verse, condemned to eat nothing but their own Cotten, and quench their Thirst with their own Ink. These, and a Thousand other Reformations, I firmly counted upon by your Encouragement; as indeed they were plainly deducible from the Precepts delivered in my Book. And, it must be owned that seven Months were a sufficient Time to correct every Vice and Folly to which* Yahoos *are subject; if their Natures had been capable of the least Disposition to Virtue or Wisdom: Yet so far have you been from answering mine Expectation in any of your Letters; that on the contrary, you are loading our Carrier every Week with Libels, and Keys, and Reflections, and Memoirs, and Second Parts; wherein I see myself accused of reflecting upon great States-Folk; of degrading human Nature, (for so they have still the Confidence to stile it) and of abusing the Female Sex. I find likewise, that the Writers of those Bundles are not agreed among themselves; for some of them will not allow me to be Author of mine own Travels; and others make me Author of Books to which I am wholly a Stranger.*

I FIND likewise, that your Printer hath been so careless as to confound the Times, and mistake the Dates of my several Voyages and Returns; neither assigning the true Year, or the true Month, or Day of the Month: And I hear the original Manuscript is all destroyed, since the Publication of my Book. Neither have I any Copy left; however, I have sent you some Corrections, which you may insert, if ever there should be a second Edition: And yet I cannot stand to them, but shall leave that Matter to my judicious and candid Readers, to adjust it as they please.

I HEAR some of our Sea-Yahoos find Fault with my Sea-Language, as not proper in many Parts, nor now in Use. I cannot help it. In my first Voyages, while I was young, I was instructed by the oldest Mariners, and learned to speak as they did. But I have since found that the Sea-Yahoos are apt, like the Land ones, to become new fangled in their Words; which the latter change every Year; insomuch, as I remember upon each Return to mine own Country, their old Dialect was so altered, that I could hardly understand the new. And I observe, when any Yahoo comes from London *out of Curiosity to visit me at mine own House, we neither of us are able to deliver our Conceptions in a Manner intelligible to the other.*

IF the Censure of Yahoos *could any Way affect me, I should have great Reason to complain, that some of them are so bold as to think my Book of Travels a meer Fiction out of mine own Brain; and have gone so far as to drop Hints, that the Houy-hnhnms, and Yahoos have no more Existence than the Inhabitants of* Utopia.

INDEED I must confess, that as to the People of Lilliput, Brobdingrag, *(for so the Word should have been spelt, and not erroneously* Brobdingnag*) and* Laputa; *I have never yet heard of any* Yahoo *so presumptuous as to dispute their Being, or the*

Facts I have related concerning them; because the Truth immediately strikes every Reader with Conviction. And, is there less Probability in my Account of the Houyhnhnms or Yahoos, when it is manifest as to the latter, there are so many Thousands even in this City, who only differ from their Brother Brutes in Houyhnhnmland, because they use a Sort of a Jabber, and do not go naked. I wrote for their Amendment, and not their Approbation. The united Praise of the whole Race would be of less Consequence to me, than the neighing of those two degenerate Houyhnhnms I keep in my Stable; because, from these, degenerate as they are, I still improve in some Virtues, without any Mixture of Vice.

DO these miserable Animals presume to think that I am so far degenerated as to defend my Veracity; Yahoo as I am, it is well known through all Houyhnhnmland, that by the Instructions and Example of my illustrious Master, I was able in the Compass of two Years (although I confess with the utmost Difficulty) to remove that infernal Habit of Lying, Shuffling, Deceiving, and Equivocating, so deeply rooted in the very Souls of all my Species; especially the Europeans.

I HAVE other Complaints to make upon this vexatious Occasion; but I forbear troubling myself on you any further. I must freely confess, that since my last Return, some Corruptions of my Yahoo Nature have revived in me by conversing with a few of your Species, and particularly those of mine own Family, by an unavoidable Necessity; else I should never have attempted so absurd a Project as that of reforming the Yahoo Race in this Kingdom; but, I have now done with all such visionary Schemes for ever.

April 2, 1727

THE PUBLISHER TO
THE READER

THE AUTHOR *of these Travels, Mr.* Lemuel Gulliver, *is my antient and intimate Friend; there is likewise some Relation between us by the Mother's Side. About three Years ago Mr.* Gulliver *growing weary of the Concourse of curious People coming to him at his House in* Redriff, *made a small Purchase of Land, with a convenient House, near* Newark, *in* Nottinghamshire, *his native Country; where he now lives retired, yet in good Esteem among his Neighbours.*

ALTHOUGH *Mr.* Gulliver *were born in* Nottinghamshire, *where his Father dwelt, yet I have heard him say, his Family came from* Oxfordshire ; *to confirm which, I have observed in the Church-Yard at* Banbury, *in that County, several Tombs and Monuments of the* Gullivers.

BEFORE *he quitted* Redriff, *he left the Custody of the following Papers in my Hands, with the Liberty to dispose of them as I should think fit. I have carefully perused them three Times; The Style is very plain and simple; and the only Fault I find is, that the Author, after the Manner of Travellers, is a little too circumstantial. There is an Air of Truth apparent through the whole; and indeed the Author was so distinguished for his Veracity, that it became a Sort of Proverb among his Neighbours at* Redriff, *when anyone affirmed a Thing, to say, it was as true as if Mr.* Gulliver *had spoke it.*

BY *the Advice of several worthy Persons, to whom, with the Author's Permission, I communicated these Papers, I now venture to send them into the World; hoping they may be, at least for some time, a better Entertainment to our young Noblemen, than the common Scribbles of Politicks and Party.*

THIS *Volume would have been at least twice as large, if I had not made bold to strike out innumerable Passages relating to the Winds and Tides, as well as to the Variations and Bearings in the several Voyages; together with the minute Descriptions of the Management of the Ship in Storms, in the Style of Sailors:*

Likewise the Account of the Longitudes and Latitudes; wherein I have Reason to apprehend that Mr. Gulliver may be a little dissatisfied: But I was resolved to fit the Work as much as possible to the general Capacity of Readers. However, if my own Ignorance in Sea-Affairs shall have led me to commit some Mistakes, I alone am answerable for them: And if any Traveller hath a Curiosity to see the whole Work at large, as it came from the Hand of the Author, I will be ready to gratify him.

As for any further Particulars relating to the Author, the Reader will receive Satisfaction from the first Pages of the Book.

RICHARD SYMPSON

PART ONE

A VOYAGE TO LILLIPUT

CHAPTER ONE

THE AUTHOR GIVETH SOME ACCOUNT OF HIMSELF AND FAMILY;
HIS FIRST INDUCEMENTS TO TRAVEL. HE IS SHIPWRECKED, AND
SWIMS FOR HIS LIFE; GETS SAFE ON SHOAR IN THE COUNTRY OF
LILLIPUT; IS MADE A PRISONER, AND CARRIED UP THE COUNTRY.

MY Father had a small Estate in *Nottinghamshire*; I was the Third of five Sons. He sent me to *Emanuel-College* in *Cambridge*, at Fourteen Years old, where I resided three Years, and applied my self close to my Studies: But the Charge of maintaining me (although I had a very scanty Allowance) being too great for a narrow Fortune; I was bound Apprentice to Mr. *James Bates*, an eminent Surgeon in *London*, with whom I continued four Years; and my Father now and then sending me small Sums of Money, I laid them out in learning Navigation and other Parts of the Mathematicks, useful to those who intend to travel, as I always believed it would be some time or other my Fortune to do. When I left Mr. *Bates*, I went down to my Father; where, by the Assistance of him and my Uncle *John*, and some other Relations, I got Forty Pounds, and a Promise of Thirty Pounds a Year to maintain me at *Leyden*: There I studied Physick two Years and seven Months, knowing it would be useful in long Voyages.

Soon after my return from *Leyden*, I was recommended by my good Master Mr. *Bates*, to be Surgeon to the *Swallow*, Captain *Abraham Pannell* Commander; with whom I continued three Years and a half, making a Voyage or two into the *Levant* and some other Parts. When I came back, I resolved to settle in *London*, to which Mr. *Bates*, my Master, encouraged me; and by him I was recommended to several Patients. I took Part of a small House in the *Old Jury*; and being advised to alter my Condition, I married Mrs. *Mary Burton*, second Daughter to Mr. *Edmond Burton*, Hosier, in *Newgate-street*, with whom I received four Hundred Pounds for a Portion.

But, my good Master *Bates* dying in two Years after, and I having few Friends my Business began to fail; for my Conscience would not suffer me to imitate the bad Practice of too many among my Brethren. Having therefore consulted with my Wife, and some of my acquaintance, I determined to go again to Sea. I was Surgeon successively in two Ships, and made Several Voyages, for six Years, to the *East* and *West-Indies*; by which I got some Addition to my Fortune. My Hours of Leisure I spent in reading the best Authors, ancient and modern; being always provided with a good Number of Books; and when I was ashore, in observing the Manners and Dispositions of the People, as well as learning their Language; wherein I had a great Facility by the Strength of my Memory.

The last of these Voyages not proving very fortunate, I grew weary of the Sea, and intended to stay at home with my Wife and Family. I removed from the *Old Jury* to *Fetter Lane*, and from thence to *Wapping*, hoping to get Business among the Sailors; but it would not turn to account. After three Years Expectation that things would mend, I accepted an advantageous Offer from Captain *William Prichard*, Master of the *Antelope*, who was making a Voyage to the *South-Sea*. We set sail from *Bristol*, *May* 4th, 1699, and our Voyage at first was very prosperous.

It would not be proper for some Reasons, to trouble the Reader with the Particulars of our Adventures in those Seas: Let it suffice to inform him, that in our Passage from thence to the *East-Indies*, we were driven by a violent Storm to the North-west of *Van Diemen's* Land. By an Observation, we found ourselves in the Latitude of 30 Degrees 2 Minutes South. Twelve of our Crew were dead by immoderate Labour, and ill Food; the rest were in a very weak Condition. On the fifth of *November*, which was the beginning of Summer in those Parts, the Weather being very hazy, the Seamen spyed a Rock, within half a Cable's length of the Ship; but the Wind was so strong, that we were driven directly upon it, and immediately split. Six of the Crew, of whom I was one, having let down the

Boat into the Sea, made a Shift to get clear of the Ship, and the Rock. We rowed by my Computation, about three Leagues, till we were able to work no longer, being already spent with Labour while we were in the Ship. We therefore trusted ourselves to the Mercy of the Waves; and in about half an Hour the Boat was overset by a sudden Flurry from the North. What became of my Companions in the Boat, as well as of those who escaped on the Rock, or were left in the Vessel, I cannot tell; but conclude they were all lost. For my own Part, I swam as Fortune directed me, and was pushed forward by Wind and Tide. I often let my Legs drop, and could feel no Bottom; But when I was almost gone, and able to struggle no longer, I found myself within my Depth; and by this Time the Storm was much abated. The Declivity was so small, that I walked near a Mile before I got to the Shore, which I conject- ured was about Eight o'Clock in the Evening. I then advanced forward near half a Mile, but could not discover any Sign of Houses or Inhabitants; at least I was in so weak a Condition, that I did not observe them. I was extremely tired, and with that, and the Heat of the Weather, and about half a Pint of Brandy that I drank as I left the Ship, I found my self much inclined to sleep. I lay down on the Grass, which was very short and soft; where I slept sounder than ever I remember to have done in my Life, and as I reckoned, above Nine Hours; for when I awaked, it was just Day-light. I attempted to rise, but was not able to stir: For as I happened to lie on my Back, I found my Arms and Legs were strongly fastened on each Side to the Ground; and my Hair, which was long and thick, tied down in the same Manner. I likewise felt several slender Ligatures across my Body, from my Armpits to my Thighs. I could only look upwards; the Sun began to grow hot, and the Light offended my Eyes. I heard a confused Noise about me, but in the Posture I lay, could see nothing except the Sky. In a little time I felt something alive and moving on my left Leg, which advancing gently forward over my Breast, came almost up to my Chin; when bending my Eyes downwards as much as I could, I perceived it to be a human Creature not six Inches high, with a Bow and Arrow in his Hands, and a Quiver at his Back. In the mean time, I felt at least Forty more of the

same Kind (as I conjectured) following the first. I was in the
utmost Astonishment, and roared so loud, that they all ran
back in a Fright; and some of them, as I was afterwards told,
were hurt with the Falls they got by leaping from my Sides
upon the Ground. However, they soon returned; and one of
them, who ventured so far as to get a full Sight of my Face,
lifting up his Hands and Eyes by way of Admiration, cryed out
in a shrill, but distinct Voice, *Hekinah Degul*: The others
repeated the same Words several times, but I then knew not
what they meant. I lay all this while, as the Reader may believe,
in great Uneasiness; At length, struggling to get loose, I had
the Fortune to break the Strings, and wrench out the Pegs
that fastened my left Arm to the Ground; for, by lifting it up
to my Face, I discovered the Methods they had taken to bind
me; and, at the same time, with a violent Pull, which gave me
excessive Pain, I a little loosened the Strings that tied down
my Hair on the left Side; so that I was just able to turn my
Head about two Inches. But the Creatures ran off a second
time, before I could seize them; whereupon there was a great
Shout in a very shrill Accent; and after it ceased, I heard one
of them cry aloud, *Tolgo Phonac*; when in an Instant I felt
above an Hundred Arrows discharged on my left Hand, which
pricked me like so many Needles; and besides, they shot
another Flight into the Air, as we do Bombs in *Europe*; whereof
many, I suppose, fell on my Body, (though I felt them not)
and some on my Face, which I immediately covered with my
left Hand. When this Shower of Arrows was over, I fell a
groaning with Grief and Pain; and then striving again to get
loose, they discharged another Volley larger than the first; and
some of them attempted with Spears to stick me in the Sides;
but by good Luck, I had on me a Buff Jerkin, which they could
not pierce. I thought it the most prudent Method to lie still,
and my Design was to continue so till Night, when my left
Hand being already loose, I could easily free myself: And as
for the Inhabitants, I had Reason to believe I might be a Match
for the greatest Armies they could bring against me, if they
were all of the same Size with him that I saw. But Fortune
disposed otherwise of me. When the People observed I was
quiet, they discharged no more Arrows: But by the Noise

increasing, I knew their Numbers were greater; and about four Yards from me, over-against my right Ear, I heard a Knocking for above an Hour, like People at work; when turning my Head that Way, as well as the Pegs and Strings would permit me, I saw a Stage erected about a Foot and a half from the Ground, capable of holding four of the Inhabitants, with two or three Ladders to mount it: From whence one of them, who seemed to be a Person of Quality, made me a long Speech, whereof I understood not one Syllable. But I should have mentioned, that before the principal Person began his Oration, he cryed out three times *Langro Dehul san*: (these Words and the former were afterwards repeated and explained to me.) Whereupon immediately about fifty of the Inhabitants came, and cut the Strings that fastened the left side of my Head, which gave me the Liberty of turning it to the right, and of observing the Person and Gesture of him who was to speak. He appeared to be of a middle Age, and taller than any of the other three who attended him; whereof one was a Page, who held up his Train, and seemed to be somewhat longer than my middle Finger; the other two stood on each side to support him. He acted every part of an Orator; and I could observe many Periods of Threatenings, and others of Promises, Pity and Kindness. I answered in a few Words, but in the most submissive Manner, lifting up my left Hand and both my eyes to the Sun, as calling him for a Witness; and being almost famished with Hunger, having not eaten a Morsel for some Hours before I left the Ship, I found the Demands of Nature so strong upon me, that I could not forbear shewing my Impatience (perhaps against the strict Rules of Decency) by putting my Finger frequently on my Mouth, to signify that I wanted Food. The *Hurgo* (for so they called a great Lord, as I afterwards learnt) understood me very well: He descended from the Stage, and commanded that several Ladders should be applied to my Sides, on which above an hundred of the Inhabitants mounted, and walked towards my Mouth laden with Baskets full of Meat, which had been provided and sent thither by the King's Orders upon the first Intelligence he received of me. I observed there was the Flesh of several Animals, but could not distinguish them by the Taste. There were Shoulders, Legs, and Loins shaped like those of Mutton, and very well dressed, but smaller than the Wings of a Lark. I ate them by two or three at a Mouthful; and took three Loaves at a time, about the bigness of Musket Bullets. They supplyed me as fast as they could, shewing a thousand Marks of Wonder and Astonishment at my Bulk and Appetite. I then made another Sign that I wanted Drink. They found by my eating that a small Quantity would not suffice me; and being a most ingenious People, they slung up with great Dexterity one of their largest Hogsheads; then rolled it towards my Hand, and beat out the Top; I drank it off at a Draught, which I might well do, for it hardly held half a Pint, and tasted like a small Wine of *Burgundy*, but much more delicious. They brought me a second Hogshead, which I drank in the same Manner, and made Signs for more, but they had none to give me. When I had performed these Wonders, they shouted for Joy, and danced upon my Breast, repeating several times as they did at first, *Hekinah Degul*. They made me a Sign that I should throw down the two Hogsheads, but first warned the People below to stand out of the Way, crying aloud, *Borach Mivola*; and when they saw the Vessels in the Air, there was an universal Shout of *Hekinah Degul*. I confess I was often tempted, while they were passing backwards and forwards on my Body, to seize Forty or Fifty of the first that came in my Reach and dash them against the Ground. But the Remembrance of what I had felt, which probably might not be the worst they could do; and the Promise of Honour I made them, for so I interpreted my submissive Behaviour, soon drove out those Imaginations. Besides, I now considered my self as bound by the Laws of Hospitality to a People who had treated me with so much Expence and Magnificence. However in my Thoughts I could not sufficiently wonder at the Intrepidity of these diminutive Mortals, who durst venture to mount and walk on my Body, while one of my Hands was at Liberty, without trembling at the very Sight of so prodigious a Creature as I must appear to them. After some time, when they observed that I made no more Demands for Meat, there appeared before me a Person of high Rank from his Imperial Majesty. His Excellency having mounted on the Small of my Right Leg,

advanced forwards up to my Face, with about a Dozen of his
Retinue; And producing his Credentials under the Signet
Royal, which he applied close to my Eyes, spoke about ten
Minutes, without any Signs of Anger, but with a kind of
determinate Resolution; often pointing forwards, which, as I
afterwards found, was towards the Capital City, about half a
Mile distant, whither it was agreed by his Majesty in Council
that I must be conveyed. I answered in few Words, but to no
Purpose, and made a Sign with my Hand that was loose,
putting it to the other, (but over his Excellency's Head, for
Fear of hurting him or his Train) and then to my own Head
and Body, to signify that I desired my Liberty. It appeared
that he understood me well enough; for he shook his Head by
way of Disapprobation, and held his Hand in a Posture to shew
that I must be carried as a Prisoner. However, he made other
Signs to let me understand that I should have Meat and Drink
enough, and very good Treatment. Whereupon I once more
thought of attempting to break my Bonds; but again, when I
felt the Smart of their Arrows upon my Face and Hands, which
were all in Blisters, and many of the Darts still sticking in them;
and observing likewise that the Number of my Enemies
encreased; I gave Tokens to let them know that they might
do with me what they pleased. Upon this, the *Hurgo* and his
Train withdrew, with much Civility and chearful Countenances.
Soon after I heard a general Shout, with frequent Repetitions
of the Words, *Peplom Selan*, and I felt great Numbers of the
People on my Left Side relaxing the Cords to such a Degree,
that I was able to turn upon my Right. But before this, they
had dawbed my Face and both my Hands with a sort of Ointment very pleasant to the Smell, which in a few Minutes
removed all the Smart of their Arrows. These Circumstances,
added to the Refreshment I had received by their Victuals and
Drink, which were very nourishing, disposed me to sleep. I
slept about eight Hours as I was afterwards assured; and it
was no Wonder; for the Physicians, by the Emperor's Order,
had mingled a Sleeping Potion in the Hogsheads of Wine.

It seems that upon the first Moment I was discovered sleeping
on the Ground after my Landing, the Emperor had early
Notice of it by an Express; and determined in Council that

I should be tyed in the Manner I have related, (which was done in the Night while I slept) that Plenty of Meat and Drink should be sent me, and a Machine prepared to carry me to the Capital City.

This Resolution perhaps may appear very bold and dangerous, and I am confident would not be imitated by any Prince in *Europe* on the like Occasion; however, in my Opinion it was extremely Prudent as well as Generous. For supposing these People had endeavoured to kill me with their Spears and Arrows while I was asleep; I should certainly have awaked with the first Sense of Smart, which might so far have rouzed my Rage and Strength, as to enable me to break the Strings wherewith I was tyed; after which, as they were not able to make Resistance, so they could expect no Mercy.

These People are the most excellent Mathematicians, and arrived to a great Perfection in Mechanicks by the Countenance and Encouragement of the Emperor, who is a renowned Patron of Learning. This Prince hath several Machines fixed on Wheels, for the Carriage of Trees and other great Weights. He often buildeth his largest Men of War, whereof some are Nine Foot long, in the Woods where the Timber grows, and has them carried on these Engines three or four Hundred Yards to the Sea. Five Hundred Carpenters and Engineers were immediately set at work to prepare the greatest Engine they had. It was a Frame of Wood raised three Inches from the Ground, about seven Foot long and four wide, moving upon twenty-two Wheels. The Shout I heard, was upon the Arrival of this Engine, which, it seems, set out in four Hours after my Landing. It was brought parallel to me as I lay. But the principal Difficulty was to raise and place me in this Vehicle. Eighty Poles, each of one Foot high, were erected for this Purpose, and very strong Cords of the bigness of Pack thread were fastened by Hooks to many Bandages, which the Workmen had girt round my Neck, my Hands, my Body, and my Legs. Nine Hundred of the strongest Men were employed to draw up these Cords by many Pullies fastened on the Poles; and thus in less than three Hours, I was raised and slung into the Engine, and there tyed fast. All this I was told; for while the whole Operation was performing, I lay in a profound Sleep, by the Force of that soporiferous Medicine infused into my Liquor. Fifteen hundred of the Emperor's largest Horses, each about four Inches and a half high, were employed to draw me towards the Metropolis, which, as I said, was half a Mile distant.

About four Hours after we began our Journey, I awaked by a very ridiculous Accident; for the Carriage being stopt a while to adjust something that was out of Order, two or three of the young Natives had the Curiosity to see how I looked when I was asleep; they climbed up into the Engine, and advancing very softly to my Face, one of them, an Officer in the Guards, put the sharp End of his Half-Pike a good way up into my left Nostril, which tickled my Nose like a Straw, and made me sneeze violently: Whereupon they stole off unperceived; and it was three Weeks before I knew the Cause of my awaking so suddenly. We made a long March the remaining Part of the Day, and rested at Night with Five Hundred Guards on each Side of me, half with Torches, and half with Bows and Arrows, ready to shoot me if I should offer to stir. The next Morning at Sunrise we continued our March, and arrived within two Hundred Yards of the City-Gates about Noon. The Emperor, and all his Court, came out to meet us; but his great Officers would by no Means suffer his Majesty to endanger his Person by mounting on my Body.

At the Place where the Carriage stopt, there stood an ancient Temple, esteemed to be the largest in the whole Kingdom; which having been polluted some Years before by an unnatural Murder, was, according to the Zeal of those People, looked upon as Prophane, and therefore had been applied to common Uses, and all the Ornaments and Furniture carried away. In this Edifice it was determined I should lodge. The great Gate fronting to the North was about four Foot high, and almost two Foot wide, through which I could easily creep. On each Side of the Gate was a small Window not above six Inches from the Ground: Into that on the Left Side, the King's Smiths conveyed fourscore and eleven Chains, like those that hang to a Lady's Watch in *Europe*, and almost as large, which were locked to my Left Leg with six and thirty Padlocks. Over against this Temple, on the other Side of the great Highway,

at twenty Foot Distance, there was a Turret at least five Foot
high. Here the Emperor ascended with many principal Lords
of his Court, to have an Opportunity of viewing me, as I was
told, for I could not see them. It was reckoned that above an
hundred thousand Inhabitants came out of the Town upon
the same Errand; and in spight of my Guards, I believe there
could not be fewer than ten thousand, at several Times, who
mounted upon my Body by the Help of Ladders. But a
Proclamation was soon issued to forbid it, upon Pain of Death.
When the Workmen found it was impossible for me to break
loose, they cut all the Strings that bound me; whereupon I
rose up with as melancholy a Disposition as ever I had in my
Life. But the Noise and Astonishment of the People at seeing
me rise and walk, are not to be expressed. The Chains that
held my left Leg were about two Yards long, and gave me not
only the Liberty of walking backwards and forwards in a
Semicircle; but being fixed within four Inches of the Gate,
allowed me to creep in, and lie at my full Length in the Temple.

CHAPTER TWO

THE EMPEROR OF LILLIPUT, ATTENDED BY SEVERAL OF THE
NOBILITY, COMES TO SEE THE AUTHOR IN HIS CONFINEMENT. THE
EMPEROR'S PERSON AND HABIT DESCRIBED. LEARNED MEN AP-
POINTED TO TEACH THE AUTHOR THEIR LANGUAGE. HE GAINS
FAVOUR BY HIS MILD DISPOSITION. HIS POCKETS ARE SEARCHED,
AND HIS SWORD AND PISTOLS TAKEN FROM HIM.

WHEN I found myself on my Feet, I looked about me,
and must confess I never beheld a more entertaining
Prospect. The Country round appeared like a continued
Garden; and the inclosed Fields, which were generally Forty
Foot square, resembled so many Beds of Flowers. These
Fields were intermingled with Woods of half a Stang, and the
tallest Trees, as I could judge, appeared to be seven Foot high.
I viewed the Town on my left Hand, which looked like the
painted Scene of a City in a Theatre.

The Emperor was already descended from the Tower, and advancing on Horseback towards me, which had like to have cost him dear; for the Beast, although very well trained, yet wholly unused to such a Sight, which appeared as if a Mountain moved before him, reared up on his hinder Feet: But that Prince, who is an excellent Horseman, kept his Seat, until his Attendants ran in, and held the Bridle, while his Majesty had Time to dismount. When he alighted, he surveyed me round with great Admiration, but kept beyond the Length of my Chains. He ordered his Cooks and Butlers, who were already prepared, to give me Victuals and Drink, which they pushed forward in a sort of Vehicles upon Wheels until I could reach them. I took these Vehicles, and soon emptied them all; twenty of them were filled with Meat, and ten with Liquor; each of the former afforded me two or three good Mouthfuls, and I emptied the Liquor of ten Vessels, which was contained in earthen Vials into one Vehicle, drinking it off at a Draught; and so I did with the rest. The Empress, and young Princes of the Blood, of both Sexes, attended by many Ladies, sate at some Distance in their Chairs; but upon the Accident that happened to the Emperor's Horse, they alighted, and came near his Person; which I am now going to describe. He is taller by almost the Breadth of my Nail, than any of his Court; which alone is enough to strike an Awe into the Beholders. His Features are strong and masculine, with an *Austrian* Lip, and arched Nose, his Complexion olive, his Countenance erect, his Body and Limbs well proportioned, all his Motions graceful, and his Deportment majestick. For the better Convenience of beholding him, I lay on my Side, so that my Face was parallel to his, and he stood but three Yards off; However, I have had him since many Times in my Hand, and therefore cannot be deceived in the Description. His Dress was very plain and simple, the Fashion of it between the *Asiatick* and the *European*; but he had on his Head a light Helmet of Gold, adorned with Jewels, and a Plume on the Crest. He held his Sword drawn in his Hand, to defend himself, if I should happen to break loose; it was almost three Inches long, the Hilt and Scabbard were Gold enriched with Diamonds. His Voice was shrill, but very clear and articulate, and I could distinctly hear it when I stood

up. The Ladies and Courtiers were all most magnificently
clad, so that the Spot they stood upon seemed to resemble a
Petticoat spread on the Ground, embroidered with Figures of
Gold and Silver. His Imperial Majesty spoke often to me, and
I returned Answers, but neither of us could understand a
Syllable. There were several of his Priests and Lawyers present
(as I conjectured by their Habits) who were commanded to
address themselves to me, and I spoke to them in as many
Languages as I had the least Smattering of, which were *High*
and *Low Dutch, Latin, French, Spanish, Italian*, and *Lingua
Franca*; but all to no purpose. After about two Hours the
Court retired, and I was left with a strong Guard, to prevent
the Impertinence, and probably the Malice of the Rabble, who
were very impatient to croud about me as near as they durst;
and some of them had the Impudence to shoot their Arrows
at me as I sate on the Ground by the Door of my House;
whereof one very narrowly missed my left Eye. But the Colonel
ordered six of the Ringleaders to be seized, and thought no
Punishment so proper as to deliver them bound into my Hands,
which some of his Soldiers accordingly did, pushing them
forwards with the But-ends of their Pikes into my Reach: I
took them all in my right Hand, put five of them into my
Coat-pocket; and as to the sixth, I made a Countenance as if
I would eat him alive. The poor Man squalled terribly, and
the Colonel and his Officers were in much Pain, especially
when they saw me take out my Penknife: But I soon put them
out of Fear; for, looking mildly, and immediately cutting the
Strings he was bound with, I set him gently on the Ground, and
away he ran. I treated the rest in the same Manner, taking
them one by one out of my Pocket; and I observed, both the
Soldiers and the People were highly obliged at this Mark of my
Clemency, which was represented very much to my Advantage
at Court.

Towards Night I got with some Difficulty into my House,
where I lay on the Ground, and continued to do so about a
Fortnight; during which time the Emperor gave Orders to
have a Bed prepared for me. Six Hundred Beds of the common
Measure were brought in Carriages, and worked up into my
House; an Hundred and Fifty of their Beds sown together

made up the Breadth and Length, and these were four double, which however kept me but very indifferently from the Hardness of the Floor, that was of smooth Stone. By the same Computation they provided me with Sheets, Blankets, and Coverlets, tolerable enough for one who had been so long enured to Hardships as I.

As the News of my Arrival spread through the kingdom, it brought prodigious Numbers of rich, idle, and curious People to see me; so that the Villages were almost emptied, and great Neglect of Tillage and Houshold Affairs must have ensued, if his Imperial Majesty had not provided by several Proclamations and Orders of State against this Inconveniency. He directed that those, who had already beheld me, should return home, and not presume to come within fifty Yards of my House, without Licence from Court; whereby the Secretaries of State got considerable Fees.

In the mean time, the Emperor held frequent Councils to debate what Course should be taken with me; and I was afterwards assured by a particular Friend, a Person of great Quality, and who was as much in the *Secret* as any; that the Court was under many Difficulties concerning me. They apprehended my breaking loose; that my Diet would be very expensive, and might cause a Famine. Sometimes they determined to starve me, or at least to shoot me in the Face and Hands with poisoned Arrows, which would soon dispatch me: But again they considered, that the Stench of so large a Carcase might produce a Plague in the Metropolis, and probably spread through the whole Kingdom. In the midst of these Consultations, several Officers of the Army went to the Door of the great Council Chamber; and two of them being admitted, gave an Account of my Behaviour to the six Criminals abovementioned; which made so favourable an Impression in the Breast of his Majesty, and the whole Board, in my Behalf, that an Imperial Commission was issued out, obliging all the Villages nine hundred Yards round the City, to deliver in every Morning six Beeves, forty Sheep, and other Victuals for my Sustenance; together with a proportionable Quantity of Bread and Wine, and other Liquors: For the due Payment of which his Majesty gave Assignments upon his Treasury. For this

Prince lives chiefly upon his own Demesnes; seldom, except upon great Occasions raising any Subsidies upon his Subjects, who are bound to attend him in his Wars at their own Expence. An Establishment was also made of Six Hundred Persons to be my Domesticks, who had Board-Wages allowed for their Maintenance, and Tents built for them very conveniently on each side of my Door. It was likewise ordered, that three hundred Taylors should make me a Suit of Cloaths after the Fashion of the Country: That, six of his Majesty's greatest Scholars should be employed to instruct me in their Language: And, lastly, that the Emperor's Horses, and those of the Nobility, and Troops of Guards, should be exercised in my Sight, to accustom themselves to me. All these Orders were duly put in Execution; and in about three Weeks I made a great Progress in Learning their Language; during which Time the Emperor frequently honoured me with his Visits, and was pleased to assist my Masters in teaching me. We began already to converse together in some Sort; and the first Words I learnt, were to express my Desire, that he would please to give me my Liberty; which I every Day repeated on my Knees. His Answer, as I could apprehend, was, that this must be a Work of Time, not to be thought on without the Advice of his Council; and that first I must *Lumos Kelmin pesso desmar lon Emposo*; that is, *Swear a Peace with him and his Kingdom*. However, that I should be used with all Kindness; and he advised me to acquire by my Patience and discreet Behaviour, the good Opinion of himself and his Subjects. He desired I would not take it ill, if he gave Orders to certain proper Officers to search me; for probably I might carry about me several Weapons, which must needs be dangerous Things, if they answered the Bulk of so prodigious a Person. I said, his Majesty should be satisfied, for I was ready to strip my self, and turn up my Pockets before him. This I delivered, part in Words, and part in Signs. He replied, that by the Laws of the Kingdom, I must be searched by two of his Officers: That he knew this could not be done without my Consent and Assistance; that he had so good an Opinion of my Generosity and Justice, as to trust their Persons in my Hands: That whatever they took from me should be returned when I left he Country, or paid for at the Rate which I would set upon hem. I took up the two Officers in my Hands, put them first nto my Coat-Pockets, and then into every other Pocket about ne, except my two Fobs, and another secret Pocket which I had no Mind should be searched, wherein I had some little Necessaries of no Consequence to any but my self. In one of my Fobs there was a Silver Watch, and in the other a small Quantity of Gold in a Purse. These Gentlemen, having Pen, Ink, and Paper about them, made an exact Inventory of every thing they saw; and when they had done, desired I would set them down, that they might deliver it to the Emperor. This Inventory I afterwards translated into *English*, and is Word for Word as follows.

Imprimis, In the right Coat-Pocket of the *Great Man Mountain* (for so I interpret the Words *Quinbus Flestrin*) after the strictest Search, we found only one great Piece of coarse Cloth, large enough to be a Foot-Cloth for your Majesty's chief Room of State. In the left Pocket, we saw a huge Silver Chest, with a Cover of the same Metal, which we, the Searchers, were not able to lift. We desired it should be opened; and one of us stepping into it, found himself up to the mid Leg in a sort of Dust, some part whereof flying up to our Faces, set us both a sneezing for several Times together. In his right Waistcoat-Pocket, we found a prodigious Bundle of white thin Substances, folded one over another, about the Bigness of three Men, tied with a strong Cable, and marked with black Figures; which we humbly conceive to be Writings; every Letter almost half as large as the Palm of our Hands. In the left there was a sort of Engine, from the Back of which were extended twenty long Poles, resembling the Pallisado's before your Majesty's Court; wherewith we conjecture the *Man Mountain* combs his Head; for we did not always trouble him with Questions, because we found it a great Difficulty to make him understand us. In the large Pocket on the right Side of his middle Cover, (so I translate the Word *Ranfu-Lo*, by which they meant my Breeches) we saw a hollow Pillar of Iron, about the Length of a Man, fastened to a strong Piece of Timber, larger than the Pillar; and upon one side of the Pillar were huge Pieces of Iron sticking out, cut into strange Figures;

which we know not what to make of. In the left Pocket,
another Engine of the same kind. In the smaller Pocket on the
right Side, were several round flat Pieces of white and red Metal,
of different Bulk: Some of the white, which seemed to be
Silver, were so large and heavy, that my Comrade and I could
hardly lift them. In the left Pocket were two black Pillars
irregularly shaped: we could not, without Difficulty, reach the
Top of them as we stood at the Bottom of his Pocket: One of
them was covered, and seemed all of a Piece; but at the upper
End of the other, there appeared a white round Substance,
about twice the bigness of our Heads. Within each of these was
inclosed a prodigious Plate of Steel; which, by our Orders, we
obliged him to shew us, because we apprehended they might
be dangerous Engines. He took them out of their Cases, and
told us, that in his own Country his Practice was to shave his
Beard with one of these, and to cut his Meat with the other.
There were two Pockets which we could not enter: These he
called his Fobs; they were two large Slits cut into the Top of
his middle Cover, but squeezed close by the Pressure of his
Belly. Out of the right Fob hung a great Silver Chain, with a
wonderful kind of Engine at the Bottom. We directed him to
draw out whatever was at the End of that Chain; which
appeared to be a Globe, half Silver, and half of some transparent
Metal: For on the transparent Side we saw certain strange
Figures circularly drawn, and thought we could touch them,
until we found our Fingers stopped with that lucid Substance.
He put this Engine to our Ears, which made an incessant Noise
like that of a Water-Mill. And we conjecture it is either some
unknown Animal, or the God that he worships: But we are
more inclined to the latter Opinion, because he assured us (if
we understood him right, for he expressed himself very imperfectly) that he seldom did any Thing without consulting it.
He called it his Oracle, and said it pointed out the Time for
every Action of his Life. From the left Fob he took out a Net
almost large enough for a Fisherman, but contrived to open and
shut like a Purse, and served him for the same Use: We found
therein several massy Pieces of yellow Metal, which if they be of
real Gold, must be of immense Value.

Having thus, in Obedience to your Majesty's Commands,

diligently searched all his Pockets ; we observed a Girdle about his Waist made of the Hyde of some prodigious Animal ; from which, on the Left Side, hung a Sword of the Length of five Men ; and on the right, a Bag or Pouch divided into two Cells ; each Cell capable of holding three of your Majesty's Subjects. In one of these Cells were several Globes or Balls of a most ponderous Metal, about the Bigness of our Heads, and required a strong Hand to lift them : The other Cell contained a Heap of certain black Grains, but of no great Bulk or Weight, for we could hold about fifty of them in the Palms of our Hands.

This is an exact Inventory of what we found about the Body of the *Man Mountain* ; who used us with great Civility, and due Respect to your Majesty's Commission. Signed and Sealed on the fourth Day of the eighty ninth Moon of your Majesty's auspicious Reign.

Clefren Frelock, Marsi Frelock.

When the Inventory was read over to the Emperor, he directed me to deliver up the several Particulars. He first called for my Scymiter, which I took out, Scabbard and all. In the mean time he ordered three thousand of his choicest Troops, who then attended him, to surround me at a Distance, with their Bows and Arrows just ready to discharge : But I did not observe it ; for my Eyes were wholly fixed upon his Majesty. He then desired me to draw my Scymiter, which, although it had got some Rust by the Sea-Water, was in most Parts exceeding bright. I did so, and immediately all the Troops gave a Shout between Terror and Surprize ; for the Sun shone clear, and the Reflexion dazzled their Eyes, as I waved the Scymiter to and fro in my Hand. His Majesty who is a most magnanimous Prince, was less daunted than I could expect ; he ordered me to return it into the Scabbard, and cast it on the Ground as gently as I could, about six Foot from the End of my Chain. The next Thing he demanded was one of the hollow Iron Pillars, by which he meant my Pocket-Pistols. I drew it out, and at his Desire, as well as I could, expressed to him the Use of it, and charging it only with Powder, which by the Closeness of my Pouch, happened to escape wetting in the

Sea, I first cautioned the Emperor not to be afraid; and
then I let it off in the Air. The Astonishment here was
much greater than at the Sight of my Scymiter. Hundreds
fell down as if they had been struck dead; and even
the Emperor, although he stood his Ground, could not
recover himself in some time. I delivered up both my Pistols
in the same Manner as I had done my Scymiter, and then my
Pouch of Powder and Bullets; begging him that the former
might be kept from Fire; for it would kindle with the smallest
Spark, and blow up his Imperial Palace into the Air. I likewise
delivered up my Watch, which the Emperor was very curious
to see; and commanded two of his tallest Yeomen of the
Guards to bear it on a Pole upon their Shoulders, as Dray-men
in *England* do a Barrel of Ale. He was amazed at the continual
Noise it made, and the Motion of the Minute-hand, which he
could easily discern; for their Sight is much more acute than
ours: I then gave up my Silver and Copper Money, my
Purse with nine large Pieces of Gold, and some smaller ones;
my Knife and Razor, my Comb and Silver Snuff-Box, my
Handkerchief and Journal Book. My Scymiter, Pistols, and
Pouch, were conveyed in Carriages to his Majesty's Stores;
but the rest of my Goods were returned me.

I had, as I before observed, one private Pocket which escaped
their Search, wherein there was a Pair of Spectacles (which I
sometimes use for the Weakness of my Eyes) a Pocket Perspective, and several other little Conveniences; which being of no
Consequence to the Emperor, I did not think my self bound
in Honour to discover; and I apprehended they might be lost
or spoiled if I ventured them out of my Possession.

CHAPTER THREE

THE AUTHOR DIVERTS THE EMPEROR AND HIS NOBILITY OF BOTH
SEXES, IN A VERY UNCOMMON MANNER. THE DIVERSIONS OF THE
COURT OF LILLIPUT DESCRIBED. THE AUTHOR HATH HIS LIBERTY
GRANTED HIM UPON CERTAIN CONDITIONS.

My Gentleness and good Behaviour had gained so far on
the Emperor and his Court, and indeed upon the Army
and People in general, that I began to conceive Hopes of getting
my Liberty in a short Time. The Natives came by Degrees
to be less apprehensive of any Danger from me. I would
sometimes lie down, and let five or six of them dance on
my Hand. And at last the Boys and Girls would venture to
come and play at Hide and Seek in my Hair. I had now made
a good Progress in understanding and speaking their Language.
The Emperor had a mind one Day to entertain me with several
of the Country Shows ; wherein they exceed all Nations I have
known, both for Dexterity and Magnificence. I was diverted
with none so much as that of the Rope-Dancers, performed
upon a slender white Thread, extended about two Foot, and
twelve Inches from the Ground.

This Diversion is only practised by those Persons, who are
Candidates for great Employments, and high Favour, at
Court. They are trained in this Art from their Youth, and are
not always of noble Birth, or liberal Education. When a great
Office is vacant, either by Death of Disgrace, (which often
happens) five or six of those Candidates petition the Emperor
to entertain his Majesty and the Court with a Dance on the
Rope ; and whoever jumps the highest without falling, succeeds
in the Office. Very often the chief Ministers themselves are
commanded to shew their Skill, and to convince the Emperor
that they have not lost their Faculty. *Flimnap*, the Treasurer,
is allowed to cut a Caper on the strait Rope, at least an Inch
higher than any other Lord in the whole Empire. I have seen
him do the Summer-set several times together, upon a Trencher

35

fixed on the rope, which is no thicker than a common Pack-thread in *England*. My Friend *Reldresal*, principal Secretary for private Affairs, is, in my Opinion, if I am not partial, the second after the Treasurer.

These Diversions are often attended with fatal Accidents, whereof great Numbers are on Record. I my self have seen two or three Candidates break a Limb. But the Danger is much greater, when the Ministers themselves are commanded to shew their Dexterity : For, by contending to excel themselves and their Fellows, they strain so far, that there is hardly one of them who hath not received a Fall ; and some of them two or three. I was assured, that a Year or two before my Arrival, *Flimnap* would have infallibly broke his Neck, if one of the *King's Cushions*, that accidentally lay on the Ground, had not weakened the Force of his Fall.

There is likewise another Diversion, which is only shewn before the Emperor and Empress, and first Minister, upon particular Occasions. The Emperor lays on a Table three fine silken Threads of six Inches long. One is Blue, the other Red, and the third Green. These Threads are proposed as Prizes, for those Persons whom the Emperor hath a mind to distinguish by a peculiar Mark of his Favour. The Ceremony is performed in his Majesty's great Chamber of State ; where the Candidates are to undergo a Tryal of Dexterity very different from the former ; and such as I have not observed the least Resemblance of in any other Country of the old or the new World. The Emperor holds a Stick in his Hands, both Ends parallel to the Horizon, while the Candidates advancing one by one, some-times leap over the Stick, sometimes creep under it backwards and forwards several times, according as the Stick is advanced or depressed. Sometimes the Emperor holds one End of the Stick, and his first Minister the other ; sometimes the Minister has it entirely to himself. Whoever performs his Part with most Agility, and holds out the longest in *leaping* and *creeping*, is rewarded with the Blue-coloured Silk ; the Red is given to the next, and the Green to the third, which they all wear girt twice round about the Middle ; and you see few great Persons about this Court, who are not adorned with one of these Girdles.

The Horses of the Army, and those of the Royal Stables, aving been daily led before me, were no longer shy, but would ome up to my very Feet, without starting. The Riders would eap them over my Hand as I held it on the Ground; and one f the Emperor's Huntsmen, upon a large Courser, took my 'oot, Shoe and all; which was indeed a prodigious Leap. I ad the good Fortune to divert the Emperor one Day, after a ery extraordinary Manner. I desired he would order several ticks of two Foot high, and the Thickness of an ordinary Cane, to be brought me; whereupon his Majesty commanded ne Master of his Woods to give Directions accordingly; and ne next Morning six Wood-men arrived with as many Carri-ges, drawn by eight Horses to each. I took nine of these ticks, and fixing them firmly in the Ground in a Quadrangular 'igure, two Foot and a half square; I took four other Sticks, nd tyed them parallel at each Corner, about two Foot from ne Ground; and then I fastened my Handkerchief to the ine Sticks that stood erect; and extended it on all Sides, till it 'as as tight as the Top of a Drum; and the four parallel ticks rising about five Inches higher than the Handkerchief, erved as Ledges on each Side. When I had finished my Work, desired the Emperor to let a Troop of his best Horse, Twenty-ur in Number, come and exercise upon this Plain. His Majesty approved of the Proposal, and I took them up one by ne in my Hands, ready mounted and armed, with the proper fficers to exercise them. As soon as they got into Order, they ivided into two Parties, performed mock Skirmishes, dis-narged blunt Arrows, drew their Swords, fled and pursued, tacked and retired; and in short discovered the best military iscipline I ever beheld. The Emperor was so much delighted, nat he ordered this Entertainment to be repeated several ays; and once was pleased to be lifted up, and give ne Word of Command; and, with great Difficulty, persuaded en the Empress her self to let me hold her in her close hair, within two Yards of the Stage, from whence she as able to take a full View of the whole Performance. It was y good Fortune that no ill Accident happened in these ntertainments; only once a fiery Horse that belonged to one the Captains, pawing with his Hoof struck a Hole in my

Handkerchief, and his Foot slipping, he over-threw his Ride
and himself; but I immediately relieved them both: Fe
covering the Hole with one Hand, I set down the Troop wit
the other, in the same Manner as I took them up. The Hors
that fell was strained in the left Shoulder, but the Rider got n
Hurt, and I repaired my Handkerchief as well as I could
However, I would not trust to the Strength of it any more i
such dangerous Enterprizes.

About two or three Days before I was set at Liberty, as I wa
entertaining the Court with these Kinds of Feats, there arrive
an Express to inform his Majesty, that some of his Subjec
riding near the Place where I was first taken up, had seen
great black Substance lying on the Ground, very oddly shape
extending its Edges round as wide as his Majesty's Bedchambe
and rising up in the Middle as high as a Man. That it was n
living Creature, as they at first apprehended; for it lay on th
Grass without Motion, and some of them had walked round
several Times: That by mounting upon each others Shoulder
they had got to the Top, which was flat and even; and stampir
upon it, they found it was hollow within: That they humb
conceived it might be something belonging to the *Man-Mou*
tain; and if his Majesty pleased, they would undertake
bring it with only five Horses. I presently knew what th
meant; and was glad at Heart to receive this Intelligence.
seems, upon my first reaching the Shore, after our Shipwrec
I was in such Confusion, that before I came to the Place whe
I went to sleep, my Hat, which I had fastened with a String
my Head while I was rowing, and had stuck on all the Time
was swimming, fell off after I came to Land; the String,
I conjecture, breaking by some Accident which I never observe
but thought my Hat had been lost at Sea. I intreated h
Imperial Majesty to give Orders it might be brought to me
soon as possible, describing to him the Use and the Nature
it: And the next Day the Waggoners arrived with it, but n
in a very good Condition; they had bored two Holes in th
Brim, within an Inch and a half of the Edge, and fastened tv
Hooks in the Holes; these Hooks were tyed by a long Co
to the Harness, and thus my Hat was dragged along for abo
half an *English* Mile: but the Ground in that Country bei

xtremely smooth and level, it received less Damage than I xpected.

Two Days after this Adventure, the Emperor having ordered at Part of his Army, which quarters in and about his Metro-olis, to be in a Readiness, took a fancy of diverting himself in very singular Manner. He desired I would stand like a *olossus*, with my Legs as far asunder as I conveniently could. e then commanded his General (who was an old experienced eader, and a great Patron of mine) to draw up the Troops in ose Order, and march them under me ; the Foot by Twenty-ur in a Breast, and the Horse by Sixteen, with Drums beating, olours flying, and Pikes advanced. This Body consisted of ree Thousand Foot, and a Thousand Horse.

I had sent so many Memorials and Petitions for my Liberty, at his Majesty at length mentioned the Matter first in the abinet, and then in a full Council ; where it was opposed by ne, except *Skyresh Bolgolam*, who was pleased, without any ovocation, to be my mortal Enemy. But it was carried against m by the whole Board, and confirmed by the Emperor. That inister was *Galbet*, or Admiral of the Realm ; very much in s Master's Confidence, and a Person well versed in Affairs, t of a morose and sour Complection. However, he was at gth persuaded to comply ; but prevailed that the Articles d Conditions upon which I should be set free, and to which must swear, should be drawn up by himself. These Articles re brought to me by *Skyresh Bolgolam* in Person, attended two under Secretaries, and several Persons of Distinction. ave made a Translation of the whole Instrument, Word for ord, as near as I was able ; which I here offer to the Publick.

OLBASTO MOMAREN EVLAME GURDILO SHEFIN MULLY ULLY UE, most Mighty Emperor of *Lilliput*, Delight and Terror of e Universe, whose Dominions extend five Thousand Blus-gs, (about twelve Miles in Circumference) to the Extremities the Globe : Monarch of all Monarchs : Taller than the ns of Men ; whose Feet press down to the Center, and whose ead strikes against the Sun : At whose Nod the Princes of e Earth shake their Knees ; pleasant as the Spring, comfort-le as the Summer, fruitful as Autumn, dreadful as Winter.

His most sublime Majesty proposeth to the *Man-Mountain*
lately arrived at our Celestial Dominions, the following Articles
which by a solemn Oath he shall be obliged to perform.

First, The *Man-Mountain* shall not depart from our Dominions, without our Licence under our Great Seal.

Secondly, He shall not presume to come into our Metropolis
without our express Order; at which time, the Inhabitants
shall have two Hours Warning, to keep within their Doors.

Thirdly, The said *Man-Mountain* shall confine his Walks to
our principal high Roads; and not offer to walk or lie down
in a Meadow, or Field of Corn.

Fourthly, As he walks the said Roads, he shall take the
utmost Care not to trample upon the Bodies of any of our
loving Subjects, their Horses, or Carriages; nor take any of
our said Subjects into his Hands, without their own Consent.

Fifthly, If an Express require extraordinary Dispatch; the
Man-Mountain shall be obliged to carry in his Pocket the
Messenger and Horse, a six Days Journey once in every
Moon, and return the said Messenger back (if so required) safe
to our Imperial Presence.

Sixthly, He shall be our Ally against our Enemies in the
Island of *Blefuscu*, and do his utmost to destroy their Fleet
which is now preparing to invade Us.

Seventhly, That the said *Man-Mountain* shall, at his Times
of Leisure, be aiding and assisting to our Workmen, in helping
to raise certain great Stones, towards covering the Wall of the
principal Park, and other our Royal Buildings.

Eighthly, That the said *Man-Mountain* shall, in two Moons
Time, deliver in an exact survey of the Circumference of our
Dominions, by a Computation of his own Paces round the
Coast.

Lastly, That upon his solemn Oath to observe all the above Articles, the said *Man-Mountain* shall have a daily Allowance of Meat and Drink, sufficient for the Support of 1728 of our Subjects; with free Access to our Royal Person, and other Marks of our Favour. Given at our Palace at *Belfaborac* the Twelfth Day of the Ninety-first Moon of our Reign.

I swore and subscribed to these Articles with great Chearfulness and Content, although some of them were not so honourable as I could have wished; which proceeded wholly from the Malice of *Skyresh Bolgolam* the High Admiral: Whereupon my Chains were immediately unlocked, and I was at full Liberty: The Emperor himself, in Person, did me the Honour to be by at the whole Ceremony. I made my Acknowledgments, by prostrating myself at his Majesty's Feet: But he commanded me to rise; and after many gracious Expressions, which, to avoid the Censure of Vanity, I shall not repeat; he added, that he hoped I should prove a useful Servant, and well deserve all the Favours he had already conferred upon me, or might do for the future.

CHAPTER FOUR

MILDENDO, THE METROPOLIS OF LILLIPUT, DESCRIBED, TOGETHER WITH THE EMPEROR'S PALACE. A CONVERSATION BETWEEN THE AUTHOR AND A PRINCIPAL SECRETARY, CONCERNING THE AFFAIRS OF THAT EMPIRE. THE AUTHOR'S OFFERS TO SERVE THE EMPEROR IN HIS WARS.

THE first Request I made after I had obtained my Liberty, was, that I might have Licence to see *Mildendo*, the Metropolis; which the Emperor easily granted me, but with a special Charge to do no Hurt, either to the Inhabitants, or their Houses. The People had Notice by Proclamation of my Design to visit the Town. The Wall which encompassed it, is two Foot and an half high, and at least eleven Inches broad, so that a Coach and Horses may be driven very safely round it;

and it is flanked with strong Towers at the Foot Distance. I stept over the great *Western* Gate, and passed very gently, and sideling through the two principal Streets, only in my short Waistcoat, for fear of damaging the Roofs and Eves of the Houses with the Skirts of my Coat. I walked with the utmost Circumspection, to avoid treading on any Stragglers, who might remain in the Streets, although the Orders were very strict, that all People should keep in their Houses, at their own Peril. The Garret Windows and Tops of Houses were so crowded with Spectators, that I thought in all my Travels I had not seen a more populous Place. The City is an exact Square, each Side of the Wall being five Hundred Foot long. The two great Streets which run cross and divide it into four Quarters, are five Foot wide. The Lanes and Alleys which I could not enter, but only viewed them as I passed, are from Twelve to Eighteen Inches. The Town is capable of holding five Hundred Thousand Souls. The Houses are from three to five Stories. The Shops and Markets are well provided.

The Emperor's Palace is in the Center of the City, where the two great Streets meet. It is inclosed by a Wall of two Foot high, and Twenty Foot distant from the Buildings. I had his Majesty's Permission to step over this Wall; and the Space being so wide between that and the Palace, I could easily view it on every Side. The outward Court is a Square of Forty Foot, and includes two other Courts: In the inmost are the Royal Apartments, which I was very desirous to see, but found it extremely difficult; for the great Gates, from one Square into another, were but Eighteen Inches high, and seven Inches wide. Now the Buildings of the outer Court were at least five Foot high; and it was impossible for me to stride over them, without infinite Damage to the Pile, although the Walls were strongly built of hewn Stone, and four Inches thick. At the same time, the Emperor had a great Desire that I should see the Magnificence of his Palace: But this I was not able to do till three Days after, which I spent in cutting down with my Knife some of the largest Trees in the Royal Park, about an Hundred Yards distant from the City. Of these Trees I made two Stools, each about three Foot high, and strong enough to bear my Weight. The People having received Notice a second time, I went again through the City to the Palace, with my two Stools in my Hands. When I came to the Side of the outer Court, I stood upon one Stool, and took the other in my Hand: This I lifted over the Roof, and gently set it down on the Space between the first and second Court, which was eight Foot wide. I then stept over the Buildings very conveniently from one Stool to the other, and drew up the first after me with a hooked Stick. By this Contrivance I got into the inmost Court; and lying down upon my Side, I applied my Face to the Windows of the middle Stories, which were left open on Purpose, and discovered the most splendid Apartments that can be imagined. There I saw the Empress and the young Princes in their several Lodgings, with their chief Attendants about them. Her Imperial Majesty was pleased to smile very graciously upon me and gave me out of the Window her Hand to kiss.

One Morning, about a Fortnight after I had obtained my Liberty, *Reldresal*, Principal Secretary (as they style him) of private Affairs, came to my House, attended only by one Servant. He ordered his Coach to wait at a Distance, and desired I would give him an Hour's Audience; which I readily consented to, on Account of his Quality, and Personal Merits, as well as of the many good Offices he had done me during my Sollicitations at Court. I offered to lie down, that he might the more conveniently reach my Ear; but he chose rather to let me hold him in my Hand during our Conversation. He began with Compliments on my Liberty; said, he might pretend to some Merit in it; but, however, added, that if it had not been for the present Situation of things at Court, perhaps I might not have obtained it so soon. For, *said he*, as flourishing a Condition as we appear to be in to Foreigners, we labour under two mighty Evils; a violent Faction at home, and the Danger of an Invasion by a most potent Enemy from abroad. As to the first, you are to understand, that for above seventy Moons past, there have been two struggling Parties in this Empire, under the Names of *Tramecksan*, and *Slamecksan*, from the high and low Heels on their Shoes, by which they distinguish themselves.

It is alleged indeed, that the high Heels are most agreeable to our ancient Constitution: But however this be, his Majesty hath determined to make use of only low Heels in the Administration of the Government, and all Offices in the Gift of the Crown; as you cannot but observe; and particularly, that his Majesty's Imperial Heels are lower at least by a *Drurr* than any of his Court; (*Drurr* is a Measure about the fourteenth Part of an Inch.) The Animosities between these two Parties run so high, that they will neither eat nor drink, nor talk with each other. We compute the *Tramecksan*, or High-Heels, to exceed us in Number; but the Power is wholly on our Side. We apprehend his Imperial Highness, the Heir to the Crown, to have some Tendency towards the High-Heels; at least we can plainly discover one of his Heels higher than the other; which gives him a Hobble in his Gait. Now, in the midst of these intestine Disquiets, we are threatened with an Invasion from the Island of *Blefuscu*, which is the other great Empire of the Universe, almost as large and powerful as this of his Majesty. For as to what we have heard you affirm, that there are other Kingdoms and States in the World, inhabited by human Creatures as large as your self, our Philosophers are in much Doubt; and would rather conjecture that you dropt from the Moon, or one of the Stars; because it is certain, that an hundred Mortals of your Bulk, would, in a short Time, destroy all the Fruits and Cattle of his Majesty's Dominions. Besides, our Histories of six Thousand Moons make no mention of any other Regions, than the two great Empires of *Lilliput* and *Blefuscu*. Which two mighty Powers have, as I was going to tell you, been engaged in a most obstinate War for six and thirty Moons past. It began upon the following Occasion. It is allowed on all Hands, that the Primitive Way of breaking Eggs before we eat them, was upon the larger End: But his present Majesty's Grand-father, while he was a Boy, going to eat an Egg, and breaking it according to the ancient Practice, happened to cut one of his Fingers. Whereupon the Emperor his Father, published an Edict, commanding all his Subjects, upon great Penalties, to break the smaller End of their Eggs. The People so highly resented this Law, that our Histories tell us, there have been six Rebellions raised on that Account; wherein one Emperor lost his Life, and another his Crown. These civil Commotions were constantly fomented by the

Monarchs of *Blefuscu*; and when they were quelled, the Exiles always fled for Refuge to that Empire. It is computed, that eleven Thousand Persons have, at several Times, suffered Death, rather than submit to break their Eggs at the smaller End. Many hundred large Volumes have been published upon this Controversy: But the Books of the *Big-Endians* have been long forbidden, and the whole Party rendered incapable by Law of holding Employments. Now the *Big-Endian* Exiles have found so much Credit in the Emperor of *Blefuscu's* Court; and so much private Assistance and Encouragement from their Party here at home, that a bloody War hath been carried on between the two Empires for six and thirty Moons with various Success; during which Time we have lost Forty Capital Ships, and a much greater Number of smaller Vessels, together with thirty thousand of our best Seamen and Soldiers; and the Damage received by the Enemy is reckoned to be somewhat greater than ours. However, they have now equipped a numerous Fleet, and are just preparing to make a Descent upon us: And his Imperial Majesty, placing great Confidence in your Valour and Strength, hath commanded me to lay this Account of his affairs before you.

I desired the Secretary to present my humble Duty to the Emperor, and to let him know, that I thought it would not become me, who was a Foreigner, to interfere with Parties; but I was ready, with the Hazard of my Life, to defend his Person and State against all Invaders.

CHAPTER FIVE

THE AUTHOR BY AN EXTRAORDINARY STRATAGEM PREVENTS AN
INVASION. A HIGH TITLE OF HONOUR IS CONFERRED UPON HIM.
AMBASSADORS ARRIVE FROM THE EMPEROR OF BLEFUSCU, AND SUE
FOR PEACE.

THE Empire of *Blefuscu*, is an Island situated to the North
North-East Side of *Lilliput*, from whence it is parted only
by a Channel of eight Hundred Yards wide. I had not yet seen
it, and upon this Notice of an intended Invasion, I avoided
appearing on that Side of the Coast, for fear of being discovered
by some of the Enemie's Ships who had received no Intelligence
of me; all intercourse between the two Empires having been
strictly forbidden during the War, upon Pain of Death; and
an Embargo laid by our Emperor upon all Vessels whatsoever.
I communicated to his Majesty a Project I had formed of seizing
the Enemie's whole Fleet; which, as our Scouts assured us,
lay at Anchor in the Harbour ready to sail with the first fair
Wind. I consulted the more experienced Seamen, upon the
Depth of the Channel, which they had often plummed; who
told me, that in the Middle at high Water it was seventy
Glumgluffs deep, which is about six Foot of *European* Measure;
and the rest of it fifty *Glumgluffs* at most. I walked to the
North-East Coast over against *Blefuscu*; where, lying down
behind a Hillock, I took out my small Pocket Perspective Glass,
and viewed the Enemy's Fleet at Anchor, consisting of about
fifty Men of War, and a great Number of Transports: I then
came back to my House, and gave Order (for which I had a
Warrant) for a great Quantity of the strongest Cable and Bars
of Iron. The Cable was about as thick as Packthread, and the
Bars of the Length and Size of a Knitting-Needle. I trebled
the Cable to make it stronger; and for the same Reason I
twisted three of the Iron Bars together, binding the Extremities
into a Hook. Having thus fixed fifty Hooks to as many Cables,
I went back to the North-East Coast, and putting off my Coat,

Shoes, and Stockings, walked into the Sea in my Leathern Jerken, about half an Hour before high Water. I waded with what Haste I could, and swam in the Middle about thirty Yards until I felt the Ground; I arrived at the Fleet in less than half an Hour. The Enemy was so frighted when they saw me, that they leaped out of their Ships, and swam to Shore; where there could not be fewer than thirty thousand Souls. I then took my Tackling, and fastning a Hook to the Hole at the Prow of each, I tyed all the Cords together at the End. While I was thus employed, the Enemy discharged several Thousand Arrows, many of which stuck in my Hands and Face; and besides the excessive Smart, gave me much Disturbance in my Work. My greatest Apprehension was for my Eyes, which I should have infallibly lost, if I had not suddenly thought of an Expedient. I kept, among other little Necessaries, a Pair of Spectacles in a private Pocket, which, as I observed before, had escaped the Emperor's Searchers. These I took out, and fastened as strongly as I could upon my Nose; and thus armed went on boldly with my Work in spight of the Enemy's Arrows; many of which struck against the Glasses of my Spectacles, but without any other Effect, further than a little to discompose them. I had now fastened all the Hooks, and taking the Knot in my Hand, began to pull; but not a Ship would stir, for they were all too fast held by their Anchors; so that the boldest Part of my Enterprize remained. I therefore let go the Cord, and leaving the Hooks fixed to the Ships, I resolutely cut with my Knife the Cables that fastened the Anchors; receiving above two hundred Shots in my Face and Hands: Then I took up the knotted End of the Cables to which my Hooks were tyed; and with great Ease drew fifty of the Enemy's largest Men of War after me.

The *Blefuscudians*, who had not the least Imagination of what I intended were at first confounded with Astonishment. They had seen me cut the Cables, and thought my Design was only to let the Ships run a-drift, or fall foul on each other: But when they perceived the whole Fleet moving in Order, and saw me pulling at the End; they set up such a Scream of Grief and Dispair, that it is almost impossible to describe or conceive. When I had got out of Danger, I stopt a while to pick

out the Arrows that stuck in my Hands and Face, and rubbed
on some of the same Ointment that was given me at my first
Arrival, as I have formerly mentioned. I then took off my
Spectacles, and waiting about an Hour until the Tyde was a
little fallen, I waded through the Middle with my Cargo, and
arrived safe at the Royal Port of *Lilliput*.

The Emperor and his whole Court stood on the Shore,
expecting the Issue of this great Adventure. They saw the
Ships move forward in a large Half-Moon, but could not
discern me, who was up to my Breast in Water. When I
advanced to the Middle of the Channel, they were yet more in
Pain because I was under Water to my Neck. The Emperor
concluded me to be drowned, and that the Enemy's Fleet was
approaching in a hostile Manner: But he was soon eased of
of his Fears; for the Channel growing shallower every Step
I made, I came in a short Time within Hearing; and holding
up the End of the Cable by which the Fleet was fastened, I
cryed in a loud Voice. *Long live the most puissant Emperor of
Lilliput!* This great Prince received me at my Landing with
all possible Encomiums, and created me a *Nardac* upon the
Spot, which is the highest Title of Honour among them.

His Majesty desired I would take some other Opportunity
of bringing all the rest of his Enemy's Ships into his Ports.
And so unmeasurable is the Ambition of Princes, that he seemed
to think of nothing less than reducing the whole Empire of
Blefuscu into a Province, and governing it by a Viceroy; of
destroying the *Big-Endian* Exiles, and compelling that People
to break the smaller End of their Eggs; by which he would
remain sole Monarch of the whole World. But I endeavoured
to divert him from this Design. And I plainly protested, that I
would never be an Instrument of bringing a free and brave
People into Slavery: And when the Matter was debated in
Council, the wisest Part of the Ministry were of my Opinion.

This open bold Declaration of mine was so opposite to the
Schemes and Politicks of his Imperial Majesty, that he could
never forgive me: He mentioned it in a very artful Manner at
Council, where, I was told, that some of the wisest appeared,
at least by their Silence, to be of my Opinion; but others, who
were my secret Enemies, could not forbear some Expressions

which by a Side-wind reflected on me. And from this Time began an Intrigue between his Majesty, and a Junta of Ministers maliciously bent against me, which broke out in less than two Months, and had like to have ended in my utter Destruction.

About three Weeks after this Exploit, there arrived a solemn Embassy from *Blefuscu*, with humble Offers of a Peace ; which was soon concluded upon Conditions very advantageous to our Emperor ; There were six Ambassadors, with a Train of about five Hundred Persons ; and their Entry was very magnificent, suitable to the Grandeur of their Master, and the Importance of their Business. When their Treaty was finished, wherein I did them several good Offices by the Credit I now had, or at least appeared to have at Court; their Excellencies, who were privately told how much I had been their Friend, made me a Visit in Form. They began with many Compliments upon my Valour and Generosity ; invited me to that Kingdom in the Emperor their Master's Name, and desired me to shew them some Proofs of my prodigious Strength.

When I had for some time entertained their Excellencies to their infinite Satisfaction and Surprize, I desired they would do me the Honour to present my most humble Respects to the Emperor their Master, the Renown of whose Virtues had so justly filled the whole World with Admiration, and whose Royal Person I resolved to attend before I returned to my own Country. Accordingly, the next time I had the Honour to see our Emperor, I desired his general Licence to wait on the *Blefuscudian* Monarch, which he was pleased to grant me, as I could plainly perceive, in a very cold Manner ; but could not guess the Reason, till I had a Whisper from a certain Person, that *Flimnap* and *Bolgolam* had represented my Intercourse with those Ambassadors, as a Mark of Disaffection, from which I am sure my Heart was wholly free.

CHAPTER SIX

OF THE INHABITANTS OF LILLIPUT; THEIR LAWS AND CUSTOMS. THE AUTHOR'S WAY OF LIVING IN THAT COUNTRY.

ALTHOUGH I intend to leave the Description of this Empire to a particular Treatise, yet in the mean time I am content to gratify the curious Reader with some general Ideas. As the common Size of the Natives is somewhat under Six Inches, so there is an exact Proportion in all other Animals, as well as Plants and Trees: For Instance, the tallest Horses and Oxen are between four and five Inches in Height, the Sheep an Inch and a half, more or less; their Geese about the Bigness of a Sparrow; and so the several Gradations downwards, till you come to the smallest, which, to my Sight, were almost invisible; but Nature hath adapted the Eyes of the *Lilliputians* to all Objects proper for their View: They see with great Exactness, but at no great Distance. And to show the Sharpness of their Sight towards Objects that are near, I have been much pleased with observing a Cook pulling a Lark, which was not so large as a common Fly; and a young Girl threading an invisible Needle with invisible Silk. Their tallest Trees are about seven Foot high; I mean some of those in the great Royal Park, the Tops whereof I could but just reach with my Fist clinched. The other Vegetables are in the same Proportion:

Their Manner of Writing is very peculiar; being neither from the Left to the Right, like the *Europeans*; nor from the Right to the Left, like the *Arabians*; nor from up to down, like the *Chinese*; nor from down to up, like the *Cascagians*; but aslant from one Corner of the Paper to the other, like Ladies in *England*.

They bury their Dead with their Heads directly downwards; because they hold an Opinion, that in eleven Thousand Moons they are all to rise again; in which Period, the Earth (which they conceive to be flat) will turn upside down, and by this Means they shall, at their Resurrection, be found ready standing on their Feet. The Learned among them confess the Absurdity of this Doctrine; but the practice still continues, in Compliance to the Vulgar.

There are some Laws and Customs in this Empire very peculiar; and if they were not so directly contrary to those of my own dear Country, I should be tempted to say a little in their Justification. It is only to be wished, that they were as well executed. The first I shall mention, relateth to Informers. All Crimes against the State, are punished here with the utmost Severity; but if the Person accused make his Innocence plainly to appear upon his Tryal, the Accuser is immediately put to an ignominious Death; and out of his Goods or Lands, the innocent Person is quadruply recompensed for the Loss of his Time, for the Danger he underwent, for the Hardship of his Imprisonment, and for all the Charges he hath been at in making his Defence. Or, if that Fund be deficient, it is largely supplyed by the Crown. The Emperor doth also confer on him some publick Mark of his Favour; and Proclamation is made of his innocence through the whole City.

They look upon Fraud as a greater Crime than Theft, and therefore seldom fail to punish it with Death: For they alledge, that Care and Vigilance, with a very common Understanding, may preserve a Man's Goods from Thieves; but Honesty hath no Fence against superior Cunning: And since it is necessary that there should be a perpetual Intercourse of buying and selling, and dealing upon Credit; where Fraud is permitted or connived at, or hath no Law to punish it, the honest Dealer is always undone, and the Knave gets the Advantage. I remember when I was once interceeding with the King for a Criminal who had wronged his Master of a great Sum of Money, which he had received by Order, and ran away with; and happening to tell his Majesty, by way of Extenuation, that it was only a Breach of Trust; the Emperor thought it monstrous in me to offer, as a Defence, the greatest Aggravation of the Crime.

Although we usually call Reward and Punishment, the two Hinges upon which all Government turns; yet I could never observe this Maxim to be put in Practice by any Nation except that of *Lilliput*. Whoever can there bring sufficient Proof that he hath strictly observed the Laws of his Country for Seventy-three Moons, hath a Claim to certain Privileges, according to his Quality and Condition of Life, with a proportionable Sum of Money out of a Fund appropriated for that Use : He likewise acquires the Title of *Snilpall*, or *Legal*, which is added to his Name, but doth not descend to his Posterity. And these People thought it a prodigious Defect of Policy among us, when I told them that our Laws were enforced only by Penalties, without any Mention of Reward. It is upon this account that the Image of Justice, in their Courts of Judicature, is formed with six Eyes, two before, as many behind, and on each Side one, to signify Circumspection ; with a Bag of Gold open in her right Hand, and a Sword sheathed in her left, to shew she is more disposed to reward than to punish.

And here it may perhaps divert the curious Reader, to give some Account of my Domestick, and my Manner of living in this Country, during a residence of nine Months and thirteen Days. Having a Head mechanically turned, and being likewise forced by Necessity, I had made for myself a Table and Chair convenient enough, out of the largest Trees in the Royal Park. Two hundred Sempstresses were employed to make me Shirts, and Linnen for my Bed and Table, all of the strongest and coarsest kind they could get ; which, however, they were forced to quilt together in several Folds ; for the thickest was some Degrees finer than Lawn. Their Linnen is usually three Inches wide, and three Foot make a Piece. The Sempstresses took my Measure as I lay on the Ground, one standing at my Neck, and another at my Mid-Leg, with a strong Cord extended, that each held by the End, while the third measured the Length of the Cord with a Rule of an Inch long. Then they measured my right Thumb, and desired no more ; for by a mathematical Computation, that twice round the Thumb is once round the Wrist, and so on to the Neck and the Waist ; and by the Help of my old Shirt, which I displayed on the Ground before them for a Pattern they fitted me exactly. Three hundred Taylors were employed in the same Manner to make me Clothes ; but they had another Contrivance for taking my Measure. I kneeled down, and they raised a Ladder from the Ground to my Neck ; upon this Ladder one of them mounted, and let fall a Plum-Line from my Collar to the Floor, which just answered the Length of my Coat; but my Waist and Arms I measured myself. When my Cloaths were finished, which was done in my House, (for the largest of theirs would not have been able to hold them) they looked like the Patchwork made by the Ladies in *England*, only that mine were all of a Colour.

I had three hundred Cooks to dress my Victuals, in little convenient Huts built about my House, where they and their Families lived, and prepared me two Dishes a-piece. I took up twenty Waiters in my Hand, and placed them on the Table; an hundred more attended below on the Ground, some with Dishes of Meat, and some with Barrels of Wine, and other Liquors, slung on their Shoulders; all which the Waiters drew up as I wanted, in a very ingenious Manner, by certain Cords, as we draw the Bucket up a Well in *Europe*. A Dish of their Meat was a good Mouthful, and a Barrel of their Liquor a reasonable Draught. Their Mutton yields to ours, but their Beef is excellent. I have had a Sirloin so large, that I have been forced to make three Bits of it; but this is rare. My Servants were astonished to see me eat it Bones and all, as in our Country we do the Leg of a Lark. Their Geese and Turkeys I usually eat at a Mouthful, and I must confess they far exceed ours. Of their smaller Fowl I could take up twenty or thirty at the End of my Knife.

One day his Imperial Majesty being informed of my Way of living, desired that himself, and his Royal Consort, with the young Princes of the Blood of both Sexes, might have the Happiness (as he was pleased to call it) of dining with me. They came accordingly, and I placed them upon Chairs of State on my Table, just over against me, with their Guards about them. *Flimnap* the Lord High Treasurer attended there likewise, with his white Staff; and I observed he often looked on me with a sour Countenance, which I would not seem to regard, but eat more than usual, in Honour to my dear Country, as well as to fill the Court with Admiration. I have some private Reasons to believe, that this Visit from his Majesty gave *Flimnap* an Opportunity of doing me ill Offices to his Master. That Minister had always been my secret Enemy, although he outwardly caressed me more than was usual to

the Moroseness of his Nature. He represented to the Emperor
the low Condition of his Treasury; that he was forced to take
up Money at great Discount; that I had cost his Majesty
about a Million and a half of *Sprugs*, (their greatest Gold
Coin, about the Bigness of a Spangle;) and upon the whole,
that it would be adviseable in the Emperor to take the first
fair Occasion of dismissing me.

CHAPTER SEVEN

THE AUTHOR BEING INFORMED OF A DESIGN TO ACCUSE HIM OF
HIGH TREASON, MAKES HIS ESCAPE TO BLEFUSCU. HIS RECEPTION
THERE.

BEFORE I proceed to give an Account of my leaving this
Kingdom, it may be proper to inform the Reader of a
private Intrigue which had been for two Months forming
against me.

I had been hitherto all my Life a Stranger to Courts, for
which I was unqualified by the Meanness of my Condition. I
had indeed heard and read enough of the Dispositions of great
Princes and Ministers; but never expected to have found such
terrible Effects of them in so remote a Country, governed, as
I thought, by very different Maxims from those in *Europe*.

When I was just preparing to pay my Attendance on the
Emperor of *Blefuscu*; a considerable Person at Court (to
whom I had been very serviceable at a time when he lay under
the highest Displeasure of his Imperial Majesty) came to my
House very privately at Night in a close Chair, and without
sending his Name, desired Admittance: The Chair-men were
dismissed; I put the Chair, with his Lordship in it, into my
Coat-Pocket; and giving Orders to a trusty Servant to say I
was indisposed and gone to sleep, I fastened the Door of my
House, placed the Chair on the Table, according to my usual
Custom, and sat down by it. After the common Salutations
were over, observing his Lordship's Countenance full of
Concern; and enquiring into the Reason, he desired I would

ear him with Patience, in a Matter that highly concerned my
Honour and my Life. His Speech was to the following Effect,
or I took Notes of it as soon as he left me.

You are to know, said he, that several Committees of Council
ave been lately called in the most private Manner on your
Account : And it is but two Days since his Majesty came to a
ull Resolution.

You are very sensible that *Skyris Bolgolam* (*Galbet*, or High
Admiral) hath been your mortal Enemy almost ever since your
Arrival. His original Reasons I know not ; but his Hatred is
much increased since your great Success against *Blefuscu*, by
which his Glory, as Admiral, is obscured. This Lord, in
Conjunction with *Flimnap* the High Treasurer, whose Enmity
against you is notorious ; *Limtoc* the General, *Lalcon* the
Chamberlain, and *Balmuff* the grand Justiciary, have prepared
Articles of Impeachment against you, for Treason, and other
capital Crimes.

In the several Debates upon this Impeachment, it must be
confessed that his Majesty gave many Marks of his great
Lenity ; often urging the Services you had done him, and
endeavouring to extenuate your Crimes. The Treasurer and
Admiral insisted that you should be put to the most painful
and ignominious Death, by setting Fire on your House at
Night ; and the General was to attend with Twenty Thousand
Men armed with poisoned Arrows, to shoot you on the Face
and Hands. Some of your Servants were to have private Orders
to strew a poisonous Juice on your Shirts and Sheets, which
would soon make you tear your own Flesh, and die in the
utmost Torture. The General came into the same Opinion ; so
that for a long time there was a Majority against you. But his
Majesty resolving, if possible, to spare your Life, at last brought
off the Chamberlain.

Upon this Incident, *Reldresal*, principal Secretary for private
Affairs, who always approved himself your true Friend, was
commanded by the Emperor to deliver his Opinion, which he
accordingly did ; and therein justified the good Thoughts you
have of him. He allowed your Crimes to be great ; but that
still there was room for Mercy, the most commendable Virtue

in a Prince, and for which his Majesty was so justly celebrated
He said, the Friendship between you and him was so wel
known to the World, that perhaps the most honourable Board
might think him partial: However, in Obedience to the
Command he had received, he would freely offer his Sentiments
That if his Majesty, in Consideration of your Services, and
pursuant to his own merciful Disposition, would please to
spare your Life, and only give order to put out both your
Eyes; he humbly conceived, that by this Expedient, Justice
might in some measure be satisfied, and all the World would
applaud the *Lenity* of the Emperor, as well as the fair and
generous Proceedings of those who have the Honour to be his
Counsellors. That the Loss of your Eyes would be no Im-
pediment to your bodily Strength, by which you might still be
useful to his Majesty. That Blindness is an Addition to Courage
by concealing Dangers from us; that the Fear you had for
your Eyes, was the greatest Difficulty in bringing over the
Enemy's Fleet; and it would be sufficient for you to see by
the Eyes of the Ministers, since the greatest Princes do no more

This Proposal was received with the utmost Disapprobation
by the whole Board. *Bolgolam*, the Admiral, could not preserve
his Temper; but rising up in Fury, said, he wondered how
the Secretary durst presume to give his Opinion for preserving
the Life of a Traytor.

The Treasurer was of the same Opinion; he shewed to
what Streights his Majesty's Revenue was reduced by the
Charge of maintaining you, which would soon grow insupport-
able: That the Secretary's Expedient of putting out your Eyes
was so far from being a Remedy against this Evil, that it would
probably increase it; as it is manifest from the common
Practice of blinding some Kind of Fowl, after which they fed
the faster, and grew sooner fat: That his sacred Majesty, and
the Council, who are your Judges, were in their own Consciences
fully convinced of your Guilt; which was a sufficient Argument
to condemn you to death, without the *formal Proofs required by
the strict Letter of the Law*.

But his Imperial Majesty fully determined against capital
Punishment, was graciously pleased to say, that since the
Council thought the Loss of your Eyes too easy a Censure,

some other may be inflicted hereafter. And your Friend the Secretary humbly desiring to be heard again, in Answer to what the Treasurer had objected concerning the great Charge his Majesty was at in maintaining you; said, that his Excellency, who had the sole Disposal of the Emperor's Revenue, might easily provide against this Evil, by gradually lessening your Establishment; by which, for want of sufficient Food, you would grow weak and faint, and lose your Appetite, and consequently decay and consume in a few Months; neither would the Stench of your Carcass be then so dangerous, when it should become more than half diminished; and immediately upon your Death, five or six Thousand of his Majesty's Subjects might, in two or three Days, cut your Flesh from your Bones, take it away by Cart-loads, and bury it in distant Parts to prevent Infection; leaving the Skeleton as a Monument of Admiration to Posterity.

In three Days your Friend the Secretary will be directed to come to your House, and read before you the Articles of Impeachment; and then to signify the great *Lenity* and Favour of his Majesty and Council; whereby you are only condemned to the Loss of your Eyes, which his Majesty doth not question you will gratefully and humbly submit to; and Twenty of his Majesty's Surgeons will attend, in order to see the Operation well performed, by discharging very sharp pointed Arrows into the Balls of your Eyes, as you lie on the Ground.

I leave to your Prudence what Measures you will take; and to avoid Suspicion, I must immediately return in as private a Manner as I came.

His Lordship did so, and I remained alone, under many Doubts and Perplexities of Mind.

At last I fixed upon a Resolution, for which it is probable I may incur some Censure, and not unjustly; for I confess I owe the preserving of my Eyes, and consequently my Liberty, to my own great Rashness and Want of Experience: Because if I had then known the Nature of Princes and Ministers, which I have since observed in many other Courts, and their Methods of treating Criminals less obnoxious than myself; I should with great Alacrity and Readiness have submitted to so *easy* a Punishment. But hurried on by the Precipitancy of Youth;

and having his Imperial Majesty's Licence to pay my Attendance upon the Emperor of *Blefuscu*; I took this Opportunity, before the three Days were elapsed, to send a Letter to my Friend the Secretary, signifying my Resolution of setting out that Morning for *Blefuscu*, pursuant to the Leave I had got; and without waiting for an Answer, I went to that Side of the Island where our Fleet lay. I seized a large Man of War, tied a Cable to the Prow, and lifting up the Anchors, I stript myself, put my Cloaths (together with my Coverlet, which I carryed under my Arm) into the Vessel; and drawing it after me, between wading and swimming, arrived at the Royal Port of *Blefuscu*, where the People had long expected me: They lent me two Guides to direct me to the Capital City, which is of the same Name; I held them in my Hands until I came within two Hundred Yards of the Gate; and desired them to signify my Arrival to one of the Secretaries, and let him know, I there waited his Majesty's Commands. I had an Answer in about an Hour, that his Majesty, attended by the Royal Family, and great Officers of the Court, was coming out to receive me. I advanced a Hundred Yards; the Emperor, and his Train, alighted from their Horses, the Empress and Ladies from their Coaches; and I did not perceive they were in any Fright or Concern. I lay on the Ground to kiss his Majesty's and the Empress's Hand. I told his Majesty, that I was come according to my Promise, and with the Licence of the Emperor my Master, to have the Honour of seeing so mighty a Monarch, and to offer him any Service in my Power, consistent with my Duty to my own Prince; not mentioning a Word of my Disgrace, because I had hitherto no regular Information of it, and might suppose myself wholly ignorant of any such Design; neither could I reasonably conceive that the Emperor would discover the Secret while I was out of his Power: Wherein, however, it soon appeared I was deceived.

I shall not trouble the Reader with the particular Account of my Reception at this Court, which was suitable to the Generosity of so great a Prince; nor of the Difficulties I was in for want of a House and Bed, being forced to lie on the Ground, wrapt up in my Coverlet.

CHAPTER EIGHT

THREE Days after my Arrival, walking out of Curiosity to
the North-East Coast of the Island ; I observed, about
half a League off, in the Sea, somewhat that looked like a Boat
overturned : I pulled off my Shoes and Stockings, and wading
two or three Hundred Yards, I found the Object to approach
nearer by Force of the Tide ; and then plainly saw it to be a
real Boat, which I supposed might, by some Tempest, have
been driven from a Ship. Whereupon I returned immediately
towards the City, and desired his Imperial Majesty to lend me
Twenty of the tallest Vessels he had left after the Loss of his
Fleet, and three Thousand Seamen under the Command of
his Vice-Admiral. This Fleet sailed round, while I went back
the shortest Way to the Coast where I first discovered the Boat ;
I found the Tide had driven it still nearer ; the Seamen were
all provided with Cordage, which I had beforehand twisted to
a sufficient Strength. When the Ships came up, I stript myself,
and waded till I came within an Hundred Yards of the Boat ;
after which I was forced to swim till I got up to it. The Seamen
threw me the End of the Cord, which I fastened to a Hole in
the fore-part of the Boat, and the other End to a Man of War :
But I found all my Labour to little Purpose ; for being out of
my Depth, I was not able to work. In this Necessity, I was
forced to swim behind, and push the Boat forwards as often as
I could, with one of my Hands ; and the Tide favouring me,
I advanced so far, that I could just hold up my Chin and feel
the Ground. I rested two or three Minutes, and then gave the
Boat another Shove, and so on till the Sea was no higher than
my Arm-pits. And now the most laborious Part being over,
I took out my other Cables which were stowed in one of the
Ships, and fastening them first to the Boat, and then to nine

of the Vessels which attended me ; the Wind being favourable, the Seamen towed, and I shoved till we arrived within forty Yards of the Shore ; and waiting till the Tide was out, I got dry to the Boat, and by the Assistance of two Thousand Men, with Ropes and Engines, I made a shift to turn it on its Bottom, and found it was but little damaged.

I shall not trouble the Reader with the Difficulties I was under by the Help of certain Paddles, which cost me ten Days making, to get my Boat to the Royal Port of *Blefuscu* ; where a mighty Concourse of People appeared upon my Arrival, full of Wonder at the Sight of so prodigious a Vessel. I told the Emperor, that my good Fortune had thrown this Boat in my Way, to carry me to some Place from whence I might return into my native Country ; and begged his Majesty's Orders for getting Materials to fit it up ; together with his Licence to depart ; which, after some kind Expostulations, he was pleased to grant.

In about a Month when all was prepared, I sent to receive his Majesty's Commands, and to take my leave. The Emperor and Royal Family came out of the Palace ; I lay down on my Face to kiss his Hand, which he very graciously gave me ; so did the Empress, and young Princes of the Blood. His Majesty presented me with fifty Purses of two hundred *Sprugs* a-piece, together with his Picture at full length, which I put immediately into one of my Gloves, to keep it from being hurt. The Ceremonies at my Departure were too many to trouble the Reader with at this time.

I stored the Boat with the Carcasses of an hundred Oxen, and three hundred Sheep, with Bread and Drink proportionable, and as much Meat ready dressed as four hundred Cooks could provide. I took with me six Cows and two Bulls alive, with as many Yews and Rams, intending to carry them into my own Country and propagate the Breed. And to feed them on board, I had a good Bundle of Hay, and a Bag of Corn. I would gladly have taken a Dozen of the Natives ; but this was a thing the Emperor would by no Means permit ; and besides a diligent Search into my Pockets, his Majesty engaged my Honour not to carry away any of his Subjects, although with their own Consent and Desire.

Having thus prepared all things as well as I was able ; I set

ail on the Twenty-fourth Day of *September* 1701, at six in the
Morning; and when I had gone about four Leagues to the
Northward, the Wind being at South-East; at six in the
Evening, I descryed a small Island about half a League to the
North West. I advanced forward, and cast Anchor on the
Lee-side of the Island, which seemed to be uninhabited. I
then took some Refreshment, and went to my Rest. I slept well,
and as I conjecture at least six Hours; for I found the Day
broke in two Hours after I awaked. It was a clear Night; I
at my Breakfast before the Sun was up; and heaving Anchor,
the Wind being favourable, I steered the same Course that I
had done the Day before, wherein I was directed by my Pocket-
Compass. My Intention was to reach, if possible, one of those
Islands, which I had reason to believe lay to the North-East of
Van Diemen's Land. I discovered nothing all that Day; but
upon the next, about three in the Afternoon, when I had by
my Computation made Twenty-four Leagues from *Blefuscu*, I
descryed a Sail steering to the South-East; my Course was
due East. I hailed her, but could get no Answer; yet I found
I gained upon her, for the Wind slackened. I made all the Sail
I could, and in half an Hour she spyed me, then hung out her
Antient, and discharged a Gun. It is not easy to express the
Joy I was in upon the unexpected Hope of once more seeing
my beloved Country, and the dear Pledges I had left in it. The
Ship slackened her Sails, and I came up with her between five
and six in the Evening, *September* 26; but my Heart leapt
within me to see her *English* Colours. I put my Cows and
Sheep into my Coat-Pockets, and got on board with all my
Cargo of Provisions. The Vessel was an *English* Merchant-man,
returning from *Japan* by the *North* and *South Seas*; the
Captain, Mr. *John Biddel* of *Deptford*, a very civil Man, and an
excellent Sailor. We were now in the Latitude of 30 Degrees
South; there were about fifty Men in the Ship; and here I
met an old Comrade of mine, one *Peter Williams*, who gave me
a good Character to the Captain. This Gentleman treated me
with Kindness and desired I would let him know what Place
I came from last, and whither I was bound; which I did in
few Words; but he thought I was raving, and that the Dangers
I underwent had disturbed my Head; whereupon I took my

black Cattle and Sheep out of my Pocket, which, after gre
Astonishment, clearly convinced him of my Veracity. I the
shewed him the Gold given me by the Emperor of *Blefusc*
together with his Majesty's Picture at full Length, and son
other Rarities of that Country. I gave him two Purses of tw
Hundred *Sprugs* each, and promised, when we arrived
England, to make him a Present of a Cow and a Sheep big wit
Young.

We arrived in the *Downs* on the 13th of *April* 1702. I had on
one Misfortune, that the Rats on board carried away one of m
Sheep; I found her Bones in a Hole, picked clean from th
Flesh. The rest of my Cattle I got safe on Shore, and s
them a grazing in a Bowling-green at *Greenwich*, where th
Fineness of the Grass made them feed very heartily, althoug
I had always feared the contrary: Neither could I possibly hav
preserved them in so long a Voyage, if the Captain had n
allowed me some of his best Bisket, which rubbed to Powde
and mingled with Water, was their constant Food. The sho
Time I continued in *England*, I made a considerable Profit b
shewing my Cattle to many Persons of Quality, and others
And before I began my second Voyage, I sold them for s
Hundred Pounds. Since my last Return, I find the Breed
considerably increased, especially the Sheep; which I hop
will prove much to the Advantage of the Woollen Manufactur
by the Fineness of the Fleeces.

I stayed but two Months with my Wife and Family; for m
insatiable Desire of seeing foreign Countries would suffer n
to continue no longer. I left fifteen Hundred Pounds with m
Wife, and fixed her in a good House at *Redriff*. My remainir
Stock I carried with me, Part in Money, and Part in Goods,
Hopes to improve my Fortunes. My eldest Uncle, *John*, ha
left me an Estate in Land, near *Epping*, of about Thirty Pound
a Year; and I had a long Lease of the *Black-Bull* in *Fetter-Lan*
which yielded me as much more: So that I was not in ar
Danger of leaving my Family upon the Parish. My Son *Johnn*
named so after his Uncle, was at the Grammar School, and
towardly Child. My Daughter *Betty* (who is now well marrie
and has Children) was then at her Needle-Work. I took Leav
of my Wife, and Boy and Girl, with Tears on both Sides; an

ent on board the *Adventure*, a Merchant-Ship of three
undred Tons, bound for *Surat*, Captain *John Nicholas* of
verpool, Commander. But my Account of this Voyage must
: referred to the second Part of my Travels.

The End of the First Part

PART TWO

A VOYAGE TO BROBDINGNAG

CHAPTER ONE

A GREAT STORM DESCRIBED. THE LONG BOAT SENT TO FETCH
WATER, THE AUTHOR GOES WITH IT TO DISCOVER THE COUNTRY
HE IS LEFT ON SHOAR, IS SEIZED BY ONE OF THE NATIVES, AND
CARRIED TO A FARMER'S HOUSE. HIS RECEPTION THERE, WITH
SEVERAL ACCIDENTS THAT HAPPENED THERE. A DESCRIPTION OF
THE INHABITANTS.

HAVING been condemned by Nature and Fortune to an
active and restless Life; in two Months after my Return
I again left my Native Country, and took Shipping in the
Downs on the 20th Day of *June* 1702, in the *Adventure*, Cap
John Nicholas, a *Cornish* Man, Commander, bound for *Sura*
We had a very prosperous Gale till we arrived at the *Cape o*
Good-hope, where we landed for fresh Water; but discovering
a Leak we unshipped our Goods, and wintered there; for the
Captain falling sick of an Ague, we could not leave the *Cap*
till the End of *March*. We then set sail, and had a good Voyage
till we passed the *Streights* of *Madagascar*; but having go
Northward of that Island, and to about five Degrees South
Latitude, the Winds, which in those Seas are observed to blow
a constant equal Gale between the North and West, from the
Beginning of *December* to the Beginning of *May*, on the 19th
of *April* began to blow with much greater Violence, and more
Westerly than usual; continuing so for twenty Days together
during which time we were driven a little to the East of the
Molucca Islands, and about three Degrees Northward of the
Line, as our Captain found by an Observation he took the 2
of *May*, at which time the Wind ceased, and it was a perfec
Calm, whereat I was not a little rejoyced. But he being a Man
well experienced in the Navigation of those Seas, bid us all

prepare against a Storm, which accordingly happened the Day
following : For a Southern Wind, called the Southern *Monsoon*,
began to set in.

Finding it was like to overblow, we took in our Spritsail, and
stood by to hand the Fore-sail; but making foul Weather, we
looked the Guns were all fast, and handed the Missen. The
Ship lay very broad off, so we thought it better spooning before
the Sea, than trying or hulling. We reeft the Foresail and set
him, we hawled aft the Foresheet; the Helm was hard a
Weather. The Ship wore bravely. We belay'd the Foredown-
all; but the Sail was split, and we hawl'd down the Yard, and
got the Sail into the Ship, and unbound all the things clear of
t. It was a very fierce Storm; the Sea broke strange and
dangerous. We hawl'd off upon the Lanniard of the Wipstaff,
and helped the Man at Helm. We would not get down our
Top-Mast, but let all stand, because she scudded before the
Sea very well, and we knew that the Top-Mast being aloft, the
Ship was the wholesomer, and made better way through the
Sea, seeing we had Sea room. When the Storm was over, we
set Fore-sail and Main-sail, and brought the Ship too. Then
we set the Missen, Maintop-Sail and the Foretop-Sail. Our
Course was East North-east, the Wind was at South-west. We
got the Star-board Tack aboard, we cast off our Weather-
braces and Lifts; we set in the Lee-braces, and hawl'd forward
by the Weather-bowlings, and hawl'd them tight, and belayed
them, and hawl'd over the Missen Tack to Windward, and kept
her full and by as near as she would lye.

During this Storm, which was followed by a strong Wind
West South-west, we were carried by my Computation about
five hundred Leagues to the East, so that the oldest Sailor on
Board could not tell in what part of the World we were. Our
Provisions held out well, our Ship was staunch, and our Crew
all in good Health; but we lay in the utmost Distress for
Water. We thought it best to hold on the same Course rather
than turn more Northerly, which might have brought us to the
North-west Parts of great *Tartary*, and into the frozen Sea.

On the 16*th* Day of *June* 1703, a Boy on the Top-mast
discovered Land. On the 17*th* we came in full View of a great
Island or Continent, (for we knew not whether) on the South-

C

side whereof was a small Neck of Land jutting out into th
Sea, and a Creek too shallow to hold a Ship of above on
hundred Tuns. We cast Anchor within a League of thi
Creek, and our Captain sent a dozen of his Men well arme
in the Long Boat, with Vessels for Water if any could b
found. I desired his leave to go with them, that I might se
the Country, and make what Discoveries I could. When w
came to Land we saw no River or Spring, nor any Sign c
Inhabitants. Our Men therefore wandered on the Shore t
find out some fresh Water near the Sea, and I walked alon
about a Mile on the other Side, where I observed the Countr
all barren and rocky. I now began to be weary, and seein
nothing to entertain my Curiosity, I returned gently dow
towards the Creek; and the Sea being full in my View, I sa
our Men already got into the Boat, and rowing for Life t
the Ship. I was going to hollow after them, although it ha
been to little purpose, when I observed a huge Creature walkin
after them in the Sea, as fast as he could: He walked not muc
deeper than his Knees, and took prodigious strides: But ou
Men had the start of him half a League, and the Sea thereabout
being full of sharp pointed Rocks, the Monster was not abl
to overtake the Boat. This I was afterwards told, for I durs
not stay to see the Issue of that Adventure; but ran as fast as
could the Way I first went; and then climbed up a steep Hil
which gave me some Prospect of the Country. I found it full
cultivated; but that which first surprized me was the Lengt
of the Grass, which in those Grounds that seemed to be kep
for Hay, was above twenty Foot high.

I fell into a high Road, for so I took it to be, although i
served to the Inhabitants only as a foot Path through a Fiel
of Barley. Here I walked on for some time, but could see littl
on either Side, it being now near Harvest, and the Corn risin
at least Forty Foot. I was an Hour walking to the end of thi
Field; which was fenced in with a Hedge of at least on
hundred and twenty Foot high, and the Trees so lofty that
could make no Computation of their Altitude. There was
Stile to pass from this Field into the next: It had four Steps
and a Stone to cross over when you came to the utmost. It wa
impossible for me to climb this Stile, because every Step wa

ix Foot high, and the upper Stone above twenty. I was endeavouring to find some Gap in the Hedge; when I discovered
one of the Inhabitants in the next Field advancing towards the
Stile, of the same Size with him whom I saw in the Sea pursuing
our Boat. He appeared as Tall as an ordinary Spire-steeple;
and took about ten Yards at every Stride, as near as I could
guess. I was struck with the utmost Fear and Astonishment,
and ran to hide my self in the Corn, from whence I saw him
at the Top of the Stile, looking back into the next Field on the
right Hand; and heard him call in a Voice many Degrees
louder than a speaking Trumpet; but the Noise was so High in
the Air, that at first I certainly thought it was Thunder. Whereupon seven Monsters like himself came towards him with
Reaping-Hooks in their Hands, each Hook about the largeness
of six Scythes. These People were not so well clad as the first,
whose Servants or Labourers they seemed to be. For, upon
some Words he spoke, they went to reap the Corn in the Field
where I lay. I kept from them at as great a Distance as I could,
but was forced to move with extream Difficulty; for the Stalks
of the Corn were sometimes not above a Foot distant, so that
I could hardly squeeze my Body betwixt them. However, I
made a shift to go forward till I came to a part of the Field
where the Corn had been laid by the Rain and Wind: Here
it was impossible for me to advance a step; for the Stalks were
so interwoven that I could not creep through, and the Beards
of the fallen Ears so strong and pointed, that they pierced
through my Cloaths into my Flesh. At the same time I heard
the Reapers not above an hundred Yards behind me. Being
quite dispirited with Toil, and wholly overcome by Grief and
Despair, I lay down between two Ridges, and heartily wished
I might there end my Days. I bemoaned my desolate Widow,
and Fatherless Children: I lamented my own Folly and
Wilfulness in attempting a second Voyage against the Advice
of all my Friends and Relations. In this terrible Agitation of
Mind I could not forbear thinking of *Lilliput*, whose Inhabitants
looked upon me as the greatest Prodigy that ever appeared in
the World; where I was able to draw an Imperial Fleet in my
Hand, and perform those other Actions which will be recorded
for ever in the Chronicles of that Empire, while Posterity shall

hardly believe them, although attested by Millions. I reflected
what a Mortification it must prove to me to appear as in-
considerable in this Nation, as one single *Lilliputian* would be
among us. But, this I conceived was to be the least of my
Misfortunes : For, as human Creatures are observed to be
more Savage and cruel in Proportion to their Bulk ; what could
I expect but to be a Morsel in the Mouth of the first among
these enormous Barbarians who should happen to seize me ?
Undoubtedly Philosophers are in the Right when they tell us,
that nothing is great or little otherwise than by Comparison :
It might have pleased Fortune to let the *Lilliputians* find some
Nation, where the People were as diminutive with respect to
them, as they were to me. And who knows but that even this
prodigious Race of Mortals might be equally overmatched in
some distant Part of the World, whereof we have yet no Discovery ?

Scared and confounded as I was, I could not forbear going
on with these Reflections ; when one of the Reapers approaching
within ten Yards of the Ridge where I lay, made me apprehend
that with the next Step I should be squashed to Death under
his Foot, or cut in two with his Reaping Hook. And therefore
when he was again about to move, I screamed as loud as Fear
could make me. Whereupon the huge Creature trod short,
and looking round about under him for some time, at last
espied me as I lay on the Ground. He considered a while with
the Caution of one who endeavours to lay hold on a small
dangerous Animal in such a Manner that it shall not be able
either to scratch or to bite him ; as I my self have sometimes
done with a *Weasel* in *England*. At length he ventured to take
me up behind by the middle between his Fore-finger and
Thumb, and brought me within three Yards of his Eyes, that
he might behold my Shape more perfectly. I guessed his
Meaning ; and my good Fortune gave me so much Presence
of Mind, that I resolved not to struggle in the least as he held
me in the Air above sixty Foot from the Ground ; although he
grievously pinched my Sides, for fear I should slip through
his Fingers. All I ventured was to raise my Eyes towards the
Sun, and place my Hands together in a supplicating Posture,
and to speak some Words in an humble melancholy Tone,

suitable to the Condition I then was in. For, I apprehended every Moment that he would dash me against the Ground, as we usually do any little hateful Animal which we have a Mind to destroy. But my good Star would have it, that he appeared pleased with my Voice and Gestures, and began to look upon me as a Curiosity; much wondering to hear me pronounce articulate Words, although he could not understand them. In the mean time I was not able to forbear Groaning and shedding Tears, and turning my Head towards my Sides; letting him know, as well as I could, how cruelly I was hurt by the Pressure of his Thumb and Finger. He seemed to apprehend my Meaning; for, lifting up the Lappet of his Coat, he put me gently into it, and immediately ran along with me to his Master, who was a substantial Farmer, and the same Person I had first seen in the Field.

The Farmer having (as I supposed by their Talk) received such an Account of me as his Servant could give him, took a piece of a small Straw, about the Size of a walking Staff, and therewith lifted up the Lappets of my Coat; which it seems he thought to be some kind of Covering that Nature had given me. He blew my Hairs aside to take a better View of my Face. He called his Hinds about him, and asked them (as I afterwards learned) whether they had ever seen in the Fields any little Creature that resembled me. He then placed me softly on the Ground upon all four; but I got immediately up, and walked slowly backwards and forwards, to let those People see I had no Intent to run away. They all sate down in a Circle about me, the better to observe my Motions. I pulled off my Hat, and made a low Bow towards the Farmer: I fell on my Knees, and lifted up my Hands and Eyes, and spoke several Words as loud as I could: I took a Purse of Gold out of my Pocket, and humbly presented it to him. He received it on the Palm of his Hand, then applied it close to his Eye, to see what it was, and afterwards turned it several times with the Point of a Pin, (which he took out of his Sleeve,) but could make nothing of it. Whereupon I made a Sign that he should place his Hand on the Ground: I then took the Purse, and opening it, poured all the Gold into his Palm. There were six *Spanish-Pieces* of four Pistoles each, besides twenty or thirty smaller

Coins. I saw him wet the Tip of his little Finger upon his Tongue, and take up one of my largest Pieces, and then another; but he seemed to be wholly ignorant what they were. He made me a Sign to put them again into my Purse, and the Purse again into my Pocket; which after offering to him several times, I thought it best to do.

The Farmer by this time was convinced I must be a rational Creature. He spoke often to me, but the Sound of his Voice pierced my Ears like that of a Water-Mill; yet his Words were articulate enough. I answered as loud as I could in several Languages; and he often laid his Ear within two Yards of me, but all in vain, for we were wholly unintelligible to each other. He then sent his Servants to their Work, and taking his Handkerchief out of his Pocket, he doubled and spread it on his Hand, which he placed flat on the Ground, with the Palm upwards, making me a Sign to step into it, as I could easily do, for it was not above a Foot in thickness. I thought it my part to obey; and for fear of falling, laid my self at full Length upon the Handkerchief, with the Remainder of which he lapped me up to the Head for further Security; and in this Manner carried me home to his House. There he called his Wife, and shewed me to her; but she screamed and ran back as Women in *England* do at the Sight of a Toad or a Spider. However, when she had a while seen my Behaviour, and how well I observed the Signs her Husband made, she was soon reconciled, and by Degrees grew extreamly tender of me.

It was about twelve at Noon, and a Servant brought in Dinner. It was only one substantial Dish of Meat (fit for the plain Condition of an Husband-Man) in a Dish of about four and twenty Foot Diameter. The Company were the Farmer and Wife, three Children, and an old Grandmother: When they were sat down, the Farmer placed me at some Distance from him on the Table, which was thirty Foot high from the Floor. I was in a terrible Fright, and kept as far as I could from the Edge, for fear of falling. The Wife minced a bit of Meat, then crumbled some Bread on a Trencher, and placed it before me. I made her a low Bow, took out my Knife and Fork, and fell to eat; which gave them exceeding Delight. The Mistress sent her Maid for a small Dram-cup, which held

about two Gallons; and filled it with Drink: I took up the
Vessel with much Difficulty in both Hands, and in a most
respectful Manner drank to her Lady-ship's Health, expressing
the Words as loud as I could in *English*; which made the
Company laugh so heartily, that I was almost deafened with
the Noise. This Liquour tasted like a small Cyder, and was not
unpleasant. Then the Master made me a Sign to come to his
Trencher side; but as I walked on the Table, being in great
surprize all the time, as the indulgent Reader will easily conceive and excuse, I happened to stumble against a Crust, and
fell flat on my Face, but received no hurt. I got up immediately,
and observing the good People to be in much Concern, I took
my Hat (which I held under my Arm out of good Manners)
and waving it over my Head, made three Huzza's, to shew I
had got no Mischief by the Fall. But advancing forwards
towards my Master (as I shall henceforth call him) his youngest
Son who sate next him, an arch Boy of about ten Years old,
took me up by the Legs, and held me so high in the Air, that
I trembled every Limb; but his Father snatched me from
him; and at the same time gave him such a Box on the left
Ear, as would have felled an *European* Troop of Horse to the
Earth; ordering him to be taken from the Table. But, being
afraid the Boy might owe me a Spight; and well remembering
how mischievous all Children among us naturally are to
Sparrows, Rabbits, young Kittens, and Puppy-Dogs; I fell
on my Knees, and pointing to the Boy, made my Master
understand, as well as I could, that I desired his Son might be
pardoned. The Father complied, and the Lad took his Seat
again; whereupon I went to him and kissed his Hand, which
my Master took, and made him stroak me gently with it.

In the Midst of Dinner my Mistress's favourite Cat leapt
into her Lap. I heard a Noise behind me like that of a Dozen
Stocking-Weavers at work; and turning my Head, I found it
proceeded from the Purring of this Animal, who seemed to be
three Times larger than an Ox, as I computed by the View of
her Head, and one of her Paws, while her Mistress was feeding
and stroaking her. The Fierceness of this Creature's Countenance altogether discomposed me; although I stood at the
further End of the Table, above fifty Foot off; and although my

Mistress held her fast for fear she might give a Spring, and seize me in her Talons. But it happened there was no Danger; for the Cat took not the least Notice of me when my Master placed me within three Yards of her. And as I have been always told, and found true by Experience in my Travels, that flying, or discovering Fear before a fierce Animal, is a certain Way to make it pursue or attack you; so I resolved in this dangerous Juncture to shew no Manner of Concern. I walked with Intrepidity five or six Times before the very Head of the Cat, and came within half a Yard of her; whereupon she drew her self back, as if she were more afraid of me: I had less Apprehension concerning the Dogs, whereof three or four came into the Room, as it is usual in Farmers Houses; one of which was a Mastiff equal in Bulk to four Elephants, and a Grey-hound somewhat taller than the Mastiff, but not so large.

When Dinner was almost done, the Nurse came in with a Child of a Year old in her Arms; who immediately spyed me, and began a Squall that you might have heard from *London-Bridge* to *Chelsea*; after the usual Oratory of Infants, to get me for a Play-thing. The Mother out of pure Indulgence took me up, and put me towards the Child, who presently seized me by the Middle, and got my Head in his Mouth, where I roared so loud that the Urchin was frighted, and let me drop; and I should infallibly have broke my Neck, if the Mother had not held her Apron under me.

When the Dinner was done, my Master went out to his Labourers; and as I could discover by his Voice and Gesture, gave his Wife a strict Charge to take Care of me. I was very much tired and disposed to sleep, which my Mistress perceiving, she put me on her own Bed, and covered me with a clean white Handkerchief, but larger and coarser than the Main Sail of a Man of War.

I slept about two Hours, and dreamed I was at home with my Wife and Children, which aggravated my Sorrows when I awaked and found my self alone in a vast Room, between two and three Hundred Foot wide, and above two Hundred high; lying in a Bed twenty Yards wide. My Mistress was gone about her household Affairs, and had locked me in. The Bed was eight Yards from the Floor. I durst not presume to call, and if I

ad, it would have been in vain with such a Voice as mine at so
reat a Distance from the Room where I lay, to the Kitchen
here the Family kept. While I was under these Circumstances,
wo Rats crept up the Curtains, and ran smelling backwards and
orwards on the Bed: One of them came up almost to my Face;
hereupon I rose in a Fright, and drew out my Hanger to
efend my self. These horrible Animals had the Boldness to
ttack me on both Sides, and one of them held his Fore-feet
t my Collar; but I had the good Fortune to rip up his Belly
efore he could do me any Mischief. He fell down at my Feet;
nd the other seeing the Fate of his Comrade, made his Escape,
ut not without one good Wound on the Back, which I gave
im as he fled, and made the Blood run trickling from him.
fter this Exploit I walked gently to and fro on the Bed, to
ecover my Breath and Loss of Spirits. These Creatures were
f the Size of a large Mastiff, but infinitely more nimble and
erce; so that if I had taken off my Belt before I went to sleep,
 must have infallibly been torn to Pieces and devoured. I
easured the Tail of the dead Rat, and found it to be two
ards long, wanting an Inch; but it went against my Stomach
 drag the Carcass off the Bed, where it lay still bleeding; I
bserved it had yet some Life, but with a strong Slash cross
e Neck, I thoroughly dispatched it.

Soon after, my Mistress came into the Room, who seeing me
l bloody, ran and took me up in her Hand. I pointed to the
ead *Rat*, smiling and making other Signs to shew I was not
urt; whereat she was extremely rejoyced, calling the Maid to
ke up the dead *Rat* with a Pair of Tongs, and throw it out of
e Window. Then she set me on a Table, where I shewed her
y Hanger all bloody, and wiping it on the Lappet of my Coat,
eturned it to the Scabbard.

CHAPTER TWO

My Mistress had a Daughter of nine Years old, a Chil
of towardly Parts for her Age, very dextrous at h
Needle, and skilful in dressing her Baby. Her Mother ar
she contrived to fit up the Baby's Cradle for me against Nigh
The Cradle was put into a small Drawer of a Cabinet, and th
Drawer placed upon a hanging Shelf for fear of the Ra
This was my Bed all the Time I stayed with those Peopl
although made more convenient by Degrees, as I began to lea
their Language, and make my Wants known. This young Gi
was so handy, that after I had once or twice pulled off n
Cloaths before her, she was able to dress and undress m
although I never gave her that Trouble when she would let n
do either my self. She made me seven Shirts, and some oth
Linnen of as fine Cloth as could be got, which indeed w
coarser than Sackcloth ; and these she constantly washed f
me with her own Hands. She was likewise my School-Mistre
to teach me the Language : When I pointed to any thing, sh
told me the Name of it in her own Tongue, so that in a fe
Days I was able to call for whatever I had a mind to. She w
very good natured, and not above forty Foot high, being litt
for her Age. She gave me the Name of *Grildrig*, which th
Family took up, and afterwards the whole Kingdom. Th
Word imports what the *Latins* call *Nanunculus*, the *Italia*
Homunceletino, and the *English Mannikin*. To her I chie
owe my Preservation in that Country : We never parted whi
I was there ; I called her my *Glumdalclitch*, or little Nurs
And I should be guilty of great Ingratitude if I omitted th
honourable Mention of her Care and Affection towards m
which I heartily wish it lay in my Power to requite as sh

74

deserves, instead of being the innocent but unhappy Instrument of her Disgrace, as I have too much Reason to fear.

It now began to be known and talked of in the Neighbourhood, that my Master had found a strange Animal in the Fields, about the Bigness of a *Splacknuck*, but exactly shaped in every Part like a human Creature ; which it likewise imitated in all its Actions ; seemed to speak in a little Language of its own, had already learned several Words of theirs, went erect upon two Legs, was tame and gentle, would come when it was called, do whatever it was bid, had the finest Limbs in the World, and a Complexion fairer than a Nobleman's Daughter of three Years old. Another Farmer who lived hard by, and was a particular Friend of my Master, came on a Visit on Purpose to inquire into the Truth of this Story. I was immediately produced, and placed upon a Table ; where I walked as I was commanded, drew my Hanger, put it up again, made my Reverence to my Master's Guest, asked him in his own Language how he did, and told him he was welcome ; just as my little Nurse had instructed me. This Man, who was old and dim-sighted, put on his Spectacles to behold me better, at which I could not forbear laughing very heartily ; for his Eyes appeared like the Full-Moon shining into a Chamber at two Windows. Our People, who discovered the Cause of my Mirth, bore me Company in Laughing ; at which the old Fellow was Fool enough to be angry and out of Countenance. He had the Character of a great Miser ; and to my Misfortune he well deserved it by the cursed Advice he gave my Master, to shew me as a Sight upon a Market-Day in the next Town, which was half an Hour's Riding, about two and twenty Miles from our House. I guessed there was some Mischief contriving, when I observed my Master and his Friend whispering long together, sometimes pointing at me ; and my Fears made me fancy that I overheard and undertood some of their Words. But, the next Morning *Glumdalclitch* my little Nurse told me the whole Matter, which she had cunningly picked out from her Mother. The poor Girl laid me on her Bosom, and fell a weeping with Shame and Grief. She apprehended some Mischief would happen to me from rude vulgar Folks, who might squeeze me to Death, or break one of my Limbs by taking me in their

Hands. She had also observed how modest I was in my Nature
how nicely I regarded my Honour; and what an Indignity I
should conceive it to be exposed for Money as a publick
Spectacle to the meanest of the People. She said, her *Papa*
and *Mamma* had promised that *Grildrig* should be hers; but
now she found they meant to serve her as they did last Year
when they pretended to give her a Lamb; and yet, as soon as
it was fat, sold it to a Butcher. For my own Part, I may truly
affirm that I was less concerned than my Nurse. I had a strong
Hope which never left me, that I should one Day recover my
Liberty.

My Master, pursuant of the Advice of his Friend, carried me
in a Box the next Market-Day to the neighbouring Town; and
took along with him his little Daughter my Nurse upon a
Pillion behind me. The Box was close on every Side, with a
little Door for me to go in and out, and a few Gimlet-holes to
let in Air. The Girl had been so careful to put the Quilt of her
Baby's Bed into it, for me to lye down on. However, I was
terribly shaken and discomposed in this Journey, although it
were but of half an Hour. For the Horse went about forty
Foot at every Step; and trotted so high, that the Agitation was
equal to the rising and falling of a Ship in a great Storm, but
much more frequent: Our Journey was somewhat further than
from *London* to St. *Albans*. My Master alighted at an Inn
which he used to frequent; and after consulting a while with
the Inn-keeper, and making some necessary Preparations, he
hired the *Grultrud*, or Cryer, to give Notice through the Town
of a strange Creature to be seen at the Sign of the Green *Eagle*,
not so big as a *Splacknuck*, (an Animal in that Country very
finely shaped, about six Foot long) and in every Part of the
Body resembling an human Creature; could speak several
Words, and perform an Hundred diverting Tricks.

I was placed upon a Table in the largest Room of the Inn,
which might be near three Hundred Foot square. My little
Nurse stood on a low Stool close to the Table, to take care of
me, and direct what I should do. My Master, to avoid a Croud,
would suffer only Thirty People at a Time to see me. I walked
about on the Table as the Girl commanded; she asked me
Questions as far as she knew my Understanding of the Language

reached, and I answered them as loud as I could. I turned about several Times to the Company, paid my humble Respects, said they were welcome; and used some other Speeches I had been taught. I took up a Thimble filled with Liquor, which *Glumdalclitch* had given me for a Cup, and drank their Health. I drew out my Hanger, and flourished with it after the Manner of Fencers in *England*. My Nurse gave me Part of a Straw, which I exercised as a Pike, having learned the Art in my Youth. I was that Day shewn to twelve Sets of Company; and as often forced to go over again with the same Fopperies, till I was half dead with Weariness and Vexation. For, those who had seen me, made such wonderful Reports, that the People were ready to break down the Doors to come in. My Master for his own Interest would not suffer any one to touch me, except my Nurse; and, to prevent Danger, Benches were set round the Table at such a Distance, as put me out of every Body's Reach. However, an unlucky School-Boy aimed a Hazel-Nut directly at my Head, which very narrowly missed me; otherwise, it came with so much Violence, that it would have infallibly knocked out my Brains; for it was almost as large as a small Pumpion: But I had the Satisfaction to see the young Rogue well beaten, and turned out of the Room.

My Master gave publick Notice, that he would shew me again the next Market-Day: And in the mean time, he prepared a more convenient Vehicle for me, which he had Reason enough to do; for I was so tired with my first Journey, and with entertaining Company eight Hours together, that I could hardly stand upon my Legs, or speak a Word. It was at least three Days before I recovered my Strength; and that I might have no rest at home, all the neighbouring Gentlemen from an Hundred Miles round, hearing of my Fame, came to see me at my Master's own House. There could not be fewer than thirty Persons with their Wives and Children; (for the Country is very populous;) and my Master demanded the Rate of a full Room whenever he shewed me at Home, although it were only to a single Family. So that for some time I had but little Ease every Day of the Week, (except *Wednesday*, which is their Sabbath) although I were not carried to the Town.

My Master finding how profitable I was like to be, resolved

to carry me to the most considerable Cities of the Kingdom. Having therefore provided himself with all things necessary for a long Journey, and settled his Affairs at Home; he took Leave of his Wife; and upon the 17th of *August* 1703, about two Months after my Arrival, we set out for the Metropolis, situated near the Middle of that Empire, and about three Thousand Miles distance from our House: My Master made his Daughter *Glumdalclitch* ride behind him. She carried me on her Lap in a Box tied about her Waist. The Girl had lined it on all Sides with the softest Cloth she could get, well quilted underneath; furnished it with her Baby's Bed, provided me with Linnen and other Necessaries; and made every thing as convenient as she could. We had no other Company but a Boy of the House, who rode after us with the Luggage.

My Master's Design was to shew me in all the Towns by the Way, and to step out of the Road for Fifty or an Hundred Miles, to any Village or Person of Quality's House where he might expect Custom. We made easy Journies of not above seven or eight Score Miles a Day: For *Glumdalclitch*, on Purpose to spare me, complained she was tired with the trotting of the Horse. She often took me out of my Box at my own Desire, to give me Air, and shew me the Country; but always held me fast by Leading-strings. We passed over five or six Rivers many Degrees broader and deeper than the *Nile* or the *Ganges*; and there was hardly a Rivulet so small as the *Thames* at *London-Bridge*. We were ten Weeks in our Journey; and I was shewn in Eighteen large Towns, besides many Villages and private Families.

On the 26th Day of *October*, we arrived at the Metropolis, called in their Language *Lorbrulgrud*, or *Pride of the Universe*. My Master took a Lodging in the principal Street of the City, not far from the Royal Palace; and put out Bills in the usual Form, containing an exact Description of my Person and Parts. I was shewn ten Times a Day to the Wonder and Satisfaction of all People. I could now speak the Language tolerably well; and perfectly understood every Word that was spoken to me. Besides, I had learned their Alphabet, and could make a shift to explain a Sentence here and there; for *Glumdalclitch* had been my Instructer while we were at home, and at leisure

Hours during our Journey. She carried a little Book in her Pocket, not much larger than a *Sanson's Atlas*; it was a common Treatise for the use of young Girls, giving a short Account of their Religion; out of this she taught me my Letters, and interpreted the Words.

CHAPTER THREE

THE AUTHOR SENT FOR TO COURT. THE QUEEN BUYS HIM OF HIS MASTER THE FARMER, AND PRESENTS HIM TO THE KING. HE DISPUTES WITH HIS MAJESTY'S GREAT SCHOLARS. AN APARTMENT AT COURT PROVIDED FOR THE AUTHOR. HE IS IN HIGH FAVOUR WITH THE QUEEN. HIS QUARRELS WITH THE QUEEN'S DWARF.

THE frequent Labours I underwent every Day, made in a few Weeks a very considerable Change in my Health: The more my Master got by me, the more unsatiable he grew. I had quite lost my Stomach, and was almost reduced to a Skeleton. The Farmer observed it; and concluding I soon must die, resolved to make as good a Hand of me as he could. While he was thus reasoning and resolving with himself; a *Slardral*, or Gentleman Usher, came from Court, commanding my Master to bring me immediately thither for the Diversion of the Queen and her Ladies. Some of the latter had already been to see me; and reported strange Things of my Beauty, Behaviour, and good Sense. Her Majesty and those who attended her, were beyond Measure delighted with my Demeanor. I fell on my Knees, and begged the Honour of kissing her Imperial Foot; but this Gracious Princess held out her little Finger towards me (after I was set on a Table) which I embraced in both my Arms, and put the Tip of it, with the utmost Respect, to my Lip. She made me some general Questions about my Country and my Travels, which I answered as distinctly and in as few Words as I could. She asked, whether I would be content to live at Court. I bowed down to the Board of the Table, and humbly answered, that I was my

Master's Slave; but if I were at my own Disposal, I should be proud to devote my Life to her Majesty's Service. She then asked my Master whether he were willing to sell me at a good Price. He, who apprehended I could not live a Month, was ready enough to part with me; and demanded a Thousand Pieces of Gold; which were ordered him on the Spot, each Piece being about the Bigness of eight Hundred Moydores: But, allowing for the Proportion of all Things between that Country and *Europe*, and the high Price of Gold among them; was hardly so great a Sum as a Thousand Guineas would be in *England*. I then said to the Queen; since I was now her Majesty's most humble Creature and Vassal, I must beg the Favour, that *Glumdalclitch*, who had always tended me with so much Care and Kindness, and understood to do it so well, might be admitted into her Service, and continue to be my Nurse and Instructor. Her Majesty agreed to my Petition; and easily got the Farmer's Consent, who was glad enough to have his Daughter preferred at Court: And the poor Girl herself was not able to hide her Joy. My late Master withdrew, bidding me farewell, and saying he had left me in a good Service; to which I replyed not a Word, only making him a slight Bow.

The Queen observed my Coldness; and when the Farmer was gone out of the Apartment, asked me the Reason. I made bold to tell her Majesty, that I owed no other Obligation to my late Master, than his not dashing out the Brains of a poor harmless Creature found by Chance in his Field; which Obligation was amply recompenced by the Gain he had made in shewing me through half the Kingdom, and the Price he had now sold me for. That the Life I had since led, was laborious enough to kill an Animal of ten Times my Strength. That my Health was much impaired by the continual Drudgery of entertaining the Rabble every Hour of the Day; and that if my Master had not thought my Life in Danger, her Majesty perhaps would not have got so cheap a Bargain. But as I was out of all fear of being ill treated under the Protection of so great and good an Empress, the Ornament of Nature, the Darling of the World, the Delight of her Subjects, the Phoenix of the Creation; so, I hoped my late Master's Apprehensions would appear to be groundless ; for I already found my Spirits to revive by the Influence of her most August Presence.

The Queen giving great Allowance for my Defectiveness in speaking, was however surprised at so much Wit and good Sense in so diminutive an Animal. She took me in her own Hand, and carried me to the King, who was then retired to his Cabinet. His Majesty, a Prince of much Gravity, and austere Countenance, not well observing my Shape at first View, asked the Queen after a cold Manner, how long it was since she grew fond of a *Splacknuck* ; for such it seems he took me to be, as I lay upon my Breast in her Majesty's right Hand. But this Princess, who hath an infinite deal of Wit and Humour, set me gently on my Feet upon the Scrutore ; and commanded me to give His Majesty an Account of my self, which I did in a very few Words ; and *Glumdalclitch*, who attended at the Cabinet Door, and could not endure I should be out of her Sight, being admitted ; confirmed all that had passed from my Arrival at her Father's House.

The King, although he be as learned a Person as any in his Dominions ; and had been educated in the Study of Philosophy, and particularly Mathematicks ; yet when he observed my Shape exactly, and saw me walk erect, before I began to speak, conceived I might be a piece of Clockwork, (which is in that Country arrived to a very great Perfection) contrived by some ingenious Artist. But, when he heard my Voice, and found what I delivered to be regular and rational, he could not conceal his Astonishment. He was by no means satisfied with the Relation I gave him of the Manner I came into his Kingdom ; but thought it a Story concerted between *Glumdalclitch* and her Father, who had taught me a Sett of Words to make me sell at a higher Price. Upon this Imagination he put several other Questions to me, and still received rational Answers, no otherwise defective than by a Foreign Accent, and an imperfect Knowledge in the Language ; with some rustick Phrases which I had learned at the Farmer's House, and did not suit the polite Style of a Court.

I applied my self to the King, and assured His Majesty, that I came from a Country which abounded with several Millions of both Sexes, and of my own Stature ; where the Animals,

Trees, and Houses were all in Proportion; and where by
Consequence I might be as able to defend my self, and to find
Sustenance, as any of his Majesty's Subjects could do here.
To this they only replied with a Smile of Contempt; saying,
that the Farmer had instructed me very well in my Lesson. The
King, who had a much better Understanding, dismissing his
learned Men, sent for the Farmer, who by good Fortune was
not yet gone out of Town: Having therefore first examined
him privately, and then confronted him with me and the
young Girl; his Majesty began to think that what we told him
might possibly be true. He desired the Queen to order, that
a particular Care should be taken of me; and was of Opinion,
that *Glumdalclitch* should still continue in her Office of tending
me, because he observed we had a great Affection for each
other. A convenient Apartment was provided for her at Court;
she had a sort of Governess appointed to take care of her
Education, a Maid to dress her, and two other Servants for
menial Offices; but, the Care of me was wholly appropriated
to her self. The Queen commanded her own Cabinet-maker
to contrive a Box that might serve me for a Bed-chamber, after
the Model that *Glumdalclitch* and I should agree upon. This
Man was a most ingenious Artist; and according to my
Directions, in three Weeks finished for me a wooden Chamber
of sixteen Foot square, and twelve High; with Sash Windows,
a Door, and two Closets, like a *London* Bed-chamber. The
Board that made the Cieling was to be lifted up and down by
two Hinges, to put in a Bed ready furnished by her Majesty's
Upholsterer; which *Glumdalclitch* took out every Day to air,
made it with her own Hands, and letting it down at Night,
locked up the Roof over me. A Nice Workman, who was
famous for little Curiosities, undertook to make me two Chairs,
with Backs and Frames, of a Substance not unlike Ivory; and
two Tables, with a Cabinet to put my Things in. The Room
was quilted on all Sides, as well as the Floor and the Cieling,
to prevent any Accident from the Carelessness of those who
carried me; and to break the Force of a Jolt when I went
in a Coach. I desired a Lock for my Door to prevent Rats and
Mice from coming in: The Smith after several Attempts made
the smallest that ever was seen among them; for I have known

a larger at the Gate of a Gentleman's House in *England*. I made a shift to keep the Key in a Pocket of my own, fearing *Glumdalclitch* might lose it. The Queen likewise ordered the thinnest Silks that could be gotten, to make me Cloaths ; not much thicker than an *English* Blanket, very cumbersome till I was accustomed to them. They were after the Fashion of the Kingdom, partly resembling the *Persian*, and partly the *Chinese* ; and are a very grave decent Habit.

The Queen became so fond of my Company, that she could not dine without me. I had a Table placed upon the same at which her Majesty eat, just at her left Elbow ; and a Chair to sit on. *Glumdalclitch* stood upon a Stool on the Floor, near my Table, to assist and take Care of me. I had an entire set of Silver Dishes and Plates, and other Necessaries, which in Proportion to those of the Queen, were not much bigger than what I have seen in a *London* Toy-shop, for the Furniture of a Baby-house : These my little Nurse kept in her Pocket, in a Silver Box, and gave me at Meals as I wanted them ; always cleaning them her self. No Person dined with the Queen but the two Princesses Royal ; the elder sixteen Years old, and the younger at that time thirteen and a Month. Her Majesty used to put a Bit of Meat upon one of my Dishes, out of which I carved for my self ; and her Diversion was to see me eat in Miniature. For the Queen (who had indeed but a weak Stomach) took up at one Mouthful, as much as a dozen *English* Farmers could eat at a Meal, which to me was for some time a very nauseous Sight. She would craunch the Wing of a Lark, Bones and all, between her Teeth, although it were nine Times as large as that of a full grown Turkey ; and put a Bit of Bread in her Mouth, as big as two twelve-penny Loaves. She drank out of a Golden Cup, above a Hogshead at a Draught. Her Knives were twice as long as a Scythe set strait upon the Handle. The Spoons, Forks, and other Instruments were all in the same Proportion. I remember when *Glumdalclitch* carried me out of Curiosity to see some of the Tables at Court, where ten or a dozen of these enormous Knives and Forks were lifted up together ; I thought I had never till then beheld so terrible a Sight.

Nothing angered and mortified me so much as the Queen's

Dwarf, who being of the lowest Stature that was ever in that Country, (for I verily think he was not full Thirty Foot high) became so insolent at seeing a Creature so much beneath him, that he would always affect to swagger and look big as he passed by me in the Queen's Antichamber, while I was standing on some Table talking with the Lords or Ladies of the Court; and he seldom failed of a smart Word or two upon my Littleness; against which I could only revenge my self by calling him *Brother*, challenging him to wrestle; and such Repartees as are usual in the Mouths of *Court Pages*. One Day at Dinner, this malicious little Cubb was so nettled with something I had said to him, that raising himself upon the Frame of her Majesty's Chair, he took me up by the Middle, as I was sitting down, not thinking any Harm, and let me drop into a large Silver Bowl of Cream; and then ran away as fast as he could. I fell over Head and Ears, and if I had not been a good Swimmer, it might have gone very hard with me; for *Glumdalclitch* in that Instant happened to be at the other End of the Room; and the Queen was in such a Fright, that she wanted Presence of Mind to assist me. But my little Nurse ran to my Relief; and took me out, after I had swallowed above a Quart of Cream. I was put to Bed; however I received no other Damage than the Loss of a Suit of Cloaths, which was utterly spoiled. The Dwarf was soundly whipped, and as a further Punishment, forced to drink up the Bowl of Cream, into which he had thrown me; neither was he ever restored to Favour: For, soon after the Queen bestowed him to a Lady of high Quality; so that I saw him no more, to my very great Satisfaction; for I could not tell to what Extremitys such a malicious Urchin might have carried his Resentment.

He had before served me a scurvy Trick, which set the Queen a laughing, although at the same time she were heartily vexed, and would have immediately cashiered him, if I had not been so generous as to intercede. Her Majesty had taken a Marrow-bone upon her Plate; and after knocking out the Marrow, placed the Bone again in the Dish erect as it stood before; the Dwarf watching his Opportunity, while *Glumdalclitch* was gone to the Side-board, mounted the Stool that she stood on to take care of me at Meals; took me up in both

Hands, and squeezing my Legs together, wedged them into the Marrow-bone above my Waist; where I stuck for some time, and made a very ridiculous Figure. I believe it was near a Minute before any one knew what was become of me; for I thought it below me to cry out. But, as Princes seldom get their Meat hot, my Legs were not scalded, only my Stockings and Breeches in a sad Condition. The Dwarf at my Entreaty had no other Punishment than a sound whipping.

I was frequently raillied by the Queen upon Account of my Fearfulness; and she used to ask me whether the People of my Country were as great Cowards as my self. The Occasion was this. The Kingdom is much pestered with Flies in Summer; and these odious Insects, each of them as big as a *Dunstable* Lark, hardly gave me any Rest while I sat at Dinner, with their continual Humming and Buzzing about my Ears. I had much ado to defend my self against these detestable Animals, and could not forbear starting when they came on my Face. It was the common Practice of the Dwarf to catch a Number of these Insects in his Hand, as School-boys do among us, and let them out suddenly under my Nose, on Purpose to frighten me, and divert the Queen. My Remedy was to cut them in Pieces with my Knife as they flew in the Air; wherein my Dexterity was much admired.

I remember one Morning when *Glumdalclitch* had set me in my Box upon a Window, as she usually did in fair Days to give me Air, (for I durst not venture to let the Box be hung on a Nail out of the Window, as we do with Cages in *England*) after I had lifted up one of my Sashes, and sat down at my Table to eat a Piece of Sweet-Cake for my Breakfast; above twenty Wasps, allured by the Smell, came flying into the Room, humming louder than the Drones of as many Bagpipes. Some of them seized my Cake, and carried it piecemeal away; others flew about my Head and Face, confounding me with the Noise, and putting me in the utmost Terror of their Stings. However I had the Courage to rise and draw my Hanger, and attack them in the Air. I dispatched four of them, but the rest got away; and I presently shut my Window. These Insects were as large as Partridges; I took out their Stings, found them an Inch and a half long, and as sharp as Needles. I carefully preserved them all, and having since shewn them with some other Curiosities in several Parts of *Europe*; upon my Return to *England* I gave three of them to *Gresham College*, and kept the fourth for my self.

CHAPTER FOUR

THE COUNTRY DESCRIBED. THE KING'S PALACE, AND SOME ACCOUNT OF THE METROPOLIS. THE AUTHOR'S WAY OF TRAVELLING. THE CHIEF TEMPLE DESCRIBED.

I NOW intend to give the Reader a short Description of this Country, as far as I travelled in it, which was not above two thousand Miles round *Lorbrulgrud* the Metropolis. For, the Queen, whom I always attended, never went further when she accompanied the King in his Progresses; and there staid till his Majesty returned from viewing his Frontiers. The whole Extent of this Prince's Dominions reacheth about six thousand Miles in Length, and from three to five in Breadth. From whence I cannot but conclude, that our Geographers of *Europe* are in a great Error, by supposing nothing but Sea between *Japan* and *California*: For it was ever my Opinion, that there must be a Balance of Earth to counterpoise the great Continent of *Tartary*; and therefore they ought to correct their Maps and Charts, by joining this vast Tract of Land to the North-west Parts of *America*; wherein I shall be ready to lend them my Assistance.

The Kingdom is a Peninsula, terminated to the North-east by a Ridge of Mountains thirty Miles high which are altogether impassable by Reason of the Volcanoes upon the Tops. Neither do the most Learned know what sort of Mortals inhabit beyond those Mountains, or whether they be inhabited at all. On the three other Sides it is bounded by the Ocean. There is not one Sea-port in the whole Kingdom; and those Parts of the Coasts into which the Rivers issue, are so full of pointed Rocks, and the Sea generally so rough, that there is no venturing with

the smallest of their Boats; so that these People are wholly
excluded from any Commerce with the rest of the World. But
the large Rivers are full of Vessels, and abound with excellent
Fish; for they seldom get any from the Sea, because the
Sea-fish are of the same Size with those in *Europe*, and consequently not worth catching; whereby it is manifest, that
Nature in the Production of Plants and Animals of so extraordinary a Bulk, is wholly confined to this Continent; of
which I leave the Reasons to be determined by Philosophers.
However, now and then they take a Whale that happens to be
dashed against the Rocks, which the common People feed on
heartily. These Whales I have known so large that a Man
could hardly carry one upon his Shoulders; and sometimes
for Curiosity they are brought in Hampers to *Lorbrulgrud*: I
saw one of them in a Dish at the King's Table, which passed
for a Rarity; but I did not observe he was fond of it; for I
think indeed the Bigness disgusted him, although I have seen
one somewhat larger in *Greenland*.

The Country is well inhabited, for it contains fifty one
Cities, near an hundred walled Towns, and a great Number
of Villages. To satisfy my curious Reader, it may be sufficient
to describe *Lorbrulgrud*. This City stands upon almost two
equal Parts on each Side the River that passes through. It
contains above eighty thousand Houses. It is in Length three
Glonglungs (which make about fifty four English Miles) and
two and a half in Breadth, as I measured it myself in the
Royal Map made by the King's Order, which was laid on the
Ground on purpose for me, and extended an hundred Feet;
I paced the Diameter and Circumference several times Bare-
foot, and computing by the Scale, measured it pretty exactly.

The King's Palace is no regular Edifice, but an Heap of
Buildings about seven Miles round: The chief Rooms are
generally two hundred and forty Foot high, and broad and long
in Proportion. A Coach was allowed to *Glumdalclitch* and me,
wherein her Governess frequently took her out to see the
Town, or go among the Shops; and I was always of the Party,
carried in my Box; although the Girl at my own Desire would
often take me out, and hold me in her Hand, that I might more
conveniently view the Houses and the People as we passed

along the Streets. I reckoned our Coach to be about a Square of *Westminster-Hall*, but not altogether so high; however, I cannot be very exact.

Beside the large Box in which I was usually carried, the Queen ordered a smaller one to be made for me, of about twelve Foot Square, and ten high, for the Convenience of Travelling; because the other was somewhat too large for *Glumdalclitch's* Lap, and cumbersom in the Coach; it was made by the same Artist, whom I directed in the whole Contrivance. This travelling Closet was an exact Square with a Window in the Middle of three of the Squares, and each Window was latticed with Iron Wire on the outside, to prevent Accidents in long Journeys. On the fourth Side, which had no Window, two strong Staples were fixed, through which the Person that carried me, when I had a Mind to be on Horseback, put in a Leathern Belt, and buckled it about his Waist. This was always the Office of some grave trusty Servant in whom I could confide, whether I attended the King and Queen in their Progresses, or were disposed to see the Gardens, or pay a Visit to some great Lady or Minister of State in the Court, when *Glumdalclitch* happened to be out of Order: For I soon began to be known and esteemed among the greatest Officers, I suppose more upon Account of their Majesty's Favour, than any Merit of my own. In Journeys, when I was weary of the Coach, a Servant on Horseback would buckle my Box, and place it on a Cushion before him; and there I had a full Prospect of the Country on three Sides from my three Windows. I had in this Closet a Field-Bed and a Hammock hung from the Ceiling, two Chairs and a Table, neatly screwed to the Floor, to prevent being tossed about by the Agitation of the Horse or the Coach. And having been long used to Sea-Voyages, those Motions, although sometimes very violent, did not much discompose me.

Whenever I had a Mind to see the Town, it was always in my Travelling-Closet; which *Glumdalclitch* held in her Lap in a kind of open Sedan, after the Fashion of the Country, born by four Men, and attended by two others in the Queen's Livery. The People who had often heard of me, were very curious to croud about the Sedan; and the Girl was complaisant enough to make the Bearers stop, and to take me in her Hand that I might be more conveniently seen.

I was very desirous to see the chief Temple, and particularly the Tower belonging to it, which is reckoned the highest in in the Kingdom. Accordingly one Day my Nurse carried me thither, but I may truly say I came back disappointed ; for, the Height is not above three thousand Foot, reckoning from the Ground to the highest Pinnacle top ; which allowing for the Difference between the Size of those People, and us in *Europe*, is no great matter for Admiration, nor at all equal in Proportion, (if I rightly remember) to *Salisbury* Steeple. But, not to detract from a Nation to which during my Life I shall acknowledge myself extremely obliged ; it must be allowed, that whatever this famous Tower wants in Height, is amply made up in Beauty and Strength. For the Walls are near an hundred Foot thick, built of hewn Stone, whereof each is about forty Foot square, and adorned on all Sides with Statues of Gods and Emperors cut in Marble larger than the Life, placed in their several Niches. I measured a little Finger which had fallen down from one of these Statues, and lay unperceived among some Rubbish ; and found it exactly four Foot and an Inch in Length. *Glumdalclitch* wrapped it up in a Handkerchief, and carried it home in her Pocket to keep among other Trinkets, of which the Girl was very fond, as Children at her Age usually are.

The King's Kitchen is indeed a noble Building, vaulted at Top, and about six hundred Foot high. The great Oven is not so wide by ten Paces as the Cupola at St. *Paul's* : For I measured the latter on purpose after my Return. But if I should describe the Kitchen-grate, the prodigious Pots and Kettles, the Joints of Meat turning on the Spits, with many other Particulars ; perhaps I should be hardly believed ; at least a severe Critick would be apt to think I enlarged a little, as Travellers are often suspected to do.

His Majesty seldom keeps above six hundred Horses in his Stables : They are generally from fifty four to sixty Foot high. But, when he goes abroad on solemn Days, he is attended for State by a Militia Guard of five hundred Horse, which indeed I thought was the most splendid Sight that could be ever beheld.

CHAPTER FIVE

SEVERAL ADVENTURES THAT HAPPENED TO THE AUTHOR. THE
AUTHOR SHEWS HIS SKILL IN NAVIGATION.

I SHOULD have lived happy enough in that Country, if my
Littleness had not exposed me to several ridiculous and
troublesome Accidents ; some of which I shall venture to relate.
Glumdalclitch often carried me into the Gardens of the Court
in my smaller Box, and would sometimes take me out of it and
hold me in her Hand, or set me down to walk. I remember,
before the Dwarf left the Queen, he followed us one Day into
those Gardens ; and my Nurse having set me down, he and I
being close together, near some Dwarf Apple-trees, I must
need shew my Wit by a silly Allusion between him and the
Trees, which happens to hold in their Language as it doth in
ours. Whereupon, the malicious Rogue watching his Opportunity, when I was walking under one of them, shook it directly
over my Head, by which a dozen Apples, each of them near as
large as a *Bristol* Barrel, came tumbling about my Ears ; one
of them hit me on the Back as I chanced to stoop, and knocked
me down flat on my Face, but I received no other Hurt ; and
the Dwarf was pardoned at my Desire, because I had given the
Provocation.

Another Day, *Glumdalclitch* left me on a smooth Grass-plot
to divert my self while she walked at some Distance with her
Governess. In the mean time, there suddenly fell such a
violent Shower of Hail, that I was immediately by the Force
of it struck to the Ground : And when I was down, the Hail-
stones gave me such cruel Bangs all over the Body, as if I had
been pelted with Tennis-Balls ; however I made a Shift to
creep on all four, and shelter my self by lying flat on my Face
on the Lee-side of a Border of Lemmon Thyme ; but so
bruised from Head to Foot, that I could not go abroad in ten
Days. Neither is this at all to be wondered at ; because Nature
in that Country observing the same Proportion through all her

Operations, a Hail-stone is near Eighteen Hundred Times as large as one in *Europe*.

But, a more dangerous Accident happened to me in the same Garden, when my little Nurse, believing she had put me in a secure Place, which I often entreated her to do, that I might enjoy my own thoughts; and having left my Box at home to avoid the Trouble of carrying it, went to another Part of the Gardens with her Governess and some Ladies of her Acquaintance. While she was absent and out of hearing, a small white Spaniel belonging to one of the chief Gardiners, having got by Accident into the Garden, happened to range near the Place where I lay. The Dog following the Scent, came directly up, and taking me in his Mouth, ran strait to his Master, wagging his Tail, and set me gently on the Ground. By good Fortune he had been so well taught, that I was carried between his Teeth without the least Hurt, or even tearing my Cloaths. But, the poor Gardiner, who knew me well, and had a great Kindness for me, was in a terrible Fright. He gently took me up in both his Hands, and asked me how I did ; but I was so amazed and out of Breath, that I could not speak a Word. In a few Minutes I came to my self, and he carried me safe to my little Nurse, who by this time had returned to the Place where she had left me, and was in cruel Agonies when I did not appear, nor answer when she called ; she severely reprimanded the Gardiner on Account of his Dog. But, the Thing was hushed up, and never known at Court ; for the Girl was afraid of the Queen's Anger ; and truly as to my self, I thought it would not be for my Reputation that such a Story should go about.

This Accident absolutely determined *Glumdalclitch* never to trust me abroad for the future out of her Sight. I had been long afraid of this Resolution ; and therefore concealed from her some little unlucky Adventures that happened in those Times when I was left by my self. Once a Kite hovering over the Garden, made a Stoop at me, and if I had not resolutely drawn my Hanger, and run under a thick Espalier, he would have certainly carried me away in his Talons. Another time, walking to the Top of a fresh Mole-hill, I fell to my Neck, in the Hole through which that Animal had cast up the Earth; and coined some Lye not worth remembering, to excuse my self for spoiling my Cloaths. I likewise broke my right Shin against the Shell of a Snail, which I happened to stumble over, as I was walking alone, and thinking on poor *England*.

I cannot tell whether I were more pleased or mortified to observe in those solitary Walks, that the smaller Birds did not appear to be at all afraid of me; but would hop about within a Yard Distance, looking for Worms, and other Food, with as much Indifference and Security as if no Creature at all were near them. I remember, a Thrush had the Confidence to snatch out of my Hand with his Bill, a Piece of Cake that *Glumdalclitch* had just given me for my Breakfast. When I attempted to catch any of these Birds, they would boldly turn against me, endeavouring to pick my Fingers, which I durst not venture within their Reach; and then they would hop back unconcerned to hunt for Worms or Snails, as they did before. But, one Day I took a thick Cudgel, and threw it with all my Strength so luckily at a Linnet, that I knocked him down, and seizing him by the Neck with both my Hands, ran with him in Triumph to my Nurse. However, the Bird who had only been stunned, recovering himself, gave me so many Boxes with his Wings on both Sides of my Head and Body, although I held him at Arms Length, and was out of the Reach of his Claws, that I was twenty Times thinking to let him go. But I was soon relieved by one of our Servants, who wrung off the Bird's Neck; and I had him next Day for Dinner by the Queen's Command. This Linnet, as near as I can remember, seemed to be somewhat larger than an *English* Swan.

The Queen, who often used to hear me talk of my Sea-Voyages, and took all Occasions to divert me when I was melancholy, asked me whether I understood how to handle a Sail or an Oar; and whether a little Exercise of Rowing might not be convenient for my Health. I answered, that I understood both very well. For although my proper Employment had been to be a Surgeon or Doctor to the Ship; yet often upon a Pinch, I was forced to work like a common Mariner. But, I could not see how this could be done in their Country, where the smallest Wherry was equal to a first Rate Man of War among us; and such a Boat as I could manage would never live in any of the Rivers: Her Majesty said, if I would contrive

Boat, her own Joyner should make it, and she would provide Place for me to sail in. The Fellow was an ingenious Workman, and by my Instructions in ten Days finished a Pleasure-Boat with all its Tackling, able conveniently to hold eight Europeans. When it was finished, the Queen was so delighted, that she ran with it in her Lap to the King, who ordered it to be put in a Cistern full of Water, with me in it, by way of Tryal; where I could not manage my two Sculls or little Oars for want of Room. But, the Queen had before contrived another Project. She ordered the Joyner to make a wooden Trough of three Hundred Foot long, fifty broad, and eight deep; which being well pitched to prevent leaking, was placed on the Floor along the Wall, in an outer Room of the Palace. It had a Cock near the Bottom, to let out the Water when it began to grow stale; and two Servants could easily fill it in half an Hour. Here I often used to row for my Diversion, as well as that of the Queen and her Ladies, who thought themselves agreeably entertained with my Skill and Agility. Sometimes I would put up my Sail, and then my Business was only to steer, while the Ladies gave me a Gale with their Fans; and when they were weary, some of the Pages would blow my Sail forward with their Breath, while I shewed my Art by steering Starboard or Larboard as I pleased. When I had done, *Glumdalclitch* always carried back my Boat into her Closet, and hung it on a Nail to dry.

In this Exercise I once met an Accident which had like to have cost me my Life. For, one of the Pages having put my Boat into the Trough; the Governess who attended *Glumdalclitch*, very officiously lifted me up to place me in the Boat; but I happened to slip through her Fingers, and should have infallibly fallen down forty Foot upon the Floor, if by the luckiest Chance in the World, I had not been stop'd by a Corking-pin that stuck in the good Gentlewoman's Stomacher; the Head of the Pin passed between my Shirt and the Waistband of my Breeches; and thus I was held by the Middle in the Air, till *Glumdalclitch* ran to my Relief.

Another time, one of the Servants, whose Office it was to fill my Trough every third Day with fresh Water; was so careless to let a huge Frog (not perceiving it) slip out of his

Pail. The Frog lay concealed till I was put into my Boat, but then seeing a resting Place, climbed up, and made it lean so much on one Side, that I was forced to balance it with all my Weight on the other, to prevent overturning. When the Frog was got in, it hopped at once half the Length of the Boat, and then over my Head, backwards and forwards, dawbing my Face and Cloaths with its odious Slime. The Largeness of its Features made it appear the most deformed Animal that can be conceived. However, I desired *Glumdalclitch* to let me deal with it alone. I banged it a good while with one of my Sculls, and at last forced it to leap out of the Boat.

But, the greatest Danger I ever underwent in that Kingdom, was from a Monkey, who belonged to one of the Clerks of the Kitchen. *Glumdalclitch* had locked me up in her Closet, while she went somewhere upon Business, or a Visit. The Weather being very warm, the Closet Window was left open, as well as the Windows and the Door of my bigger Box, in which I usually lived, because of its Largeness and Conveniency. As I sat quietly meditating at my Table, I heard something bounce in at the Closet Window, and skip about from one Side to the other; whereat, although I were much alarmed, yet I ventured to look out, but not stirring from my Seat; and then I saw this frolicksome Animal, frisking and leaping up and down, till at last he came to my Box, which he seemed to view with great Pleasure and Curiosity, peeping in at the Door and every Window. I retreated to the farther Corner of my Room, or Box; but the Monkey looking in at every Side, put me into such a Fright, that I wanted Presence of Mind to conceal my self under the Bed, as I might easily have done. After some time spent in peeping, grinning, and chattering, he at last espyed me; and reaching one of his Paws in at the Door, as a Cat does when she plays with a Mouse, although I often shifted Place to avoid him; he at length seized the Lappet of my Coat (which being made of that Country Silk, was very thick and strong) and dragged me out. He took me up in his right Fore-foot, and held me. When I offered to struggle, he squeezed me so hard, that I thought it more prudent to submit. I have good Reason to believe that he took me for a young one of his own Species, by his often stroaking my Face very gently with his other Paw. In these Diversions he was interrupted by a Noise at the Closet Door, as if some Body were opening it ; whereupon he suddenly leaped up to the Window at which he had come in, and thence upon the Leads and Gutters, walking upon three Legs, and holding me in the fourth, till he clambered up to a Roof that was next to ours. I heard *Glumdalclitch* give a Shriek at the Moment he was carrying me out. The poor Girl was almost distracted : That Quarter of the Palace was all in an Uproar ; the Servants ran for Ladders ; the Monkey was seen by Hundreds in the Court, sitting upon the Ridge of a Building, holding me like a Baby in one of his Fore-Paws. Some of the People threw up Stones, hoping to drive the Monkey down ; but this was strictly forbidden, or else very probably my Brains had been dashed out.

The Ladders were now applied, and mounted by several Men ; which the Monkey observing, and finding himself almost encompassed ; not being able to make Speed enough with his three Legs, let me drop on a Ridge-Tyle, and made his Escape. Here I sat for some time five Hundred Yards from the Ground, expecting every Moment to be blown down by the Wind, or to fall by my own Giddiness, and come tumbling over and over from the Ridge to the Eves. But an honest Lad, one of my Nurse's Footmen, climbed up, and putting me into his Breeches Pocket, brought me down safe.

CHAPTER SIX

SEVERAL CONTRIVANCES OF THE AUTHOR TO PLEASE THE KING AND
QUEEN. HE SHEWS HIS SKILL IN MUSICK.

I USED to attend the King's Levee once or twice a Week, and had often seen him under the Barber's Hand, which indeed was at first very terrible to behold. For, the Razor was almost twice as long as an ordinary Scythe. His Majesty, according to the Custom of the Country, was only shaved twice a Week. I once prevailed on the Barber to give me some of the Suds and Lather, out of which I picked Forty or Fifty of the strongest Stumps of Hair, I then took a Piece of fine Wood, and cut it like the Back of Comb, making several Holes in it at equal Distance, with as small a Needle as I could get from *Glumdalclitch*. I fixed in the Stumps so artificially, scraping and sloping them with my Knife towards the Points, that I made a very tolerable Comb ; which was a seasonable Supply, my own being so much broken in the Teeth, that it was almost useless : Neither did I know any Artist in that Country so nice and exact, as would undertake to make me another.

And this puts me in mind of an Amusement wherein I spent many of my leisure Hours. I desired the Queen's Woman to save for me the Combings of her Majesty's Hair, whereof in time I got a good Quantity ; and consulting with my Friend the Cabinet-maker, who had received general Orders to do little Jobbs for me ; I directed him to make two Chair-frames, no larger than those I had in my Box, and then to bore little Holes with a fine Awl round those Parts where I designed the Backs and Seats ; through these Holes I wove the strongest Hairs I could pick out, just after the Manner of Cane-chairs in *England*. When they were finished, I made a Present of them to her Majesty, who kept them in her Cabinet, and used to shew them for Curiosities ; as indeed they were the Wonder of every one who beheld them. The Queen would have had me sit upon one of these Chairs, but I absolutely refused to obey her; protesting I would rather dye a Thousand Deaths than place a dishonourable Part of my Body on those precious Hairs that once adorned her Majesty's Head. Of these Hairs (as I had always a Mechanical Genius) I likewise made a neat little Purse about five Foot long, with her Majesty's Name decyphered in Gold Letters ; which I gave to *Glumdalclitch*, by the Queen's Consent.

The King, who delighted in Musick, had frequent Consorts at Court, to which I was sometimes carried, and set in my Box on a Table to hear them : But, the Noise was so great, that I could hardly distinguish the Tunes. I am confident, that all the Drums and Trumpets of a Royal Army, beating and sounding together just at your Ears, could not equal it. My Practice was to have my Box removed from the Places where the Performers sat, as far as I could ; then to shut the Doors and

Windows of it, and draw the Window-Curtains ; after which I found their Musick not disagreeable.

I had learned in my Youth to play a little upon the Spinet ; Glumdalclitch kept one in her Chamber, and a Master attended twice a Week to teach her : I call it a Spinet, because it somewhat resembled that Instrument, and was play'd upon in the same Manner. A Fancy came into my Head, that I would entertain the King and Queen with an *English* Tune upon this Instrument. But this appeared extremely difficult : For, the Spinet was near sixty Foot long, each Key being almost a Foot wide ; so that, with my Arms extended. I could not reach to above five Keys ; and to press them down required a good smart stroak with my Fist, which would be too great a Labour, and to no purpose. The Method I contrived was this. I prepared two round Sticks about the Bigness of common Cudgels ; they were thicker at one End than the other ; and I covered the thicker End with a Piece of a Mouse's Skin, that by rapping on them, I might neither Damage the Tops of the Keys, nor interrupt the Sound. Before the Spinet, a Bench was placed about four Foot below the Keys, and I was put upon the Bench. I ran sideling upon it that way and this, as fast as I could, banging the proper Keys with my two Sticks ; and made a shift to play a Jigg to the great Satisfaction of both their Majesties.

CHAPTER SEVEN

THE KING AND QUEEN MAKE A PROGRESS TO THE FRONTIERS. THE AUTHOR ATTENDS THEM. THE MANNER IN WHICH HE LEAVES THE COUNTRY VERY PARTICULARLY RELATED. HE RETURNS TO ENGLAND.

I HAD always a strong Impulse that I should some time recover my Liberty, although it were impossible to conjecture by what Means, or to form any Project with the least Hope of succeeding. The Ship in which I sailed was the first ever known to be driven within Sight of that Coast ; and the King had given strict Orders, that if at any Time another

appeared, it should be taken ashore, and with all its Crew and
Passengers brought in a Tumbril to *Lorbrulgrud*. I was
indeed treated with much Kindness; I was the Favourite
of a great King and Queen, and the Delight of the whole Court;
but it was upon such a Foot as ill became the Dignity of human
Kind. I could never forget those domestick Pledges I had left
behind me. I wanted to be among People with whom I could
converse upon even Terms; and walk about the Streets and
Fields without Fear of being trod to Death like a Frog or young
Puppy. But, my Deliverance came sooner than I expected, and
in a Manner not very common: The whole Story and Circumstances of which I shall faithfully relate.

I had now been two Years in this Country; and, about the
Beginning of the third, *Glumdalclitch* and I attended the King
and Queen in Progress to the South Coast of the Kingdom. I
was carried as usual in my Travelling-Box, which, as I have
already described, was a very convenient Closet of twelve Foot
wide. I had ordered a Hammock to be fixed by silken Ropes
from the four Corners at the Top; to break the Jolts, when a
Servant carried me before him on Horseback, as I sometimes
desired; and would often sleep in my Hammock while we
were upon the Road. On the Roof of my Closet, set not directly
over the Middle of the Hammock, I ordered the Joiner to cut
out a Hole of a Foot square to give me Air in hot Weather as I
slept; which Hole I shut at pleasure with a Board that drew
backwards and forwards through a Groove.

When we came to our Journey's End, the King thought
proper to pass a few Days at a Palace he hath near *Flanflasnic*,
a City within eighteen *English* Miles of the Sea-side. *Glumdalclitch* and I were much fatigued: I had gotten a small
Cold; but the poor Girl was so ill as to be confined to her
Chamber. I longed to see the Ocean, which must be the only
Scene of my Escape, if ever it should happen. I pretended to
be worse than I really was; and desired leave to take the
fresh Air of the Sea, with a Page whom I was very fond of,
and who had sometimes been trusted with me. I shall never
forget with what Unwillingness *Glumdalclitch* consented; nor
the strict Charge she gave the Page to be careful of me; bursting
at the same time into a Flood of Tears, as if she had some

Foreboding of what was to happen. The Boy took me out in my Box about Half an Hour's Walk from the Palace, towards the Rocks on the Sea-Shore. I ordered him to set me down; and lifting up one of my Sashes, cast many a wistful melancholy Look towards the Sea. I found myself not very well; and told the Page that I had a Mind to take a Nap in my Hammock, which I hoped would do me good. I got in, and the Boy shut the Window close down, to keep out the Cold. I soon fell asleep: And all I can conjecture is, that while I slept, the Page, thinking no Danger could happen, went among the Rocks to look for Birds Eggs. I found my self suddenly awaked with a violent Pull upon the Ring which was fastned at the Top of my Box for the Conveniency of Carriage. I felt the Box raised very high in the Air, and then born forward with prodigious Speed. The first Jolt had like to have shaken me out of my Hammock; but afterwards the Motion was easy enough. I called out several times as loud as I could raise my Voice, but all to no purpose. I looked towards my Windows, and could see nothing but the Clouds and Sky. I heard a Noise just over my Head like the clapping of Wings; and then began to perceive the woeful Condition I was in; that some Eagle had got the Ring of my Box in his Beak, with an Intent to let it fall on a Rock, like a Tortoise in a Shell, and then pick out my Body and devour it. For the Sagacity and Smell of this Bird enable him to discover his Quarry at a great Distance, although better concealed than I could be within a two Inch Board.

In a little time I observed the Noise and flutter of Wings to increase very fast; and my Box was tossed up and down like a Sign-post in a windy Day. I heard several Bangs or Buffets, as I thought, given to the Eagle (for such I am certain it must have been that held the Ring of my Box in his Beak) and then all on a sudden felt my self falling perpendicularly down for above a Minute; but with such incredible Swiftness that I almost lost my Breath. My Fall was stopped by a terrible Squash, that sounded louder to my Ears than the Cataract of Niagara; after which I was quite in the Dark for another Minute, and then my Box began to rise so high that I could see Light from the Tops of my Windows. I now perceived that I was fallen into the Sea. My Box, by the Weight of my

Body, the Goods that were in, and the broad Plates of Iron
fixed for Strength at the four Corners of the Top and Bottom,
floated about five Foot deep in Water. I did then, and do now
suppose, that the Eagle which flew away with my Box was
pursued by two or three others, and forced to let me drop
while he was defending himself against the Rest, who hoped
to share in the Prey. The Plates of Iron fastned at the Bottom
of the Box, (for those were the strongest) preserved the Balance
while it fell; and hindred it from being broken on the Surface
of the Water. Every Joint of it was well grooved, and the Door
did not move on Hinges, but up and down like a Sash; which
kept my Closet so tight that very little Water came in. I got
with much Difficulty out of my Hammock, having first ventured
to draw back the Slip board on the Roof already mentioned
contrived on purpose to let in Air; for want of which I found
my self almost stifled.

How often did I then wish my self with my dear *Glumdalclitch*,
from whom one single Hour had so far divided me! And I
may say with Truth, that in the midst of my own Misfortune,
I could not forbear lamenting my poor Nurse, the Grief she
would suffer for my Loss, the Displeasure of the Queen, and
the Ruin of her Fortune. Perhaps many Travellers have not
been under greater Difficulties and Distress than I was at this
Juncture; expecting every Moment to see my Box dashed in
Pieces, or at least overset by the first violent Blast, or a rising
Wave. A Breach in one single Pane of Glass would have been
immediate Death: Nor could any thing have preserved the
Windows but the strong Lattice Wires placed on the outside
against Accidents in Travelling. I saw the Water ooze in at
several Crannies, although the Leaks were not considerable;
and I endeavoured to stop them as well as I could. I was not
able to lift up the Roof of my Closet, which otherwise I certainly
should have done, and sat on the Top of it, where I might at
least preserve myself from being shut up, as I may call it, in
the Hold. Or, if I escaped these Dangers for a Day or two,
what could I expect but a miserable Death of Cold and Hunger!
I was four Hours under these Circumstances, expecting and
indeed wishing every Moment to be my last.

I have already told the Reader, that there were two strong

Staples fixed upon the Side of my Box which had no Window,
and into which the Servant, who used to carry me on Horseback, would put a Leathern Belt, and buckle it about his Waist.
Being in this disconsolate State, I heard, or at least thought I
I heard some kind of grating Noise on that Side of my Box
where the Staples were fixed; and soon after I began to fancy
that the Box, was pulled, or towed along in the Sea; for I now
and then felt a sort of tugging, which made the Waves rise near
the Tops of my Windows, leaving me almost in the Dark. This
gave me some faint Hopes of Relief, although I were not able
to imagine how it could be brought about. I ventured to
unscrew one of my Chairs, which were always fastned to the
Floor; and having made a hard shift to screw it down again
directly under the Slipping-board that I had lately opened; I
mounted on the Chair, and putting my Mouth as near as I
could to the Hole, I called for Help in a loud Voice, and in all
the Languages I understood. I then fastned my Handkerchief
to a Stick I usually carried, and thrusting it up the Hole, I
waved it several times in the Air; that if any Boat or Ship
were near, the Seamen might conjecture some unhappy Mortal
to be shut up in the Box.

I found no Effect from all I could do, but plainly perceived
my Closet to be moved along; and in the Space of an Hour,
or better, that Side of the Box where the Staples were, and had
no Window, struck against something that was hard. I apprehended it to be a Rock, and found my self tossed more than
ever. I plainly heard a Noise upon the Cover of my Closet,
like that of a Cable, and the grating of it as it passed through
the Ring. I then found my self hoisted up by Degrees at least
three Foot higher than I was before. Whereupon, I again
thrust up my Stick and Handkerchief, calling for Help till I
was almost hoarse. In return to which, I heard a great Shout
repeated three times, giving me such Transports of Joy as are
not to be conceived but by those who feel them. I now heard
a trampling over my Head; and somebody calling through
the Hole with a loud Voice in the *English* Tongue: *If there be
any Body below, let them speak.* I answered, I was an *Englishman*,
drawn by ill Fortune into the greatest Calamity that ever any
Creature underwent; and begged, by all that was moving,

to be delivered out of the Dungeon I was in. The Voice replied, I was safe, for my Box was fastned to their Ship; and the Carpenter should immediately come, and saw an Hole in the Cover, large enough to pull me out. I answered, that was needless, and would take up too much Time; for there was no more to be done, but let one of the Crew put his Finger into the Ring, and take the Box out of the Sea into the Ship, and so into the Captain's Cabbin. Some of them upon hearing me talk so wildly, thought I was mad; others laughed; for indeed it never came into my Head, that I was now got among People of my own Stature and Strength. The Carpenter came, and in a few Minutes sawed a Passage about four Foot square; then let down a small Ladder, upon which I mounted, and from thence was taken into the Ship in a very weak Condition.

The Sailors were all in Amazement, and asked me a thousand Questions, which I had no Inclination to answer. I was equally confounded at the Sight of so many Pigmies; for such I took them to be, after having so long accustomed my Eyes to the monstrous Objects I had left. But the Captain, Mr. *Thomas Wilcocks*, an honest worthy *Shropshire* Man, observing I was ready to faint, took me into his Cabbin, gave me a Cordial to comfort me, and made me *turn in* upon his own Bed; advising me to take a little Rest, of which I had great need. Before I went to sleep I gave him to understand, that I had some valuable Furniture in my Box too good to be lost; a fine Hammock, an handsome Field-Bed, two Chairs, a Table and a Cabinet: That my Closet was hung on all Sides, or rather quilted with Silk and Cotton: That if he would let one of the Crew bring my Closet into his Cabbin, I would open it before him, and shew him my Goods. The Captain hearing me utter these Absurdities, concluded I was raving: However, (I suppose to pacify me) he promised to give Order as I desired; and going upon Deck, sent some of his Men down into my Closet, from whence (as I afterwards found) they drew up all my Goods, and stripped off the Quilting; but the Chairs, Cabinet and Bed-sted being screwed to the Floor, were damaged by the Ignorance of the Seamen, who tore them up by Force. Then they knocked off some of the Boards for the Use of the Ship; and when they had got all they had a Mind for, let the Hulk drop into the Sea,

which by Reason of many Breaches made in the Bottom and
Sides, sunk *to rights*. And indeed I was glad not to have been
a Spectator of the Havock they made ; because I am confident
it would have sensibly touched me, by bringing former Passages
into my Mind, which I had rather forget.

I slept some Hours, but perpetually disturbed with Dreams
of the Place I had left, and the Dangers I had escaped. However,
upon waking I found my self much recovered. It was now
about eight a Clock at Night, and the Captain ordered Supper
immediately, thinking I had already fasted too long. He
entertained me with great Kindness, observing me not to look
wildly, or talk inconsistently ; and when we were left alone,
desired I would give him a Relation of my Travels, and by
what Accident I came to be set adrift in that monstrous wooden
Chest. He said, that about twelve a Clock at Noon, as he was
looking through his Glass, he spied it at a Distance, and thought
it was a Sail, which he had a Mind to make ; being not much
out of his Course, in hopes of buying some Biscuit, his own
beginning to fall short. That, upon coming nearer, and finding
his Error, he sent out his Long-boat to discover what I was ;
that his Men came back in a Fright, swearing they had seen a
swimming House. That he laughed at their Folly, and went
himself in the Boat, ordering his Men to take a strong Cable
along with them. That the Weather being calm, he rowed
round me several times, observed my Windows, and the Wire
Lattices that defended them. That he discovered two Staples
upon one Side, which was all of Boards, without any Passage
for Light. He then commanded his Men to row up to that
Side ; and fastning a Cable to one of the Staples, ordered his
Men to tow my Chest (as he called it) towards the Ship. When
it was there, he gave Directions to fasten another Cable to the
Ring fixed in the Cover, and to raise up my Chest with Pullies,
which all the Sailors were not able to do above two or three
Foot. He said, they saw my Stick and Handkerchief thrust
out of the Hole, and concluded, that some unhappy Man must
be shut up in the Cavity. I asked whether he or the Crew had
seen any prodigious Birds in the Air about the Time he first
discovered me : To which he answered, that discoursing this
Matter with the Sailors while I was asleep, one of them said

he had *observed* three Eagles flying towards the North; but remarked nothing of their being larger than the usual Size; which I suppose must be imputed to the great Height they were at: And he could not guess the Reason of my Question. I then asked the Captain how far he reckoned we might be from Land; he said, by the best Computation he could make, we were at least an hundred Leagues. I assured him, that he must be mistaken by almost half; for I had not left the Country from whence I came, above two Hours before I dropt into the Sea. Whereupon he began again to think that my Brain was disturbed, of which he gave me a Hint, and advised me to go to Bed in a Cabin he had provided. I assured him I was well refreshed with his good Entertainment and Company, and as much in my Senses as ever I was in my Life. He then grew serious, and desired to ask me freely whether I were not troubled in Mind by the Consciousness of some enormous Crime, for which I was punished at the Command of some Prince, by exposing me in that Chest; as great Criminals in other Countries have been forced to Sea in a leaky Vessel without Provisions: For, although he should be sorry to have taken so ill a Man into his Ship, yet he would engage his Word to set me safe on Shore in the first Port where we arrived. He added, that his Suspicions were much increased by some very absurd Speeches I had delivered at first to the Sailors, and afterwards to himself, in relation to my Closet or Chest, as well as by my odd Looks and Behaviour while I was at Supper.

I begged his Patience to hear me tell my Story; which I faithfully did from the last Time I left *England*, to the Moment he first discovered me. And, as Truth always forceth its Way into rational Minds; so, this honest worthy Gentleman, who had some Tincture of Learning, and very good Sense, was immediately convinced of my Candor and Veracity. But, further to confirm all I had said, I entreated him to give Order that my Cabinet should be brought, of which I kept the Key in my Pocket, (for he had already informed me how the Seamen disposed of my Closet) I opened it in his Presence, and shewed him the small Collection of Rarities I made in the Country from whence I had been so strangely delivered. There was the

Comb I had contrived out of the Stumps of the King's Beard ; and another of the same Materials, but fixed into a paring of her Majesty's Thumb-nail, which served for the Back. There was a Collection of Needles and Pins from a Foot to half a Yard long. Four Wasp-Stings, like Joyners Tacks : Some Combings of the Queen's Hair : A Gold Ring which one Day she made me a Present of in a most obliging Manner, taking it from her little Finger, and throwing it over my Head like a Collar. I desired the Captain would please to accept this Ring in Return of his Civilities ; which he absolutely refused. I shewed him a Corn that I had cut off with my own Hand from a Maid of Honour's Toe ; it was about the Bigness of a *Kentish Pippin*, and grown so hard, that when I returned to *England*, I got it hollowed into a Cup and set in Silver. Lastly, I desired him to see the Breeches I had then on, which were made of a Mouse's Skin.

I could force nothing on him but a Footman's Tooth, which I observed him to examine with great Curiosity, and found he had a Fancy for it. He received it with abundance of Thanks, more than such a Trifle could deserve. It was drawn by an unskilful Surgeon in a Mistake from one of *Glumdalclitch's* Men, who was afflicted with the Tooth-ach ; but it was as sound as any in his Head. I got it cleaned, and put it into my Cabinet. It was about a Foot long, and four Inches in Diameter.

The Captain was very well satisfied with this plain Relation I had given him ; and said, he hoped when we returned to *England*, I would oblige the World by putting it in Paper, and making it publick. He said, he wondered at one Thing very much ; which was, to hear me speak so loud ; asking me whether the King or Queen of that Country were thick of Hearing. I told him it was what I had been used to for above two Years past ; and that I admired as much at the Voices of him and his Men, who seemed to me only to whisper, and yet I could hear them well enough. But, when I spoke in that Country, it was like a Man talking in the Street to another looking out from the Top of a Steeple, unless when I was placed on a Table, or held in any Person's Hand. I told him, I had likewise observed another Thing ; that when I first got into the Ship, and the Sailors stood all about me, I thought they were the most little con-

temptible Creatures I had ever beheld. For, indeed, while
was in that Prince's Country, I could never endure to look in
Glass after my Eyes had been accustomed to such prodigiou
Objects; because the Comparison gave me so despicable
Conceit of my self. The Captain said, that while we were
Supper, he observed me to look at every thing with a Sort
Wonder; and that I often seemed hardly able to contain m
Laughter; which he knew not well how to take, but impute
it to some Disorder in my Brain. I answered, it was very true
and I wondered how I could forbear, when I saw his Dish
of the Size of a Silver Three-pence, a Leg of Pork hardly
Mouthful, a Cup not so big as a Nutshell: And so I went o
describing the rest of his Household stuff and Provisions aft
the same Manner. For although the Queen had ordered
little Equipage of all Things necessary for me while I was
her Service; yet my Ideas were wholly taken up with what
saw on every Side of me; and I winked at my own Littlenes
as People do at their own Faults. The Captain understood m
Raillery very well, and merrily replied with the old *Engli*
Proverb, that he doubted, my Eyes were bigger than my Bell
for he did not observe my Stomach so good, although I ha
fasted all Day: And continuing his Mirth, protested he wou
have gladly given an Hundred Pounds to have seen my Clos
in the Eagle's Bill, and afterwards in its Fall from so great a
Height into the Sea; which would certainly have been a mo
astonishing Object, worthy to have the Description of
transmitted to future Ages.

The Captain having been at *Tonquin*, was in his Return
England driven North Eastward to the Latitude of 44 Degree
and of Longitude 143. But meeting a Trade Wind two Da
after I came on board him, we sailed Southward a long Tim
and coasting *New-Holland*, kept our Course West-south-wes
and then South-south-west till we doubled the *Cape of Goo*
hope. Our Voyage was very prosperous, but I shall not troub
the Reader with a Journal of it. The Captain called in at on
or two Ports, and sent in his Longboat for Provisions and fres
Water; but I never went out of the Ship till we came int
the *Downs*, which was on the 3d Day of *June* 1706, about nin
Months after my Escape. I offered to leave my Goods i

Security for Payment of my Freight; but the Captain protested he would not receive one Farthing. We took kind Leave of each other; and I made him promise he would come to see me at my House in *Redriff*. I hired a Horse and Guide for five Shillings, which I borrowed of the Captain.

As I was on the Road; observing the Littleness of the Houses, the Trees, the Cattle and the People, I began to think my self in *Lilliput*. I was afraid of trampling on every Traveller I met; and often called aloud to have them stand out of the Way; so that I had like to have gotten one or two broken Heads for my Impertinence.

When I came to my own House, for which I was forced to inquire, one of the Servants opening the Door, I bent down to go in (like a Goose under a Gate) for fear of striking my Head. My Wife ran out to embrace me, but I stooped lower than her Knees, thinking she could otherwise never be able to reach my Mouth. My Daughter kneeled to ask me Blessing, but I could not see her till she arose; having been so long used to stand with my Head and Eyes erect to above Sixty Foot; and then I went to take her up with one Hand, by the Waist. I looked down upon the Servants, and one or two Friends who were in the House, as if they had been Pigmies, and I a Giant. I told my Wife, she had been too thrifty; for I found she had starved herself and her Daughter to nothing. In short, I behaved my self so unaccountably, that they were all of the Captain's Opinion when he first saw me; and concluded I had lost my Wits. This I mention as an Instance of the great Power of Habit and Prejudice.

In a little Time I and my Family and Friends came to a right Understanding: But my Wife protested I should never go to Sea any more; although my evil Destiny so ordered, that she had not Power to hinder me; as the Reader may know hereafter. In the mean Time, I here conclude the second Part of my unfortunate Voyages.

The End of the Second Part

PART THREE

A VOYAGE TO LAPUTA, BALNI-BARBI, LUGGNAGG, GLUBBDUBDRIB, AND JAPAN

CHAPTER ONE

THE AUTHOR SETS OUT ON HIS THIRD VOYAGE. IS TAKEN BY
PYRATES. THE MALICE OF A DUTCHMAN. HIS ARRIVAL AT AN
ISLAND. HE IS RECEIVED INTO LAPUTA.

I HAD not been at home above ten Days, when Captain
William Robinson, a *Cornish* Man, Commander of the
Hopewell, a stout Ship of three Hundred Tuns, came to my
House. I had formerly been Surgeon of another Ship where
he was Master, and a fourth Part Owner, in a Voyage to the
Levant. He had always treated me more like a Brother than an
inferior Officer ; and hearing of my Arrival made me a Visit,
as I apprehended only out of Friendship, for nothing passed
more than what is usual after long Absence. But repeating his
Visits often, expressing his Joy to find me in good Health,
asking whether I were now settled for Life, adding that he
intended a Voyage to the *East-Indies*, in two Months, at last
plainly invited me, although with some Apologies, to be Surgeon
of the Ship. That I should have another Surgeon under me
besides our two Mates ; that my Sallary should be double to
the usual Pay ; and that having experienced my Knowledge in
Sea-Affairs to be at least equal to his, he would enter into any
Engagement to follow my Advice, as much as if I had Share in
the Command.

He said so many other obliging things, and I knew him to be
so honest a Man, that I could not reject his Proposal ; the

Thirst I had of seeing the World, notwithstanding my past Misfortunes, continuing as violent as ever. The only Difficulty that remained, was to persuade my Wife, whose Consent however I at last obtained, by the Prospect of Advantage she proposed to her Children.

We set out the 5th Day of *August*, 1706, and arrived at Fort St. *George*, the 11th of *April* 1707. We stayed there three Weeks to refresh our Crew, many of whom were sick. From hence we went to *Tonquin*, where the Captain resolved to continue some time ; because many of the Goods he intended to buy were not ready, nor could he expect to be dispatched in several Months. Therefore in hopes to defray some of the Charges he must be at, he bought a Sloop, loaded it with several Sorts of Goods, wherewith the *Tonquinese* usually trade to the neighbouring Islands ; and putting Fourteen Men on Board, whereof three were of the Country, he appointed me Master of the Sloop, and gave me Power to traffick, while he transacted his Affairs at *Tonquin*.

We had not sailed above three Days, when a great Storm arising, we were driven five days to the North-North-East, and then to the East ; after which we had fair Weather, but still with a pretty strong Gale from the West. Upon the tenth Day we were chased by two Pyrates, who soon overtook us ; for my Sloop was so deep loaden, that she sailed very slow ; neither were we in a Condition to defend our selves.

We were boarded about the same Time by both the Pyrates, who entered furiously at the Head of their Men ; but finding us all prostrate upon our Faces, (for so I gave Order), they pinioned us with strong Ropes, and setting a Guard upon us, went to search the Sloop.

I observed among them a *Dutchman*, who seemed to be of some Authority, although he were not Commander of either Ship. He knew us by our Countenances to be *Englishmen*, and jabbering to us in his own Language, swore we should be tyed Back to Back, and thrown into the Sea. I spoke *Dutch* tolerably well ; I told him who we were, and begged him in Consideration of our being Christians and Protestants, of neighbouring Countries, in strict Alliance, that he would move the Captains to take some Pity on us. This inflamed his Rage ; he repeated his Threatnings, and turning to his Companions, spoke with great Vehemence, in the *Japanese* Language, as I suppose; often using the Word *Christianos*.

The largest of the two Pyrate Ships was commanded by a *Japanese* Captain, who spoke a little *Dutch*, but very imperfectly. He came up to me, and after several Questions, which I answered in great Humility, he said we should not die. I made the Captain a very low Bow, and then turning to the *Dutchman*, said, I was sorry to find more Mercy in a Heathen, than in a Brother Christian. But I had soon Reason to repent those foolish Words; for that malicious Reprobate, having often endeavoured in vain to persuade both the Captains that I might be thrown into the Sea, (which they would not yield to after the Promise made me, that I should not die) however prevailed so far as to have a Punishment inflicted on me, worse in all human Appearance than Death it self. My Men were sent by an equal Division into both the Pyrate-Ships, and my Sloop new manned. As to my self, it was determined that I should be set a-drift, in a small Canoe, with Paddles and a Sail, and four Days Provisions; which last the *Japanese* Captain was so kind to double out of his own Stores, and would permit no Man to search me. I got down into the Canoe, while the *Dutchman* standing up on the Deck, loaded me with all the Curses and injurious Terms his Language could afford.

About an Hour before we saw the Pyrates, I had taken an Observation, and found we were in the Latitude of 46 N. and of Longitude 183. When I was at some Distance from the Pyrates, I discovered by my Pocket-Glass several Islands to the South-East. I set up my Sail, the Wind being fair, with a Design to reach the nearest of those Islands, which I made a Shift to do in about three Hours. It was all rocky; however I got many Birds Eggs; and striking Fire, I kindled some Heath and dry Sea Weed, by which I roasted my Eggs. I eat no other Supper, being resolved to spare my Provisions as much as I could. I passed the Night under the Shelter of a Rock, strowing some Heath under me, and slept pretty well.

The next Day I sailed to another Island, and thence to a third and fourth, sometimes using my Sail, and sometimes my Paddles. But not to trouble the Reader with a particular

Account of my Distresses; let it suffice, that on the 5th Day, I arrived at the last Island in my Sight, which lay South-South-East to the former.

This Island was at a greater Distance than I expected, and I did not reach it in less than five Hours. I encompassed it almost round before I could find a convenient Place to land in, which was a small Creek, about three Times the Wideness of my Canoe. I found the Island to be all rocky, only a little intermingled with Tufts of Grass, and sweet smelling Herbs. I took out my small Provisions, and after having refreshed myself, I secured the Remainder in a Cave, whereof there were great Numbers. I gathered Plenty of Eggs upon the Rocks, and got a Quantity of dry Sea-weed, and parched Grass, which I designed to kindle the next Day, and roast my Eggs as well as I could. (For I had about me my Flint, Steel, Match, and Burning-glass.) I lay all Night in the Cave where I had lodged my Provisions. My Bed was the same dry Grass and Sea-weed which I intended for Fewel. I slept very little; for the Disquiets of my Mind prevailed over my Wearyness, and kept me awake. I considered how impossible it was to preserve my Life, in so desolate a Place; and how miserable my End must be. Yet I found my self so listless and desponding, that I had not the Heart to rise; and before I could get Spirits enough to creep out of my Cave, the Day was far advanced. I walked a while among the Rocks, the Sky was perfectly clear, and the Sun so hot, that I was forced to turn my Face from it: When all on a Sudden it became obscured, as I thought, in a Manner very different from what happens by the Interposition of a Cloud. I turned back, and perceived a vast Opake Body between me and the Sun, moving forwards towards the Island: It seemed to be about two Miles high, and hid the Sun six or seven Minutes, but I did not observe the Air to be much colder, or the Sky more darkned, than if I had stood under the Shade of a Mountain. As it approached nearer over the Place where I was, it appeared to be a firm Substance, the Bottom flat, smooth, and shining very bright from the Reflexion of the Sea below. I stood upon a Height about two Hundred Yards from the Shoar, and saw this vast Body descending almost to a Parallel with me, at less than an *English* Mile Distance. I

took out my Pocket-Perspective, and could plainly discover
Numbers of People moving up and down the Sides of it, which
appeared to be sloping, but what those People were doing, I
was not able to distinguish.

The natural Love of Life gave me some inward Motions of
Joy ; and I was ready to entertain a Hope, that this Adventure
might some Way or other help to deliver me from the desolate
Place and Condition I was in. But, at the same Time, the Reader
can hardly conceive my Astonishment, to behold an Island in
the Air, inhabited by Men, who were able (as it should seem)
to raise, or sink, or put in a progressive Motion, as they pleased.
But not being, at that Time, in a Disposition to philosophise
upon this Phaenomenon, I rather chose to observe what Course
the Island would take ; because it seemed for a while to stand
still. Yet soon after it advanced nearer ; and I could see the
Sides of it, encompassed with several Gradations of Galleries
and Stairs, at certain Intervals, to descend from one to the
other. In the lowest Gallery, I beheld some People fishing with
long Angling Rods, and others looking on. I waved my Cap,
(for my Hat was long since worn out), and my Handkerchief
towards the Island ; and upon its nearer Approach, I called
and shouted with the utmost Strength of my Voice ; and then
looking circumspectly, I beheld a Crowd gathered to that Side
which was most in my View. I found by their pointing towards
me and to each other, that they plainly discovered me, although
they made no Return to my Shouting : But I could see four
or five Men running in great Haste up the Stairs to the Top of
the Island, who then disappeared. I happened rightly to
conjecture, that these were sent for Orders to some Person in
Authority upon this Occasion.

The Number of People increased ; and in less than Half an
Hour, the Island was moved and raised in such a Manner, that
the lowest Gallery appeared in a Parallel of less than an Hundred
Yards Distance from the Height where I stood. I then put my
self in the most supplicating Postures, and spoke in the humblest
Accent, but received no Answer. Those who stood nearest
over-against me, seemed to be Persons of Distinction, as I
supposed by their Habit. They conferred earnestly with each
other, looking often upon me. At length one of them called

out in a clear, polite, smooth Dialect, not unlike in Sound to the *Italian*; and therefore I returned an Answer in that Language, hoping at least that the Cadence might be more agreeable to his Ears. Although neither of us understood the other, yet my Meaning was easily known, for the People saw the Distress I was in.

They made Signs for me to come down from the Rock, and go towards the Shoar, which I accordingly did; and the flying Island being raised to a convenient Height, the Verge directly over me, a Chain was let down from the lowest Gallery, with a Seat fastned to the Bottom, to which I fixed my self, and was drawn up by Pullies.

CHAPTER TWO

THE HUMOURS AND DISPOSITIONS OF THE LAPUTIANS DESCRIBED. AN ACCOUNT OF THEIR LEARNING. OF THE KING AND HIS COURT. THE AUTHOR'S RECEPTION THERE. THE INHABITANTS SUBJECT TO FEARS AND DISQUIETUDES. AN ACCOUNT OF THE WOMEN.

AT my alighting I was surrounded by a Crowd of People, but those who stood nearest seemed to be of better Quality. They beheld me with all the Marks and Circumstances of Wonder; neither indeed was I much in their Debt; having never till then seen a Race of Mortals so singular in their Shapes, Habits, and Countenances. Their Heads were all reclined to the Right, or the Left; one of their Eyes turned inward, and the other directly up to the Zenith. Their outward Garments were adorned with the Figures of Suns, Moons, and Stars, interwoven with those of Fiddles, Flutes, Harps, Trumpets, Harpsicords, and many more Instruments of Musick, unknown to us in *Europe*. I observed here and there many in the Habit of Servants, with a blown Bladder fastned like a Flail to the End of a short Stick, which they carried in their Hands. In each Bladder was a small Quantity of dried Pease, or little Pebbles, (as I was afterwards informed.) With these Bladders they now and then flapped the Mouths and Ears of those who stood near them, of which Practice I could not then conceive the Meaning. It seems, the Minds of these People are so taken up with intense Speculations, that they neither can speak, or attend to the Discourses of others, without being rouzed by some external Taction upon the Organs of Speech and Hearing; for which Reason, those Persons who are able to afford it, always keep a *Flapper*, (the Original is *Climenole*) in their Family, as one of their Domesticks; nor ever walk abroad or make Visits without him. And the Business of this Officer is, when two or more Persons are in Company, gently to strike with his Bladder the Mouth of him who is to speak, and the Right Ear of him or them to whom the Speaker addresseth himself. This *Flapper* is likewise employed diligently to attend his Master in his Walks, and upon Occasion to give him a soft Flap on his Eyes; because he is always so wrapped up in Cogitation, that he is in manifest Danger of falling down every Precipice, and bouncing his Head against every Post; and in the Streets, of jostling others, or being jostled himself into the Kennel.

It was necessary to give the Reader this Information, without which he would be at the same Loss with me, to understand the Proceedings of these People, as they conducted me up the Stairs, to the Top of the Island, and from thence to the Royal Palace. While we were ascending, they forgot several Times what they were about, and left me to my self, till their Memories were again rouzed by their *Flappers*; for they appeared altogether unmoved by the Sight of my foreign Habit and Countenance, and by the Shouts of the Vulgar, whose Thoughts and Minds were more disengaged.

At last we entered the Palace, and proceeded into the Chamber of Presence; where I saw the King seated on his Throne, attended on each Side by Persons of prime Quality. Before the Throne, was a large Table filled with Globes and Spheres, and Mathematical Instruments of all Kinds. His Majesty took not the least Notice of us, although our Entrance were not without sufficient Noise, by the Concourse of all Persons belonging to the Court. But, he was then deep in a Problem, and we attended at least an Hour, before he could solve it. There stood by him on each Side, a young Page, with Flaps in their Hands; and when they saw that he was at Leisure, one of them gently struck his Mouth, and the other his Right Ear; at which he started like one awaked on the sudden, and looking towards me, and the Company I was in, recollected the Occasion of our coming, whereof he had been informed before. He spoke some Words; whereupon immediately a young Man with a Flap came up to my Side, and flapt me gently on the Right Ear; but I made Signs as well as I could, that I had no Occasion for such an Instrument; which as I afterwards found, gave his Majesty and the whole Court a very mean Opinion of my Understanding. The King, as far as I could conjecture, asked me several Questions, and I addressed myself to him in all the Languages I had. When it was found, that I could neither understand nor be understood, I was conducted by his Order to an Apartment in his Palace, (this Prince being distinguished above all his Predecessors for his Hospitality to Strangers,) where two Servants were appointed to attend me. My Dinner was brought, and four Persons of Quality, whom I remembered to have seen very near the King's Person, did me the Honour to dine with me. We had two Courses, of three Dishes each. In the first Course, there was a Shoulder of Mutton, cut into an Æquilateral Triangle; a Piece of Beef into a Rhomboides; and a Pudding into a Cycloid. The second Course was two Ducks, trussed up into the Form of Fiddles; Sausages and Puddings resembling Flutes and Haut-boys, and a Breast of Veal in the Shape of a Harp. The Servants cut our Bread into Cones, Cylinders, Parallelograms, and several other Mathematical Figures.

While we were at Dinner, I made bold to ask the Names of several Things in their Language; and those noble Persons, by the Assistance of their *Flappers*, delighted to give me Answers, hoping to raise my Admiration of their great Abilities, if I could be brought to converse with them. I was soon able to call for Bread, and Drink, or whatever else I wanted.

After Dinner my Company withdrew, and a Person was sent to me by the King's Order, attended by a *Flapper*. He brought with him Pen, Ink, and Paper, and three or four Books; giving me to understand by Signs, that he was sent to teach me the Language. We sat together four Hours, in which Time I wrote down a great Number of Words in Columns, with the Trans-

lations over against them. I likewise made a Shift to learn
several short Sentences. For my Tutor would order one of my
Servants to fetch something, to turn about, to make a Bow, to
sit, or stand, or walk, and the like. Then I took down the
Sentence in Writing. He shewed me also in one of his Books,
the Figures of the Sun, Moon, and Stars, the Zodiack, the
Tropics and Polar Circles, together with the Denominations of
many Figures of Planes and Solids. He gave me the Names
and Descriptions of all the Musical Instruments, and the
general Terms of Art in playing on each of them. After he had
left me, I placed all my Words with their Interpretations in
alphabetical Order. And thus in a few Days, by the Help of a
very faithful Memory, I got some Insight into their Language.

Those to whom the King had entrusted me, observing how
ill I was clad, ordered a Taylor to come next Morning, and
take my Measure for a Suit of Cloths. This Operator did his
Office after a different Manner from those of his Trade in
Europe. He first took my Altitude by a Quadrant, and then
with Rule and Compasses, described the Dimensions and Out-
Lines of my whole Body; all which he entred upon Paper,
and in six Days brought my Cloths very ill made, and quite out
of Shape, by happening to mistake a Figure in the Calculation.
But my Comfort was, that I observed such Accidents very
frequent, and little regarded.

During my Confinement for want of Cloaths, and by an
Indisposition that held me some Days longer, I much enlarged
my Dictionary; and when I went next to Court, was able to
understand many Things the King spoke, and to return him
some Kind of Answers. His Majesty had given Orders, that
the Island should move North-East and by East, to the vertical
Point over *Lagado*, the Metropolis of the whole Kingdom,
below upon the firm Earth. It was about Ninety Leagues
distant, and our Voyage lasted four Days and an Half. I was
not in the least sensible of the progressive Motion made in the
Air by the Island. On the second Morning, about Eleven
o'Clock, the King himself in Person, attended by his Nobility,
Courtiers, and Officers, having prepared all their Musical
Instruments, played on them for three Hours without Inter-
mission; so that I was quite stunned with the Noise; neither

could I possibly guess the Meaning, till my Tutor informed me. He said, that the People of their Island had their Ears adapted to hear the Musick of the Spheres, which always played at certain Periods ; and the Court was now prepared to bear their Part in whatever Instrument they most excelled.

In our Journey towards *Lagado* the Capital City, his Majesty ordered that the Island should stop over certain Towns and Villages, from whence he might receive the Petitions of his Subjects. And to this Purpose, several Packthreads were let down with small Weights at the Bottom. On these Packthreads the People strung their Petitions, which mounted up directly like the Scraps of Paper fastned by School-boys at the End of the String that holds their Kite. Sometimes we received Wine and Victuals from below, which were drawn up by Pullies.

The Knowledge I had in Mathematicks gave me great Assistance in acquiring their Phraseology, which depended much upon that Science and Musick ; and in the latter I was not unskilled. Their Ideas are perpetually conversant in Lines and Figures. If they would, for Example, praise the Beauty of a Woman, or any other Animal, they describe it by Rhombs, Circles, Parallelograms, Ellipses, and other Geometrical Terms ; or else by Words of Art drawn from Musick, needless here to repeat. I observed in the King's Kitchen all Sorts of Mathematical and Musical Instruments, after the Figures of which they cut up the Joynts that were served to his Majesty's Table.

These People are under continual Disquietudes, never enjoying a Minute's Peace of Mind ; and their Disturbances proceed from Causes which very little affect the rest of Mortals. Their Apprehensions arise from several Changes they dread in the Celestial Bodies. For instance ; that the Earth by the continual Approaches of the Sun towards it, must in Course of Time be absorbed or swallowed up. That the Face of the Sun will by Degrees be encrusted with its own Effluvia, and give no more Light to the World. That, the Earth very narrowly escaped a Brush from the Tail of the last Comet, which would have infallibly reduced it to Ashes ; and that the next, which they have calculated for One and Thirty Years hence, will probably destroy us. For, if in its Perihelion it should approach within a certain Degree of the Sun, (as by their Calculations they have

Reason to dread) it will conceive a Degree of Heat ten Thousand Times more intense than that of red hot glowing Iron; and in its Absence from the Sun, carry a blazing Tail Ten Hundred Thousand and Fourteen Miles long; through which if the Earth should pass at the Distance of one Hundred Thousand Miles from the *Nucleus*, or main Body of the Comet, it must in its Passage be set on Fire, and reduced to Ashes. That the Sun daily spending its Rays without any Nutriment to supply them, will at last be wholly consumed and annihilated; which must be attended with the Destruction of this Earth, and of all the Planets that receive their Light from it.

They are so perpetually alarmed with the Apprehensions of these and the like impending Dangers, that they can neither sleep quietly in their Beds, nor have any Relish for the common Pleasures or Amusements of Life. When they meet an Acquaintance in the Morning, the first Question is about the Sun's Health; how he looked at his Setting and Rising, and what Hopes they have to avoid the Stroak of the approaching Comet. This Conversation they are apt to run into with the same Temper that Boys discover, in delighting to hear terrible Stories of Sprites and Hobgoblins, which they greedily listen to, and dare not go to Bed for fear.

In about a Month's Time I had made a tolerable Proficiency in their Language, and was able to answer most of the King's Questions, when I had the Honour to attend him. His Majesty discovered not the least Curiosity to enquire into the Laws, Government, History, Religion, or Manners of the Countries where I had been; but confined his Questions to the State of Mathematicks, and received the Account I gave him, with great Contempt and Indifference, though often rouzed by his *Flapper* on each Side.

CHAPTER THREE

A PHÆNOMENON SOLVED BY MODERN PHILOSOPHY AND ASTRONOMY. THE LAPUTIANS' GREAT IMPROVEMENTS IN THE LATTER. THE KING'S METHOD OF SUPPRESSING INSURRECTIONS.

I DESIRED Leave of this Prince to see the Curiosities of the Island; which he was graciously pleased to grant, and ordered my Tutor to attend me. I chiefly wanted to know to what Cause in Art or in Nature, it owed its several Motions; whereof I will now give a philosophical Account to the Reader.

The flying or floating Island is exactly circular; its Diameter 7837 Yards, or about four Miles and an Half, and consequently contains ten Thousand Acres. It is three Hundred Yards thick. The Bottom, or under Surface, which appears to those who view it from below, is one even regular Plate of Adamant, shooting up to the Height of about two Hundred Yards. Above it lye the several Minerals in their usual Order; and over all is a Coat of rich Mould ten or twelve Foot deep. The Declivity of the upper Surface, from the Circumference to the Center, is the natural Cause why all the Dews and Rains which fall upon the Island, are conveyed in small Rivulets towards the Middle, where they are emptied into four large Basons, each of about Half a Mile in Circuit, and two Hundred Yards distant from the Center. From these Basons the Water is continually exhaled by the Sun in the Day-time, which effectually prevents their overflowing. Besides, as it is in the Power of the Monarch to raise the Island above the Region of Clouds and Vapours, he can prevent the falling of Dews and Rains whenever he pleases. For the highest Clouds cannot rise above two Miles, as Naturalists agree, at least they were never known to do so in that Country.

At the Center of the *Island* there is a Chasm about fifty Yards in Diameter, from whence the Astronomers descend into a large Dome, which is therefore called *Flandona Gagnole*, or the *Astronomers Cave* ; situated at the Depth of an Hundred Yards beneath the upper Surface of the Adamant. In this Cave are Twenty Lamps continually burning, which from the Reflection of the Adamant cast a strong Light into every Part. The Place is stored with great Variety of Sextants, Quadrants, Telescopes, Astrolabes, and other Astronomical Instruments. But the greatest Curiosity, upon which the Fate of the Island depends, is a Load-stone of a prodigious Size, in Shape resembling a Weaver's Shuttle. It is in Length six Yards, and in the thickest Part at least three Yards over. This Magnet is sustained by a very strong Axle of Adamant, passing through its Middle, upon which it plays, and is poized so exactly that the weakest Hand can turn it. It is hooped round with an hollow Cylinder of Adamant, four Foot deep, as many thick, and twelve Yards in Diameter, placed horizontally, and supported by Eight Adamantine Feet, each Six Yards high. In the Middle of the Concave Side there is a Groove Twelve Inches deep, in which the Extremities of the Axle are lodged, and turned round as there is Occasion.

This Stone cannot be moved from its Place by any Force, because the Hoop and its Feet are one continued Piece with that Body of Adamant which constitutes the Bottom of the Island.

By Means of this Load-stone, the Island is made to rise and fall, and move from one Place to another. For, with respect to that Part of the Earth over which the Monarch presides, the Stone is endued at one of its Sides with an attractive Power, and at the other with a repulsive. Upon placing the Magnet erect with its attracting End towards the Earth, the Island descends ; but when the repelling Extremity points downwards, the Island mounts directly upwards. When the Position of the Stone is oblique, the Motion of the Island is so too. For in this Magnet the Forces always act in Lines parallel to its Direction.

But it must be observed, that this Island cannot move beyond the Extent of the Dominions below ; nor can it rise above the Height of four Miles. For which the Astronomers (who have written large Systems concerning the Stone) assign the following Reason : That the Magnetick Virtue does not extend beyond the Distance of four Miles, and that the Mineral which acts upon the Stone in the Bowels of the Earth, and in the Sea about six Leagues distant from the Shoar, is not diffused through the whole Globe, but terminated with the Limits of the King's Dominions : And it was easy from the great Advantage of such a superior Situation, for a Prince to bring under his Obedience whatever Country lay within the Attraction of that Magnet.

When the Stone is put parallel to the Plane of the Horizon, the Island standeth still ; for in that Case, the Extremities of it being at equal Distance from the Earth, act with equal Force, the one in drawing downwards, the other in pushing upwards ; and consequently no Motion can ensue.

This Load-stone is under the Care of certain Astronomers, who from Time to Time give it such Positions as the Monarch directs. They spend the greatest Part of their Lives in observing the celestial Bodies, which they do by the Assistance of Glasses, far excelling ours in Goodness. For, although their largest Telescopes do not exceed three Feet, they magnify much more than those of a Hundred with us, and shew the Stars with greater Clearness. This Advantage hath enabled them to extend their Discoveries much farther than our Astronomers in *Europe*. They have made a Catalogue of ten Thousand fixed Stars, whereas the largest of ours do not contain above one third Part of that Number. They have likewise discovered two lesser Stars, or *Satellites*, which revolve about *Mars* ; whereof the innermost is distant from the Center of the primary Planet exactly three of his Diameters, and the outermost five ; the former revolves in the Space of ten Hours, and the latter in Twenty-one and an Half ; so that the Squares of their periodical Times, are very near in the same Proportion with the Cubes of their Distance from the Center of *Mars* ; which evidently shews them to be governed by the same Law of Gravitation, that influences the other heavenly Bodies.

They have observed Ninety-three different Comets, and settled their Periods with great Exactness. If this be true, (and they affirm it with great Confidence) it is much to be wished that their Observations were made publick ; whereby the Theory of Comets, which at present is very lame and defective, might be brought to the same Perfection with other Parts of Astronomy.

If any Town should engage in Rebellion or Mutiny, fall into violent Factions, or refuse to pay the usual Tribute; the King hath two Methods of reducing them to Obedience. The first and the mildest Course is by keeping the Island hovering over such a Town, and the Lands about it; whereby he can deprive them of the Benefit of the Sun and the Rain, and consequently afflict the Inhabitants with Dearth and Diseases. And if the Crime deserve it, they are at the same time pelted from above with great Stones, against which they have no Defence, but by creeping into Cellars or caves, while the Roofs of their Houses are beaten to Pieces. But if they still continue obstinate, or offer to raise Insurrections; he proceeds to the last Remedy, by letting the Island drop directly upon their Heads, which makes a universal Destruction both of Houses and Men. However, this is an Extremity to which the Prince is seldom driven, neither indeed is he willing to put it in Execution; nor dare his Ministers advise him to an Action, which as it would render them odious to the People, so it would be a great Damage to their own Estates that lie all below; for the Island is the King's Demesn.

But there is still indeed a more weighty Reason, why the Kings of this Country have been always averse from executing so terrible an Action, unless upon the utmost Necessity. For if the Town intended to be destroyed should have in it any tall Rocks, as it generally falls out in the larger Cities; a Situation probably chosen at first with a View to prevent such a Catastrophe: Or if it abound in high Spires or Pillars of Stone, a sudden Fall might endanger the Bottom or under Surface of the Island, which although it consist as I have said, of one entire Adamant two hundred Yards thick, might happen to crack by too great a Choque, or burst by approaching too near the Fires from the Houses below; as the Backs both of Iron and Stone will often do in our Chimneys. Of all this the People are well apprized, and understand how far to carry their Obstinacy, where their Liberty or Property is concerned. And the King, when he is highest provoked, and most determined to press a City to Rubbish, orders the Island to descend with

great Gentleness, out of a Pretence of Tenderness to his People,
but indeed for fear of breaking the Adamantine Bottom; in
which Case it is the Opinion of all their Philosophers, that the
Load-stone could no longer hold it up, and the whole Mass
would fall to the Ground.

By a fundamental Law of this Realm, neither the King nor
either of his two elder Sons, are permitted to leave the Island;
nor the Queen till she is past Child-bearing.

CHAPTER FOUR

THE AUTHOR LEAVES LAPUTA, IS CONVEYED TO BALNIBARBI, ARRIVES
AT THE METROPOLIS. A DESCRIPTION OF THE METROPOLIS AND
THE COUNTRY ADJOINING. THE AUTHOR HOSPITABLY RECEIVED BY
A GREAT LORD. HIS CONVERSATION WITH THAT LORD.

ALTHOUGH I cannot say that I was ill treated in this Island,
yet I must confess I thought my self too much neglected,
not without some Degree of Contempt. For neither Prince
nor People appeared to be curious in any Part of Knowledge,
except Mathematicks and Musick, wherein I was far their
inferior, and upon that Account very little regarded.

On the other Side, after having seen all the Curiosities of the
Island, I was very desirous to leave it, being heartily weary of
those People. They were indeed excellent in two Sciences for
which I have great Esteem, and wherein I am not unversed;
but at the same time so abstracted and involved in Speculation,
that I never met with such disagreeable Companions. I
conversed only with Women, Tradesmen, *Flappers*, and Court-
Pages, during two Months of my Abode there; by which at
last I rendered my self extremely contemptible; yet these
were the only People from whom I could ever receive a reasonable Answer.

There was a great Lord at Court, nearly related to the King,
and for that Reason alone used with Respect. He was universally reckoned the most ignorant and stupid Person among
them. He had performed many eminent Services to the Crown,

had great natural and acquired Parts, adorned with Integrity and Honour; but so ill an Ear for Musick, that his Detractors reported he had been often known to beat Time in the wrong Place; neither could his Tutors without extreme Difficulty teach him to demonstrate the most easy Proposition in the Mathematicks. He was pleased to shew me many Marks of Favour, often did me the Honour of a Visit, desired to be informed in the Affairs of *Europe*, the Laws and Customs, the Manners and Learning of the several Countries where I had travelled. He listened to me with great Attention, and made very wise Observations on all I spoke. He had two *Flappers* attending him for State, but never made use of them except at Court, and in Visits of Ceremony; and would always command them to withdraw when we were alone together.

I intreated this illustrious Person to intercede in my Behalf with his Majesty for Leave to depart; which he accordingly did, as he was pleased to tell me, with Regret: For, indeed he had made me several Offers very advantageous, which however I refused with Expressions of the highest Acknowledgment.

On the 16th Day of *February*, I took Leave of his Majesty and the Court. The King made me a Present to the Value of about two Hundred Pounds *English*; and my Protector his Kinsman as much more, together with a Letter of Recommendation to a Friend of his in *Lagado*, the Metropolis: The Island being then hovering over a Mountain about two Miles from it, I was let down from the lowest Gallery, in the same Manner as I had been taken up.

The Continent, as far as it is subject to the Monarch of the *Flying Island*, passeth under the general Name of *Balnibarbi*; and the Metropolis, as I said before, is called *Lagado*. I felt some little Satisfaction in finding my self on firm Ground. I walked to the City without any Concern, being clad like one of the Natives, and sufficiently instructed to converse with them. I soon found out the Person's House to whom I was recommended; presented my Letter from his Friend the Grandee in the Island, and was received with much Kindness. This great Lord, whose Name was *Munodi*, ordered me an Apartment in his own House, where I continued during my Stay, and was entertained in a most hospitable Manner.

The next Morning after my Arrival he took me in his Chariot to see the Town, which is about half the Bigness of *London*; but the Houses very strangely built, and most of them out of Repair. The People in the Streets walked fast, looked wild, their Eyes fixed, and were generally in Rags. We passed through one of the Town Gates, and went about three Miles into the Country, where I saw many Labourers working with several Sorts of Tools in the Ground, but was not able to conjecture what they were about; neither did I observe any Expectation either of Corn or Grass, although the Soil appeared to be excellent. I could not forbear admiring at these odd Appearances both in Town and Country; and I made bold to desire my Conductor, that he would be pleased to explain to me what could be meant by so many busy Heads, Hands and Faces, both in the Streets and the Fields, because I did not discover any good Effects they produced; but on the contrary, I never knew a Soil so unhappily cultivated, Houses so ill contrived and so ruinous, or a People whose Countenances and Habit expressed so much Misery and Want.

This Lord *Munodi* was a Person of the first Rank, and had been some Years Governor of *Lagado*; but by a Cabal of Ministers was discharged for Insufficiency. However the King treated him with Tenderness, as a well-meaning Man, but of a low contemptible Understanding.

When I gave that free Censure of the Country and its Inhabitants, he made no further Answer than by telling me, that I had not been long enough among them to form a Judgment; and that the different Nations of the World had different Customs; with other common Topicks to the same Purpose. But when we returned to his Palace, he asked me how I liked the Building, what Absurdities I observed, and what Quarrel I had with the Dress or Looks of his Domesticks. This he might safely do; because every Thing about him was magnificent, regular and polite. I answered, that his Excellency's Prudence, Quality, and Fortune, had exempted him from those Defects which Folly and Beggary had produced in others. He said, if I would go with him to his Country House about Twenty Miles distant, where his Estate lay, there would be more Leisure for this Kind of Conversation. I told his Excellency, that I was entirely at his Disposal; and accordingly we set out next Morning.

During our Journey, he made me observe the several Methods used by Farmers in managing their Lands; which to me were wholly unaccountable: For except in some very few Places, I could not discover one Ear of Corn, or Blade of Grass. But, in three Hours travelling, the Scene was wholly altered; we came into a most beautiful Country; Farmers Houses at small Distances, neatly built, the Fields enclosed, containing Vineyards, Corn-grounds and Meadows. Neither do I remember to have seen a more delightful Prospect. His Excellency observed my Countenance to clear up; he told me with a Sigh, that there his Estate began, and would continue the same till we should come to his House. That his Countrymen ridiculed and despised him for managing his Affairs no better, and for setting so ill an Example to the Kingdom; which however was followed by very few, such as were old and wilful, and weak like himself.

We came at length to the House, which was indeed a noble Structure, built according to the best Rules of ancient Architecture. The Fountains, Gardens, Walks, Avenues, and Groves were all disposed with exact Judgment and Taste. I gave due Praises to every Thing I saw, whereof his Excellency took not the least Notice till after Supper; when, there being no third Companion, he told me with a very melancholy Air, that he doubted he must throw down his Houses in Town and Country, to rebuild them after the present Mode; destroy all his Plantations, and cast others in such a Form as modern Usage required; and give the same Directions to all his Tenants, unless he would submit to incur the Censure of Pride, Singularity, Affectation, Ignorance, Caprice; and perhaps encrease his Majesty's Displeasure.

The Sum of his Discourse was to this Effect. That about Forty Years ago, certain Persons went up to *Laputa*, either upon Business or Diversion; and after five Months Continuance, came back with a very little Smattering in Mathematicks, but full of Volatile Spirits acquired in that Airy Region. That these Persons upon their Return, began to dislike the Management of every Thing below; and fell into Schemes of putting all Arts, Sciences, Languages, and Mechanics upon a new Foot. To this End they procured a Royal Patent for erecting an Academy of PROJECTORS in *Lagado* : And the Humour prevailed so strongly among the People, that there is not a Town of any Consequence in the Kingdom without such an Academy. In these Colleges, the Professors contrive new Rules and Methods of Agriculture and Building, and new Instruments and Tools for all Trades and Manufactures, whereby, as they undertake, one Man shall do the Work of Ten; a Palace may be built in a Week, of Materials so durable as to last for ever without repairing. All the Fruits of the Earth shall come to Maturity at whatever Season we think fit to chuse, and increase an Hundred Fold more than they do at present; with innumerable other happy Proposals. The only Inconvenience is, that none of these Projects are yet brought to Perfection; and in the mean time, the whole Country lies miserably waste, the Houses in Ruins, and the People without Food or Cloaths. By all which, instead of being discouraged, they are Fifty Times more violently bent upon prosecuting their Schemes, driven equally on by Hope and Despair : That, as for himself, being not of an enterprizing Spirit, he was content to go on in the old Forms; to live in the Houses his Ancestors had built, and act as they did in every Part of Life without Innovation. That, some few other Persons of Quality and Gentry had done the same; but were looked on with an Eye of Contempt and ill Will, as Enemies of Art, ignorant, and ill Commonwealthsmen, preferring their own Ease and Sloth before the general Improvement of their Country.

CHAPTER FIVE

THE Continent of which this Kingdom is a part, extends
itself, as I have Reason to believe, Eastward to that
unknown Tract of *America*, Westward of *California*, and
North to the Pacifick Ocean, which is not above an hundred
and fifty Miles from *Lagado* ; where there is a good Port and
much Commerce with the great Island of *Luggnagg* ; situated
to the North-West about 29 Degrees North Latitude, and 140
Longitude. This Island of *Luggnagg* stands South Eastwards
of *Japan*, about an hundred Leagues distant. There is a strict
Alliance between the *Japanese* Emperor and the King of *Luggnagg*, which affords frequent Opportunities of sailing from one
Island to the other. I determined therefore to direct my Course
this Way, in order to my Return to *Europe*. I hired two Mules
with a Guide to shew me the Way, and carry my small Baggage.
I took leave of my noble Protector, who had shewn me so much
Favour, and made me a generous Present at my Departure.

My Journey was without any Accident or Adventure worth
relating. When I arrived at the Port of *Maldonada*, (for so it is
called) there was no Ship in the Harbour bound for *Luggnagg*,
nor like to be in some Time. The Town is about as large as
Portsmouth. I soon fell into some Acquaintance, and was very
hospitably received. A Gentleman of Distinction said to me,
that since the Ships bound for *Luggnagg* could not be ready in
less than a Month, it might be no disagreeable Amusement for
me to take a Trip to the little Island of *Glubbdubdrib*, about five
Leagues off to the South-West. He offered himself and a
Friend to accompany me, and that I should be provided with
a small convenient Barque for the Voyage.

GLUBBDUBDRIB, as nearly as I can interpret the Word,
signifies the Island of *Sorcerers or Magicians*. It is about one

third as large as the Isle of *Wight*, and extreamly fruitful : It is governed by the Head of a certain Tribe, who are all Magicians. This Tribe marries only among each other ; and the eldest in Succession is Prince or Governor. He hath a noble Palace, and a Park of about three thousand Acres, surrounded by a Wall of hewn Stone twenty Foot high. In this Park are several small Inclosures for Cattle, Corn and Gardening.

The Governor and his Family are served and attended by Domesticks of a Kind somewhat unusual. By his Skill in Necromancy, he hath Power of calling whom he pleaseth from the Dead, and commanding their Service for twenty four Hours, but no longer ; nor can he call the same Persons up again in less than three Months, except upon very extraordinary Occasions.

When we arrived at the Island, which was about Eleven in the Morning, one of the Gentlemen who accompanied me, went to the Governor, and desired Admittance for a Stranger, who came on purpose to have the Honour of attending on his Highness. This was immediately granted, and we all three entered the Gate of the Palace between two Rows of Guards, armed and dressed after a very antick Manner, and something in their Countenances that made my Flesh creep with a Horror I cannot express. We passed through several Apartments between Servants of the same Sort, ranked on each Side as before, till we came to the Chamber of Presence, where after three profound Obeysances, and a few general Questions, we were permitted to sit on three Stools near the lowest Step of his Highness's Throne. He understood the Language of *Balnibarbi*, although it were different from that of his Island. He desired me to give him some Account of my Travels ; and to let me see that I should be treated without Ceremony, he dismissed all his Attendants with a Turn of his Finger, at which to my great Astonishment they vanished in an Instant, like Visions in a Dream, when we awake on a sudden. I could not recover myself in some Time, till the Governor assured me that I should receive no Hurt. I had the Honour to dine with the Governor, where a new Set of Ghosts served up the Meat, and waited at Table. I now observed myself to be less terrified than I had been in the Morning. I stayed till Sun-set, but

E

humbly desired his Highness to excuse me for not accepting his Invitation of lodging in the Palace. My two Friends and I lay at a private House in the Town adjoining, which is the Capital of this little Island; and the next Morning we returned to pay our Duty to the Governor, as he was pleased to command us.

After this Manner we continued in the Island for ten Days, most Part of every Day with the Governor, and at Night in our Lodging. I soon grew so familiarized to the Sight of Spirits, that after the third or fourth Time they gave me no Emotion at all; or if I had any Apprehensions left, my Curiosity prevailed over them. For his Highness the Governor ordered me to call up whatever Persons I would chuse to name, and in whatever Numbers among all the Dead from the Beginning of the World to the present Time, and command them to answer any Questions I should think fit to ask; with this Condition, that my Questions must be confined within the Compass of the Times they lived in. And one Thing I might depend upon, that they would certainly tell me Truth; for Lying was a Talent of no Use in the lower World.

I made my humble Acknowledgments to his Highness for so great a Favour. We were in a Chamber, from whence there was a fair Prospect into the Park. And because my first Inclination was to be entertained with Scenes of Pomp and Magnificence, I desired to see *Alexander* the Great, at the Head of his Army just after the Battle of *Arbela*; which upon a Motion of the Governor's Finger immediately appeared in a large Field under the Window, where we stood. *Alexander* was called up into the Room: It was with great Difficulty that I understood his *Greek*, and had but little of my own. He assured me upon his Honour that he was not poisoned, but dyed of a Fever by excessive Drinking.

Next I saw *Hannibal* passing the *Alps*, who told me he had not a Drop of Vinegar in his Camp.

I saw *Cæsar* and *Pompey* at the Head of their Troops just ready to engage. I saw the former in his last great Triumph. I desired that the Senate of *Rome* might appear before me in one large Chamber, and a modern Representative, in Counterview, in another. The first seemed to be an Assembly of

Heroes and Demy-Gods; the other a Knot of Pedlars, Pick-pockets, Highwaymen and Bullies. The Governor at my Request gave the Sign for *Cæsar* and *Brutus* to advance towards us. I was struck with a profound Veneration at the Sight of *Brutus*; and could easily discover the most consummate Virtue, the greatest Intrepidity, and Firmness of Mind, the truest Love of his Country, and general Benevolence for Mankind in every Lineament of his Countenance. I observed with much Pleasure, that these two Persons were in good Intelligence with each other; and *Cæsar* freely confessed to me, that the greatest Actions of his own Life were not equal by many Degrees to the Glory of taking it away.

CHAPTER SIX

THE AUTHOR'S RETURN TO MALDONADA. SAILS TO THE KINGDOM OF LUGGNAGG. THE AUTHOR CONFINED. HE IS SENT FOR TO COURT. THE MANNER OF HIS ADMITTANCE. THE KING'S GREAT LENITY TO HIS SUBJECTS.

THE Day of our Departure being come, I took leave of his Highness the Governor of *Glubbdubdrib*, and returned with my two Companions to *Maldonada*, where after a Fort-night's waiting, a Ship was ready to sail for *Luggnagg*. The two Gentlemen and some others were so generous and kind as to furnish me with Provisions, and see me on Board. I was a Month in Voyage. We had one violent Storm, and were under a Necessity of steering Westward to get into the Trade-Wind, which holds for above sixty Leagues. On the 21st of *April*, 1708, we sailed in the River of *Clumegnig*, which is a Sea-port Town, at the South-East Point of *Luggnagg*. We cast Anchor within a League of the Town, and made a Signal for a Pilot. Two of them came on Board in less than half an Hour, by whom we were guided between certain Shoals and Rocks, which are very dangerous in the Passage, to a large Basin, where a Fleet may ride in Safety within a Cable's Length of the Town-Wall.

Some of our Sailors, whether out of Treachery or Inadvertence, had informed the Pilots that I was a Stranger and a great Traveller, whereof these gave Notice to a Custom-House Officer, by whom I was examined very strictly upon my landing. This Officer spoke to me in the Language of *Balnibarbi*, which by the Force of much Commerce is generally understood in that Town, especially by Seamen, and those employed in the Customs. I gave him a short Account of some Particulars, and made my Story as plausible and consistent as I could; but I thought it necessary to disguise my Country, and call my self a *Hollander*; because my Intentions were for *Japan*, and I knew the *Dutch* were the only *Europeans* permitted to enter into that Kingdom. The Officer said, I must be confined till he could receive Orders from Court, for which he would write immediately, and hoped to receive an Answer in a Fortnight. I was carried to a convenient Lodging, with a Centry placed at the Door; however I had the Liberty of a large Garden, and was treated with Humanity enough, being maintained all the Time at the King's Charge. I was invited by several Persons, chiefly out of Curiosity, because it was reported I came from Countries very remote, of which they had never heard.

I hired a young Man who came in the same Ship to be an Interpreter; he was a Native of *Luggnagg*, but had lived some Years at *Maldonada*, and was a perfect Master of both Languages. By his Assistance I was able to hold a Conversation with those that came to visit me; but this consisted only of their Questions and my Answers.

The Dispatch came from Court about the Time we expected. It contained a Warrant for conducting me and my Retinue to *Traldragdubh* or *Trildrogdrib*, (for it is pronounced both Ways as near as I can remember) by a Party of Ten Horse. All my Retinue was that poor Lad for an Interpreter, whom I persuaded into my Service. At my humble Request we had each of us a Mule to ride on. A Messenger was dispatched half a Day's Journey before us, to give the King Notice of my Approach, and to desire that his Majesty would please to appoint a Day and Hour, when it would be his gracious Pleasure that I might have the Honour to *lick the Dust before his Footstool*. This is the Court Style, and I found it to be more than Matter

Form : For upon my Admittance two Days after my Arrival, was commanded to crawl upon my Belly, and lick the Floor I advanced ; but on account of my being a Stranger, Care as taken to have it so clean that the Dust was not offensive. owever, this was a peculiar Grace, not allowed to any but ersons of the highest Rank, when they desire an Admittance : ay, sometimes the Floor is strewed with Dust on purpose, hen the Person to be admitted happens to have powerful nemies at Court : And I have seen a great Lord with his louth so crammed, that when he had crept to the proper istance from the Throne, he was not able to speak a Word. either is there any Remedy, because it is capital for those ho receive an Audience to spit or wipe their Mouths in his lajesty's Presence.

When I had crept within four Yards of the Throne, I ised my self gently upon my Knees, and then striking my orehead seven Times against the Ground, I pronounced the llowing Words, as they had been taught me the Night before, *kpling Gloffthrobb Squutserumm blhiop Mlashnalt Zwin odbalkguffh Slhiophad Gurdlubh Asht*. This is the Compliment tablished by the Laws of the Land for all Persons admitted the King's Presence. It may be rendered into *English* thus : *lay your cœlestial Majesty out-live the Sun, eleven Moons and half*. To this the King returned some Answer, which though I could not understand, yet I replied as I had been rected ; *Fluft drin Yalerick Dwuldum prastrad mirplush*, hich properly signifies, *My Tongue is in the Mouth of my riend* ; and by this Expression was meant that I desired ave to bring my Interpreter ; whereupon the young Man ready mentioned was accordingly introduced ; by whose ntervention I answered as many Questions as his Majesty uld put in above an Hour. I spoke in the *Balnibarbian* ongue, and my Interpreter delivered my Meaning in that of *uggnagg*.

The King was much delighted with my Company, and dered his *Bliffmarklub* or High Chamberlain to appoint a dging in the Court for me and my Interpreter, with a daily llowance for my Table, and a large Purse of Gold for my mmon Expences.

I stayed three Months in this Country out of perfect Obedience to his Majesty, who was pleased highly to favour me, and
made me very honourable Offers. But I thought it more
consistent with Prudence and Justice to pass the Remainder of
my Days with my Wife and Family.

CHAPTER SEVEN

THE LUGGNUGGIANS COMMENDED. A PARTICULAR DESCRIPTION OF
THE STRULDBRUGS, WITH MANY CONVERSATIONS BETWEEN THE
AUTHOR AND SOME EMINENT PERSONS UPON THAT SUBJECT.

THE *Luggnuggians* are a polite and generous People, and
although they are not without some Share of that Pride
which is peculiar to all *Eastern* Countries, yet they shew
themselves courteous to Strangers, especially such who are
countenanced by the Court. I had many Acquaintance
among Persons of the best Fashion, and being always attended
by my Interpreter, the Conversation we had was not disagreeable.

One Day in much good Company, I was asked by a Person
of Quality, whether I had seen any of their *Struldbrugs* or
Immortals. I said I had not; and desired he would explain to
me what he had meant by such an Appellation, applyed to a
mortal Creature. He told me, that sometimes, although very
rarely, a Child happened to be born in a Family with a red
circular Spot in the Forehead, directly over the left Eye-brow,
which was an infallible Mark that it should never dye. The
Spot, as he described it, was about the Compass of a Silver
Threepence, but in the Course of Time grew larger, and
changed its Colour; for at Twelve Years old it became green,
so continued till Five and Twenty, then turned to a deep blue;
at Five and Forty it grew coal black, and as large as an *English*
Shilling; but never admitted any farther Alteration. He said
these Births were so rare, that he did not believe there could
be above Eleven Hundred *Struldbrugs* of both Sexes in the

ole Kingdom, of which he computed about Fifty in the
etropolis, and among the rest a young Girl born about three
ars ago. That, these Productions were not peculiar to any
mily but a meer Effect of Chance; and the Children of the
ruldbrugs themselves, were equally mortal with the rest of
: People.

I freely own myself to have been struck with inexpressible
light upon hearing this Account: And the Person who gave
me happening to understand the *Balnibarbian* Language,
ich I spoke very well, I could not forbear breaking out into
pressions perhaps a little too extravagant. I cryed out as in
Rapture; Happy Nation, where every Child hath at least a
ance for being immortal! Happy People who enjoy so many
ing Examples of antient Virtue, and have Masters ready to
truct them in the Wisdom of all former Ages! But, happiest
yond all Comparison are those excellent *Struldbrugs*, who
ng born exempt from that universal Calamity of human
ture, have their Minds free and disingaged, without the
:ight and Depression of Spirits caused by the continual
prehension of Death. I discovered my Admiration that I
l not observed any of these illustrious Persons at Court; the
ck Spot on the Fore-head, being so remarkable a Distinction,
t I could not have easily overlooked it: And it was impossible
t his Majesty, a most judicious Prince, should not provide
1self with a good Number of such wise and able Counsellors.
t perhaps the Virtue of those Reverend Sages was too strict
the corrupt and libertine Manners of a Court. And we often
l by Experience, that young Men are too opinionative and
atile to be guided by the sober Dictates of their Seniors.
wever, since the King was pleased to allow me Access to his
yal Person, I was resolved upon the very first Occasion to
iver my Opinion to him on this Matter freely, and at large
the Help of my Interpreter; and whether he would please
take my Advice or no, yet in one Thing I was determined,
t his Majesty having frequently offered me an Establishment
this Country, I would with great Thankfulness accept the
vour, and pass my Life here in the Conversation of those
periour Beings the *Struldbrugs*, if they would please to admit

The Gentleman to whom I addressed my Discourse, becau[se] (as I have already observed) he spoke the Language of *Balnib[e]bi*, said to me with a Sort of a Smile, which usually ariseth fr[om] Pity to the Ignorant, that he was glad of any Occasion to ke[ep] me among them, and desired my Permission to explain to t[he] Company what I had spoke. He did so; and they talk[ed] together for some time in their own Language, whereof [I] understood not a Syllable, neither could I observe by th[eir] Countenances what Impression my Discourse had made [on] them. After a short Silence, the same Person told me, that [his] Friends and mine (so he thought fit to express himself) w[ere] very much pleased with the judicious Remarks I had made [on] the great Happiness and Advantages of immortal Life; and th[ey] were desirous to know in a particular Manner, what Sche[me] of Living I should have formed to myself, if it had fallen to [my] Lot to have been born a *Struldbrug*.

I answered, it was easy to be eloquent on so copious a[nd] delightful a Subject, especially to me who have been often [used] to amuse myself with Visions of what I should do if I wer[e a] King, a General, or a great Lord: And upon this very C[ase] I had frequently run over the whole System how I sho[uld] employ myself, and pass the Time if I were sure to live [for] ever.

That, if it had been my good Fortune to come into [the] World a *Struldbrug*; as soon as I could discover my o[wn] Happiness by understanding the Difference between Life a[nd] Death, I would first resolve by all Arts and Methods whatsoe[ver] to procure myself Riches: In the Pursuit of which, by Th[rift] and Management, I might reasonably expect in about t[wo] Hundred Years, to be the wealthiest Man in the Kingdom. [In] the second Place, I would from my earliest Youth apply mys[elf] to the Study of Arts and Sciences, by which I should arrive [in] time to excel all others in Learning. Lastly, I would carefu[lly] record every Action and Event of Consequence that happen[ed] in the Publick, impartially draw the Characters of the seve[ral] Successions of Princes, and great Ministers of State; with [my] own Observations on every Point. I would exactly set down [the] several Changes in Customs, Languages, Fashions of Dre[ss,] Dyet and Diversions. By all which Acquirements, I should [

a living Treasury of Knowledge and Wisdom, and certainly become the Oracle of the Nation.

I would never marry after Threescore, but live in an hospitable Manner, yet still on the saving Side. I would entertain myself in forming and directing the Minds of hopeful young Men, by convincing them from my own Remembrance, Experience and Observation, fortified by numerous Examples, of the Usefulness of Virtue in publick and private Life. But, my choice and constant Companions should be a Sett of my own immortal Brotherhood, among whom I would elect a Dozen from the most ancient down to my own Contemporaries. Where any of these wanted Fortunes, I would provide them with convenient Lodges round my own Estate, and have some of them always at my Table, only mingling a few of the most valuable among you Mortals, whom Length of Time would harden me to lose with little or no Reluctance, and treat your Posterity after the same Manner; just as a Man diverts himself with the annual Succession of Pinks and Tulips in his Garden, without regretting the Loss of those which withered the preceding Year.

These *Struldbrugs* and I would mutually communicate our Observations and Memorials through the Course of Time; remark the several Gradations by which Corruption steals into the World, and oppose it in every Step, by giving perpetual Warning and Instruction to Mankind; which, added to the strong Influence of our own Example, would probably prevent that continual Degeneracy of human Nature, so justly complained of in all Ages.

Add to all this, the Pleasure of seeing the various Revolutions of States and Empires; the Changes in the lower and upper World; antient Cities in Ruins, and obscure Villages become the Seats of Kings. Famous Rivers lessening into shallow Brooks; the Ocean leaving one Coast dry, and overwhelming another: The Discovery of many Countries yet unknown. Barbarity over-running the politest Nations, and the most barbarous becoming civilized. I should then see the Discovery of the *Longitude*, the *perpetual Motion*, the *universal Medicine*, and many other great Inventions brought to the utmost Perfection.

What wonderful Discoveries should we make in Astronomy, by outliving and confirming our own Predictions; by observing the Progress and Returns of Comets, with the Changes of Motion in the Sun, Moon and Stars.

At last the same Gentleman who had been my Interpreter, said, he was desired by the rest to set me right in a few Mistakes, which I had fallen into through the common Imbecility of human Nature, and upon that Allowance was less answerable for them. That, this Breed of *Struldbrugs* was peculiar to their Country, for there were no such People either in *Balnibarbi* or *Japan*, where he had the Honour to be Ambassador from his Majesty, and found the Natives in both those Kingdoms very hard to believe that the Fact was possible; and it appeared from my Astonishment when he first mentioned the Matter to me, that I received it as a Thing wholly new, and scarcely to be credited. That in the two Kingdoms abovementioned, where during his Residence he had conversed very much, he observed long Life to be the universal Desire and Wish of Mankind. That, whoever had one Foot in the Grave, was sure to hold back the other as strongly as he could. That the oldest had still Hopes of living one Day longer, and looked on Death as the greatest Evil, from which Nature always prompted him to retreat; only in this Island of *Luggnagg*, the Appetite for living was not so eager, from the continual Example of the *Struldbrugs* before their Eyes.

That the System of Living contrived by me was unreasonable and unjust, because it supposed a Perpetuity of Youth, Health, and Vigour, which no Man could be so foolish to hope, however extravagant he might be in his Wishes. That, the Question therefore was not whether a Man would chuse to be always in the Prime of Youth, attended with Prosperity and Health; but how he would pass a perpetual Life under all the usual Disadvantages which old Age brings along with it. For although few Men will avow their Desires of being immortal upon such hard Conditions, yet in the two Kingdoms before mentioned of *Balnibarbi* and *Japan*, he observed that every Man desired to put off Death for sometime longer, let it approach ever so late; and he rarely heard of any Man who died willingly, except he were incited by the Extremity of Grief or Torture.

And he appealed to me whether in those Countries I had travelled as well as my own, I had not observed the same general Disposition.

After this Preface, he gave me a particular Account of the *Struldbrugs* among them. He said they commonly acted like Mortals, till about Thirty Years old, after which by Degrees they grew melancholy and dejected, increasing in both till they came to Fourscore. This he learned from their own Confession; for otherwise there not being above two or three of that Species born in an Age, they were too few to form a general Observation by. When they came to Fourscore Years, which is reckoned the Extremity of living in this Country, they had not only all the Follies and Infirmities of other old Men, but many more which arose from the dreadful Prospect of never dying. They were not only opinionative, peevish, covetous, morose, vain, talkative; but uncapable of Friendship, and dead to all natural Affection, which never descended below their Grand-children. Envy and impotent Desires, are their prevailing Passions. But those Objects against which their Envy seems principally directed, are the Vices of the younger Sort, and the Deaths of the old. By reflecting on the former, they find themselves cut off from all Possibility of Pleasure; and whenever they see a Funeral, they lament and repine that others are gone to an Harbour of Rest, to which they themselves never can hope to arrive. They have no Remembrance of any thing but what they learned and observed in their Youth and middle Age, and even that is very imperfect: And for the Truth or Particulars of any Fact, it is safer to depend on common Traditions than upon their best Recollections. The least miserable among them, appear to be those who turn to Dotage, and entirely lose their Memories; these meet with more Pity and Assistance, because they want many bad Qualities which abound in others.

They are despised and hated by all Sorts of People: When one of them is born, it is reckoned ominous, and their Birth is recorded very particularly; so that you may know their Age by consulting the Registry, which however hath not been kept above a Thousand Years past, or at least hath been destroyed by Time or publick Disturbances. But the usual Way of computing how old they are, is, by asking them what Kings or great Persons they can remember, and then consulting History ; for infallibly the last Prince in their Mind did not begin his Reign after they were Fourscore Years old.

They were the most mortifying Sight I ever beheld ; and the Women more horrible than the Men. Besides the usual Deformities in extreme old Age, they acquired an additional Ghastliness in Proportion to their Number of Years, which is not to be described ; and among half a Dozen I soon distingui- shed which was the eldest, although there were not above a Century or two between them.

The Reader will easily believe, that from what I had heard and seen, my keen Appetite for Perpetuity of Life was much abated. I grew heartily ashamed of the pleasing Visions I had formed ; and thought no Tyrant could invent a Death into which I would not run with Pleasure from such a Life. The King heard of all that had passed between me and my Friends upon this Occasion, and raillied me very pleasantly ; wishing I would send a Couple of *Struldbrugs* to my own Country, to arm our People against the Fear of Death ; but this it seems is forbidden by the fundamental Laws of the Kingdom ; or else I should have been well content with the Trouble and Expence of transporting them.

CHAPTER EIGHT

THE AUTHOR LEAVES LUGGNAGG AND SAILS TO JAPAN. FROM THENCE HE RETURNS IN A DUTCH SHIP TO AMSTERDAM, AND FROM AMSTERDAM TO ENGLAND.

THERE is indeed a perpetual Commerce between this King- dom and the great Empire of *Japan* ; and it is very probable that the *Japanese* Authors may have given some Account of the *Struldbrugs* ; but my Stay in *Japan* was so short, and I was so entirely a Stranger to the Language, that I was not qualified to make any Enquiries. But I hope the *Dutch* upon this Notice will be curious and able enough to supply my Defects.

His Majesty having often pressed me to accept some Employment in his Court, and finding me absolutely determined to return to my Native Country; was pleased to give me his Licence to depart; and honoured me with a Letter of Recommendation under his own Hand to the Emperor of *Japan*. He likewise presented me with four Hundred forty-four large Pieces of Gold (this Nation delighting in even Numbers) and a red Diamond which I sold in *England* for Eleven Hundred Pounds.

On the 6th Day of *May*, 1709, I took a solemn Leave of his Majesty, and all my Friends. This Prince was so gracious as to order a Guard to conduct me to *Glanguenstald*, which is a Royal Port to the *South-West* Part of the Island. In six Days I found a Vessel ready to carry me to *Japan*; and spent fifteen Days in the Voyage. We landed at a small Port-Town called *Xamoschi*, situated on the *South-East* Part of *Japan*. The Town lies on the *Western* Part, where there is a narrow Streight, leading *Northward* into a long Arm of the Sea, upon the *North-West* Part of which *Yedo* the Metropolis stands. At landing I shewed the Custom-House Officers my Letter from the King of *Luggnagg* to his Imperial Majesty: They knew the Seal perfectly well; it was as broad as the Palm of my Hand. The Impression was, *A King lifting up a lame Beggar from the Earth.* The Magistrates of the Town hearing of my Letter, received me as a publick Minister; they provided me with Carriages and Servants, and bore my Charges to *Yedo*, where I was admitted to an Audience, and delivered my Letter; which was opened with great Ceremony, and explained to the Emperor by an Interpreter, who gave me Notice of his Majesty's Order, that I should signify my Request; and whatever it were, it should be granted for the sake of his Royal Brother of *Luggnagg*. This Interpreter was a Person employed to transact Affairs with the *Hollanders*: He soon conjectured by my Countenance that I was an *European*, and therefore repeated his Majesty's Commands in *Low-Dutch*, which he spoke perfectly well. I answered, (as I had before determined) that I was a *Dutch* Merchant, shipwrecked in a very remote Country, from whence I travelled by Sea and Land to *Luggnagg*, and then took Shipping for *Japan*, where I knew my Countrymen often traded,

and with some of these I hoped to get an Opportunity c
returning into *Europe* : I therefore most humbly entreated hi
Royal Favour to give Order, that I should be conducted i
Safety to *Nangasac*. To this I added another Petition, that fo
the sake of my Patron the King of *Luggnagg*, his Majesty woul
condescend to excuse my performing the Ceremony impose
on my Countrymen, of *trampling upon the Crucifix* ; becaus
I had been thrown into his Kingdom by my Misfortune
without any Intention of trading. When this latter Petitio
was interpreted to the Emperor, he seemed a little surprised
and said, he believed I was the first of my Countrymen wh
ever made any Scruple in this Point ; and that he began t
doubt whether I were a real *Hollander* or no ; but rathe
suspected I must be a Christian. However, for the Reasons
had offered, but chiefly to gratify the King of *Luggnagg*, by a
uncommon Mark of his Favour, he would comply with th
singularity of my Humour ; but the Affair must be manage
with Dexterity, and his Officers should be commanded to l
me pass as it were by Forgetfulness. For he assured me, that
the Secret should be discovered by my Countrymen, the *Dutc*
they would cut my Throat in the Voyage. I returned m
Thanks by the Interpreter for so unusual a Favour ; and son
Troops being at that Time on their March to *Nangasac*, t
Commanding Officer had Orders to convey me safe thithe
with particular Instructions about the Business of the *Crucifi*.

On the 9th Day of *June*, 1709, I arrived at *Nangasac*, aft
a very long and troublesome Journey. I soon fell into Compar
of some *Dutch* Sailors belonging to the *Amboyna* of *Amsterdar*
a stout Ship of 450 Tuns. I have lived long in *Holland*, pursuir
my Studies at *Leyden*, and I spoke *Dutch* well : The Seame
soon knew from whence I came last ; they were curious
enquire into my Voyages and Course of Life. I made up
Story as short and probable as I could, but concealed t
greatest Part. I knew many Persons in *Holland* ; I was ab
to invent Names for my Parents, whom I pretended to l
obscure People in the Province of *Guelderland*. I would ha
given the Captain (one *Theodorus Vangrult*) what he pleased
ask for my Voyage to *Holland* ; but, understanding I was
Surgeon, he was contented to take half the usual Rate,

Condition that I would serve him in the Way of my Calling. Before we took Shipping, I was often asked by some of the Crew, whether I had performed the Ceremony above-mentioned? I evaded the Question by general Answers, that I had satisfied the Emperor and Court in all Particulars. However, a malicious Rogue of a Skipper went to an Officer, and pointing to me, told him, I had not yet *trampled on the Crucifix*: But the other, who had received Instructions to let me pass, gave the Rascal twenty Strokes on the Shoulders with a Bamboo; after which I was no more troubled with such Questions.

Nothing happened worth mentioning in this Voyage. We sailed with a fair Wind to the *Cape of Good Hope*, where we staid only to take in fresh Water. On the 16th of *April* we arrived safe at *Amsterdam*, having lost only three Men by Sickness in the Voyage, and a fourth who fell from the Fore-mast into the Sea, not far from the Coast of *Guinea*. From *Amsterdam* I soon after set sail for *England* in a small Vessel belonging to that City.

On the 20th of *April*, 1710, we put in at the *Downs*. I landed the next Morning, and saw once more my Native Country after an Absence of five Years and six Months compleat. I went strait to *Redriff*, whither I arrived the same Day at two in the Afternoon, and found my Wife and Family in good Health.

The End of the Third Part

PART FOUR

A VOYAGE TO THE COUNTRY OF THE HOUYHNHNMS

CHAPTER ONE

THE AUTHOR SETS OUT AS CAPTAIN OF A SHIP. HIS MEN CONSPIRE
AGAINST HIM, CONFINE HIM A LONG TIME TO HIS CABBIN, SET
HIM ON SHORE IN AN UNKNOWN LAND. HE TRAVELS UP INTO THE
COUNTRY. THE YAHOOS, A STRANGE SORT OF ANIMAL, DESCRIBED.
THE AUTHOR MEETS TWO HOUYHNHNMS.

I CONTINUED at home with my Wife and Children about five
Months in a very happy Condition, if I could have learned
the Lesson of knowing when I was well. I left my poor Wife
and accepted an advantageous Offer made me to be Captain of
the *Adventure*, a stout Merchant-man of 350 Tuns: For I
understood Navigation well, and being grown weary of a
Surgeon's Employment at Sea, which however I could exercise
upon Occasion, I took a skilful young Man of that Calling,
one *Robert Purefoy*, into my Ship. We set sail from *Portsmouth*
upon the 7th Day of *September*, 1710; on the 14th we met
with Captain *Pocock* of *Bristol*, at *Tenariff*, who was going to
the Bay of *Campeachy*, to cut Logwood. On the 16th he was
parted from us by a Storm: I heard since my Return, that his
Ship foundered, and none escaped, but one Cabbin-Boy. He
was an honest Man, and a good Sailor, but a little too positive
in his own Opinions, which was the Cause of his Destruction,
as it hath been of several others. For if he had followed my
Advice, he might at this Time have been safe at home with
his Family as well as my self.

I had several Men died in my Ship of Calentures, so that I was
forced to get Recruits out of *Barbadoes*, and the *Leeward
Islands*, where I touched by the Direction of the Merchants

who employed me; which I had soon too much Cause to repent; for I found afterwards that most of them had been Buccaneers. I had fifty Hands on Board; and my Orders were, that I should trade with the *Indians* in the *South-Sea*, and make what Discoveries I could. These Rogues whom I had picked up, debauched my other Men, and they all formed a Conspiracy to seize the Ship and secure me; which they did one Morning, rushing into my Cabbin, and binding me Hand and Foot, threatening to throw me overboard, if I offered to stir. I told them, I was their Prisoner, and would submit. This they made me swear to do, and then unbound me, only fastening one of my Legs with a Chain near my Bed; and placed a Centry at my Door with his Piece charged, who was commanded to shoot me dead if I attempted my Liberty. They sent me down Victuals and Drink, and took the Government of the Ship to themselves. Their Design was to turn Pirates, and plunder the *Spaniards*, which they could not do, till they got more Men. But first they resolved to sell the Goods in the Ship, and then go to *Madagascar* for Recruits, several among them having died since my Confinement. They sailed many Weeks, and traded with the *Indians*; but I knew not what Course they took, being kept close Prisoner in my Cabbin, and expecting nothing less than to be murdered, as they often threatened me.

Upon the 9th Day of *May*, 1711, one *James Welch* came down to my Cabbin; and said he had Orders from the Captain to set me ashore. I expostulated with him, but in vain; neither would he so much as tell me who their new Captain was. They forced me into the Long-boat, letting me put on my best Suit of Cloaths, which were as good as new, and a small Bundle of Linnen, but no Arms except my Hanger; and they were so civil as not to search my Pockets, into which I conveyed what Money I had, with some other little Necessaries. They rowed about a League; and then set me down on a Strand. I desired them to tell me what Country it was: They all swore, they knew no more than my self, but said, that the Captain (as they called him) was resolved, after they had sold the Lading, to get rid of me in the first Place where they discovered Land. They pushed off immediately, advising me to make haste, for fear of being overtaken by the Tide; and bade me farewell.

In this desolate Condition I advanced forward, and soon got upon firm Ground, where I sat down on a Bank to rest my self, and consider what I had best to do. When I was a little refreshed, I went up into the Country, resolving to deliver my self to the first Savages I should meet; and purchase my Life from them by some Bracelets, Glass Rings, and other Toys, which Sailors usually provide themselves with in those Voyages, and whereof I had some about me: The Land was divided by long Rows of Trees, not regularly planted, but naturally growing; there was great Plenty of Grass, and several Fields of Oats. I walked very circumspectly for fear of being surprised, or suddenly shot with an Arrow from behind, or on either Side. I fell into a beaten Road, where I saw many Tracks of human Feet, and some of Cows, but most of Horses. At last I beheld several Animals in a Field, and one or two of the same Kind sitting in Trees. Their Shape was very singular, and deformed, which a little discomposed me, so that I lay down behind a Thicket to observe them better. Some of them coming forward near the Place where I lay, gave me an Opportunity of distinctly marking their Form. Their Heads and Breasts were covered with a thick Hair, some frizzled and others lank; they had Beards like Goats, and a long Ridge of Hair down their Backs, and the fore Parts of their Legs and Feet; but the rest of their Bodies were bare, so that I might see their Skins, which were of a brown Buff Colour. They climbed high Trees, as nimbly as a Squirrel, for they had strong extended Claws before and behind, terminating on sharp Points, hooked. They would often spring, and bound, and leap with prodigious Agility. The Females were not so large as the Males; they had long lank Hair on their Heads, and only a Sort of Down on the rest of their Bodies. The Hair of both Sexes was of several Colours, brown, red, black and yellow. Upon the whole, I never beheld in all my Travels so disagreeable an Animal, or one against which I naturally conceived so strong an Antipathy. So that thinking I had seen enough, full of Contempt and Aversion, I got up and pursued the beaten Road, hoping it might direct me to the Cabbin of some *Indian*. I had not gone far when I met one of these Creatures full in my Way, and coming up directly to me. The ugly Monster, when he saw me, distorted several Ways every Feature of his Visage, and stared as at an Object he had never seen before; then approaching nearer, lifted up his fore Paw, whether out of Curiosity or Mischief, I could not tell: But I drew my Hanger, and gave him a good Blow with the flat Side of it; for I durst not strike him with the Edge, fearing the Inhabitants might be provoked against me, if they should come to know, that I had killed or maimed any of their Cattle. When the Beast felt the Smart, he drew back, and roared so loud, that a Herd of at least forty came flocking about me from the next Field, howling and making odious Faces; but I ran to the Body of a Tree, and leaning my Back against it, kept them off, by waving my Hanger.

In the Midst of this Distress, I observed them all to run away on a sudden as fast as they could; at which I ventured to leave the Tree, and pursue the Road, wondering what it was that could put them into this Fright. But looking on my Left-Hand, I saw a Horse walking softly in the Field; which my Persecutors having sooner discovered, was the Cause of their Flight. The Horse started a little when he came near me, but soon recovering himself, looked full in my Face with manifest Tokens of Wonder: He viewed my Hands and Feet, walking round me several times. I would have pursued my Journey, but he placed himself directly in the Way, yet looking with a very mild Aspect, never offering the least Violence. We stood gazing at each other for some time; at last I took the Boldness to reach my Hand towards his Neck, with a Design to stroak it; using the common Style and Whistle of Jockies when they are going to handle a strange Horse. But, this Animal seeming to receive my Civilities with Disdain, shook his Head, and bent his Brows, softly raising up his Left Fore-Foot to remove my Hand. Then he neighed three or four times, but in so different a Cadence, that I almost began to think he was speaking to himself in some Language of his own.

While He and I were thus employed, another Horse came up; who was applying himself to the first in a very formal Manner, they gently struck each others Right Hoof before, neighing several times by Turns, and varying the Sound, which seemed to be almost articulate. They went some Paces off, as if it were to confer together, walking Side by Side, backward and forward, like Persons deliberating upon some Affair of Weight; but often turning their Eyes towards me, as it were to watch that I might not escape. I was amazed to see such Actions and Behaviour in Brute Beasts; and concluded with myself, that if the Inhabitants of this Country were endured with a proportionable Degree of Reason, they must needs be the wisest People upon Earth. This Thought gave me so much Comfort, that I resolved to go forward untill I could discover some House or Village, or meet with any of the Natives; leaving the two Horses to discourse together as they pleased. But the first, who was a Dapple-Grey, observing me to steal off, neighed after me in so expressive a Tone, that I fancied myself to understand what he meant; whereupon I turned back, and came near him, to expect his farther Commands; but concealing my Fear as much as I could; for I began to be in some Pain, how this Adventure might terminate; and the Reader will easily believe I did not much like my present Situation.

The two Horses came up close to me, looking with great Earnestness upon my Face and Hands. The grey Steed rubbed my Hat all round with his Right Fore-hoof, and discomposed it so much, that I was forced to adjust it better, by taking it off, and settling it again; whereat both he and his Companion (who was a brown Bay) appeared to be much surprized; the latter felt the Lappet of my Coat, and finding it to hang loose about me, they both looked with new Signs of Wonder. He stroked my Right Hand, seeming to admire the Softness, and Colour; but he squeezed it so hard between his Hoof and his Pastern, that I was forced to roar; after which they both touched me with all possible Tenderness. They were under great Perplexity about my Shoes and Stockings, which they felt very often, neighing to each other, and using various Gestures, not unlike those of a Philosopher, when he would attempt to solve some new and difficult Phænomenon.

Upon the whole, the Behaviour of these Animals was so orderly and rational, so acute and judicious, that I at last concluded, they must needs be Magicians, who had thus metamorphosed themselves upon some Design; and seeing a Stranger in the Way, were resolved to divert themselves with him ; or perhaps were really amazed at the Sight of a Man so very different in Habit, Feature and Complexion from those who might probably live in so remote a Climate. Upon the Strength of this Reasoning, I ventured to address them in the following Manner : Gentlemen, if you be Conjurers, as I have good Cause to believe, you can understand any Language ; therefore I make bold to let your Worships know, that I am a poor distressed *Englishman*, driven by his Misfortunes upon your Coast ; and I entreat one of you, to let me ride upon his Back, as if he were a real Horse, to some House or Village, where I can be relieved. In return of which Favour, I will make you a Present of this Knife and Bracelet, (taking them out of my Pocket.) The two Creatures stood silent while I spoke, seeming to listen with great Attention ; and when I had ended, they neighed frequently towards each other, as if they were engaged in serious Conversation. I plainly observed, that their Language expressed the Passions very well, and the Words might with little Pains be resolved into an Alphabet more easily than the *Chinese*.

I could frequently distinguish the Word *Yahoo*, which was repeated by each of them several times ; and although it were impossible for me to conjecture what it meant, yet while the two Horses were busy in Conversation, I endeavoured to practice this Word upon my Tongue ; and as soon as they were silent, I boldly pronounced *Yahoo* in a loud Voice, imitating, at the same time, as near as I could, the Neighing of a Horse ; at which they were both visibly surprized, and the Grey repeated the same Word twice, as if he meant to teach me the right Accent, wherein I spoke after him as well as I could, and found myself perceivably to improve every time, although very far from any Degree of Perfection. Then the Bay tried me with a second Word, much harder to be pronounced ; but reducing it to the *English Orthography*, may be spelt thus, *Houyhnhnm*. I did not succeed in this so well as the former, but after two or three farther Trials, I had better Fortune ; and they both appeared amazed at my Capacity.

After some farther Discourse, which I then conjectured might relate to me, the two Friends took their Leaves, with the same Compliment of striking each other's Hoof ; and the

Grey made me Signs that I should walk before him; wherein I thought it prudent to comply, till I could find a better Director. When I offered to slacken my Pace, he would cry *Hhuun*, *Hhuun*; I guessed his Meaning, and gave him to understand, as well as I could, that I was weary, and not able to walk faster; upon which, he would stand a while to let me rest.

CHAPTER TWO

THE AUTHOR CONDUCTED BY A HOUYHNHNM TO HIS HOUSE. THE HOUSE DESCRIBED. THE AUTHOR'S RECEPTION. THE FOOD OF THE HOUYHNHNMS. THE AUTHOR IN DISTRESS FOR WANT OF MEAT, IS AT LAST RELIEVED. HIS MANNER OF FEEDING IN THAT COUNTRY.

HAVING travelled about three Miles, we came to a long Kind of Building, made of Timber, stuck in the Ground, and wattled a-cross; the Roof was low, and covered with Straw. I now began to be a little comforted; and took out some Toys, which Travellers usually carry for Presents to the Savage *Indians* of *America* and other Parts, in hopes the People of the House would be thereby encouraged to receive me kindly. The Horse made me a Sign to go in first; it was a large Room with a smooth Clay Floor, and a Rack and Manger extending the whole Length on one Side. There were three Nags, and two Mares, not eating, but some of them sitting down upon their Hams, which I very much wondered at; but wondered more to see the rest employed in domestick Business: The last seemed but ordinary Cattle; however this confirmed my first Opinion, that a People who could so far civilize brute Animals, must needs excel in Wisdom all the Nations of the World. The Grey came in just after, and thereby prevented any ill Treatment, which the others might have given me. He neighed to them several times in a Style of Authority, and received Answers.

Beyond this Room there were three others, reaching the Length of the House, to which you passed through three Doors, opposite to each other, in the Manner of a Vista: We went

through the second Room towards the third; here the Grey
walked in first, beckoning me to attend: I waited in the second
Room, and got ready my Presents, for the Master and Mistress
of the House: They were two Knives, three Bracelets of false
Pearl, a small Looking Glass and a Bead Necklace. The Horse
neighed three or four Times, and I waited to hear some answers
in a human Voice, but I heard no other Returns than in the
same Dialect, only one or two a little shriller than his. I began
to think that this House must belong to some Person of great
Note among them, because there appeared so much Ceremony
before I could gain Admittance. But, that a Man of Quality
should be served all by Horses, was beyond my Comprehension.
I feared my Brain was disturbed by my Sufferings and Misfortunes: I roused my self, and looked about me in the Room
where I was left alone; this was furnished as the first, only
after a more elegant Manner. I rubbed my Eyes often, but the
same Objects still occurred. I pinched my Arms and Sides, to
awake my self, hoping I might be in a Dream. I then absolutely
concluded, that all these Appearances could be nothing else
but Necromancy and Magick. But I had no Time to pursue
these Reflections; for the Grey Horse came to the Door, and
made me a Sign to follow him into the third Room; where I
saw a very comely Mare, together with a Colt and Fole, sitting
on their Haunches, upon Mats of Straw, not unartfully made,
and perfectly neat and clean.

The Mare soon after my Entrance, rose from her Mat, and
coming up close, after having nicely observed my Hands and
Face, gave me a most contemptuous Look; then turning to
the Horse, I heard the Word *Yahoo* often repeated betwixt
them; the meaning of which Word I could not then com-
prehend, although it were the first I had learned to pronounce;
but I was soon better informed, to my everlasting Mortification:
For the Horse beckoning to me with his Head, and repeating
the Word *Hhuun, Hhuun,* as he did upon the Road, which I
understood was to attend him, led me out into a kind of Court,
where was another Building at some Distance from the House.
Here we entered, and I saw three of those detestable Creatures,
which I first met after my landing, feeding upon Roots, and
the Flesh of some Animals, which I afterwards found to be that

of Asses and Dogs, and now and then a Cow dead by Accident
or Disease. They were all tied by the Neck with strong Wyths,
fastened to a Beam; they held their Food between the Claws
of their fore Feet, and tore it with their Teeth.

The Master Horse ordered a Sorrel Nag, one of his Servants,
to untie the largest of these Animals, and take him into a Yard.
The Beast and I were brought close together; and our Countenances diligently compared, both by Master and Servant,
who thereupon repeated several Times the Word *Yahoo*. My
Horror and Astonishment are not to be described, when I
observed, in this abominable Animal, a perfect human Figure;
the Face of it indeed was flat and broad, the Nose depressed,
the Lips large, and the Mouth wide: But these Differences
are common to all savage Nations, where the Lineaments of the
Countenance are distorted by the Natives suffering their Infants
to lie grovelling on the Earth, or by carrying them on their
Backs, nuzzling with their Face against the Mother's Shoulders.
The Fore-feet of the *Yahoo* differed from my Hands in nothing
else, but the Length of the Nails, the Coarseness and Brownness
of the Palms, and the Hairiness on the Backs. There was the
same Resemblance between our Feet, with the same Differences,
which I knew very well, although the Horses did not, because
of my Shoes and Stockings; the same in every Part of our
Bodies, except as to Hairiness and Colour, which I have already
described.

The great Difficulty that seemed to stick with the two
Horses, was, to see the rest of my Body so very different from
that of a *Yahoo*, for which I was obliged to my Cloaths, whereof
they had no Conception: The Sorrel Nag offered me a Root,
which he held (after their Manner, as we shall describe in its
proper Place) between his Hoof and Pastern; I took it in my
Hand, and having smelt it, returned it to him again as civilly
as I could. He brought out of the *Yahoo's* Kennel a Piece of
Ass's Flesh, but it smelt so offensively that I turned from it
with loathing; he then threw it to the *Yahoo*, by whom it was
greedily devoured. He afterwards shewed me a Wisp of Hay,
and a Fettlock full of Oats; but I shook my Head, to signify
that neither of these were Food for me. And indeed, I now
apprehended, that I must absolutely starve, if I did not get to

some of my own Species: For as to those filthy *Yahoos*, although there were few greater Lovers of Mankind, at that time, than myself; yet I confess I never saw any sensitive Being so detestable on all Accounts; and the more I came near them, the more hateful they grew, while I stayed in that Country. This the Master Horse observed by my Behaviour, and therefore sent the *Yahoo* back to his Kennel. He then put his Fore-hoof to his Mouth, at which I was much surprized, although he did it with Ease, and with a Motion that appear'd perfectly natural; and made other Signs to know what I would eat; but I could not return him such an Answer as he was able to apprehend; and if he had understood me, I did not see how it was possible to contrive any way for finding myself Nourishment. While we were thus engaged, I observed a Cow passing by; whereupon I pointed to her, and expressed a Desire to let me go and milk her. This had its Effect; for he led me back into the House, and ordered a Mare-servant to open a Room, where a good Store of Milk lay in Earthen and Wooden Vessels, after a very orderly and cleanly Manner. She gave me a large Bowl full, of which I drank very heartily, and found myself well refreshed.

About Noon I saw coming towards the House a Kind of Vehicle, drawn like a Sledge by four *Yahoos*. There was in it an old Steed, who seemed to be of Quality; he alighted with his Hind-feet forward, having by Accident got a Hurt in his Left Fore-foot. He came to dine with our Horse, who received him with great Civility. They dined in the best Room, and had Oats boiled in Milk for the second Course, which the old Horse eat warm, but the rest cold. Their Mangers were placed circular in the Middle of the Room, and divided into several Partitions, round which they sat on their Haunches upon Bosses of Straw. In the Middle was a large Rack with Angles answering to every Partition of the Manger. So that each Horse and Mare eat their own Hay, and their own Mash of Oats and Milk, with much Decency and Regularity. The Behaviour of the young Colt and Fole appeared very modest; and that of the Master and Mistress extremely chearful and complaisant to their Guest. The Grey ordered me to stand by him; and much Discourse passed between him and his Friend concerning me, as I found by the Stranger's often looking on me, and the frequent Repetition of the Word *Yahoo*.

I happened to wear my Gloves; which the Master Grey observing, seemed perplexed; discovering Signs of Wonder what I had done to my Fore-feet; he put his Hoof three or four times to them, as if he would signify, that I should reduce them to their former Shape, which I presently did, pulling off both my Gloves and putting them into my Pocket. This occasioned farther Talk, and I saw the Company was pleased with my Behaviour, whereof I soon found the good Effects. I was ordered to speak the few Words I understood; and while they were at Dinner, the Master taught me the Names for Oats, Milk, Fire, Water, and some others; which I could readily pronounce after him; having from my Youth a great Facility in learning Languages.

When Dinner was done, the Master Horse took me aside, and by Signs and Words made me understand the Concern he was in, that I had nothing to eat. Oats in their Tongue are called *Hlunnh*. This Word I pronounced two or three times; for although I had refused them at first, yet upon second Thoughts, I considered that I could contrive to make a Kind of Bread, which might be sufficient with Milk to keep me alive, till I could make my Escape to some other Country, and to Creatures of my own Species. The Horse immediately ordered a white Mare-servant of his Family to bring me a good Quantity of Oats in a Sort of wooden Tray. These I heated before the Fire as well as I could, and rubbed them till the Husks came off, which I made a shift to winnow from the Grain; I ground and beat them between two Stones, then took Water, and made them into a Paste or Cake, which I toasted at the Fire, and eat warm with Milk. It was at first a very insipid Diet, although common enough in many Parts of *Europe*, but grew tolerable by Time; and having been often reduced to hard Fare in my Life, this was not the first Experiment I had made how easily Nature is satisfied. And I cannot but observe, that I never had one Hour's Sickness, while I staid in this Island. It is true, I sometimes made a shift to catch a Rabbet, or Bird, by Springes made of *Yahoos* Hairs; and I often gathered wholesome Herbs, which I boiled, or eat as Salades with my Bread; and now and then, for a Rarity, I made a little Butter, and drank the Whey. I was at first at a great Loss for Salt; but Custom soon reconciled the Want of it; and I am confident that the frequent Use of Salt among us is an Effect of Luxury, and was first introduced only as a Provocative to Drink; except where it is necessary for preserving of Flesh in long Voyages, or in Places remote from great Markets. For we observe no Animal to be fond of it but Man: And as to myself, when I left this Country, it was a great while before I could endure the Taste of it in any thing that I eat.

When it grew towards Evening, the Master Horse ordered a Place for me to lodge in; it was but Six Yards from the House, and separated from the Stable of the *Yahoos*. Here I got some Straw, and covering myself with my own Cloaths, slept very sound. But I was in a short time better accommodated, as the Reader shall know hereafter, when I come to treat more particularly about my Way of living.

CHAPTER THREE

THE AUTHOR STUDIOUS TO LEARN THE LANGUAGE, THE HOUYHN-HNM HIS MASTER ASSISTS IN TEACHING HIM. THE LANGUAGE DESCRIBED. SEVERAL HOUYHNHNMS OF QUALITY COME OUT OF CURIOSITY TO SEE THE AUTHOR. HE GIVES HIS MASTER A SHORT ACCOUNT OF HIS VOYAGE.

My principal Endeavour was to learn the Language, which my Master (for so I shall henceforth call him) and his Children, and every Servant of his House were desirous to teach me. For they looked upon it as a Prodigy, that a brute Animal should discover such Marks of a rational Creature. I pointed to every thing, and enquired the Name of it, which I wrote down in my *Journal Book* when I was alone, and corrected my bad Accent, by desiring those of the Family to pronounce it often. In this Employment, a Sorrel Nag, one of the under Servants, was very ready to assist me.

The Curiosity and Impatience of my Master were so great

that he spent many Hours of his Leisure to instruct me. He was convinced (as he afterwards told me) that I must be a *Yahoo*, but my Teachableness, Civility and Cleanliness astonished him; which were Qualities altogether so opposite to those Animals. He was most perplexed about my Cloaths, reasoning sometimes with himself, whether they were a Part of my Body; for I never pulled them off till the Family were asleep, and got them on before they waked in the Morning. My Master was eager to learn from whence I came; how I acquired those Appearances of Reason, which I discovered in all my Actions; and to know my Story from my own Mouth, which he hoped he should soon do by the great Proficiency I made in learning and pronouncing their Words and Sentences.

In about ten Weeks time I was able to understand most of his Questions; and in three Months could give him some tolerable Answers. He was extremely curious to know from what Part of the Country I came, and how I was taught to imitate a rational Creature; because the *Yahoos*, (whom he saw I exactly resembled in my Head, Hands and Face, that were only visible,) with some Appearance of Cunning, and the strongest Disposition to Mischief, were observed to be the most unteachable of all Brutes. I answered; that I came over the Sea, from a far Place, with many others of my own Kind, in a great hollow Vessel made of the Bodies of Trees: That, my Companions forced me to land on this Coast, and then left me to shift for myself. It was with some Difficulty, and by the Help of many Signs, that I brought him to understand me. He replied, That I must needs be mistaken, or that I *said the thing which was not*. (For they have no Word in their Language to express Lying or Falshood.) He knew it was impossible that there could be a Country beyond the Sea, or that a Parcel of Brutes could move a wooden Vessel whither they pleased upon Water. He was sure no *Houyhnhnm* alive could make such a Vessel, or would trust *Yahoos* to manage it.

The Word *Houyhnhnm*, in their Tongue, signifies a *Horse*; and in its Etymology, *the Perfection of Nature*. I told my Master, that I was at a Loss for Expression, but would improve as fast as I could; and hoped in a short time I should be able to tell him Wonders: He was pleased to direct his own Mare,

is Colt and Fole, and the Servants of the Family to take all
Opportunities of instructing me; and every Day for two or
three Hours, he was at the same Pains himself: Several Horses
and Mares of Quality in the Neighbourhood came often to our
House, upon the Report spread of a wonderful *Yahoo*, that
could speak like a *Houyhnhnm*, and seemed in his Words and
Actions to discover some Glimmerings of Reason. These
delighted to converse with me; they put many Questions, and
received such Answers, as I was able to return. By all which
Advantages, I made so great a Progress, that in five Months
from my Arrival, I understood whatever was spoke, and could
express myself tolerably well.

The *Houyhnhnms* who came to visit my Master, out of a
Design of seeing and talking with me, could hardly believe me
to be a right *Yahoo*, because my Body had a different Covering
from others of my Kind. They were astonished to observe me
without the usual Hair or Skin, except on my Head, Face and
Hands: but I discovered that Secret to my Master, upon an
Accident, which happened about a Fortnight before.

I have already told the Reader, that every Night when the
Family were gone to Bed, it was my Custom to strip and cover
myself with my Cloaths: It happened one Morning early,
that my Master sent for me, by the Sorrel Nag, who was his
Valet; when he came, I was fast asleep, my Cloaths fallen off
on one Side, and my Shirt above my Waste. I awaked at the
Noise he made, and observed him to deliver his Message in
some Disorder; after which he went to my Master, and in a
great Fright gave him a very confused Account of what he had
seen: This I presently discovered; for going as soon as I was
dressed, to pay my Attendance upon his Honour, he asked me
the Meaning of what his Servant had reported; that I was not
the same Thing when I slept as I appeared to be at other
times; that his Valet assured him, some Part of me was white,
some yellow, at least not so white, and some brown.

I had hitherto concealed the Secret of my Dress, in order to
distinguish myself as much as possible, from that cursed Race
of *Yahoos*; but now I found it in vain to do so any longer.
Besides, I considered that my Cloaths and Shoes would soon
wear out, which already were in a declining Condition, and

must be supplied by some Contrivance from the Hides o
Yahoos, or other Brutes ; whereby the whole Secret would b
known. I therefore told my Master, that in the Country from
whence I came, those of my Kind always covered their Bodie
with the Hairs of certain Animals prepared by Art, as well fo
Decency, as to avoid Inclemencies of Air both hot and cold
of which, as to my own Person I would give him immediat
Conviction, if he pleased to command me ; only desiring hi
Excuse, if I did not expose those Parts that Nature taught u
to conceal. He said, my Discourse was all very strange, bu
especially the last Part ; for he could not understand wh
Nature should teach us to conceal what Nature had given
That neither himself nor Family were ashamed of any Part
of their Bodies ; but however I might do as I pleased. Where
upon, I first unbuttoned my Coat, and pulled it off. I did th
same with my Waste-coat ; I drew off my Shoes, Stocking
and Breeches. I let my Shirt down to my Waste, and drew u
the Bottom, fastening it like a Girdle about my Middle to hid
my Nakedness.

My Master observed the whole Performance with grea
Signs of Curiosity and Admiration. He took up all my Cloath
in his Pastern, one Piece after another, and examined then
diligently ; he then stroaked my Body very gently, and looke
round me several Times ; after which he said, it was plain
must be a perfect *Yahoo* ; but that I differed very much from
the rest of my Species, in the Whiteness, and Smoothness o
my Skin, my want of Hair in several Parts of my Body, th
Shape and Shortness of my Claws behind and before, and m
Affectation of walking continually on my two hinder Feet. H
desired to see no more ; and gave me leave to put on m
Cloaths again, for I was shuddering with Cold.

I expressed my Uneasiness at his giving me so often th
Appellation of *Yahoo*, an odious Animal, for which I had s
utter an Hatred and Contempt. I begged he would forbea
applying that Word to me, and take the same Order in hi
Family, and among his Friends whom he suffered to see me
I requested likewise, that the Secret of my having a fals
Covering to my Body might be known to none but himself
at least as long as my present Cloathing should last : For a

what the Sorrel Nag his Valet had observed, his Honour
might command him to conceal it.

All this my Master very graciously consented to; and thus
the Secret was kept till my Cloaths began to wear out, which
I was forced to supply by several Contrivances, that shall
hereafter be mentioned.

Every Day when I waited on him, beside the Trouble he
was at in teaching, he would ask me several Questions concerning my self, which I answered as well as I could; and by those
Means he had already received some general Ideas, although
very imperfect. It would be tedious to relate the several Steps,
by which I advanced to a more regular Conversation: But
the first Account I gave of my self in any Order and Length,
was to this Purpose:

That, I came from a very far Country, as I already had
attempted to tell him, with about fifty more of my own Species;
that we travelled upon the Seas, in a great hollow Vessel made
of Wood, and larger than his Honour's House. I described the
Ship to him in the best Terms I could; and explained by the
Help of my Handkerchief displayed, how it was driven forward
by the Wind. That, upon a Quarrel among us, I was set on
Shoar on this Coast, where I walked forward without knowing
whither, till he delivered me from the Persecution of those
execrable *Yahoos*. He asked me, Who made the Ship, and how
was possible that the *Houyhnhnms* of my Country would
leave it to the Management of Brutes? My Answer was, that
I durst proceed no farther in my Relation, unless he would
give me his Word and Honour that he would not be offended;
and then I would tell him the Wonders I had so often promised.
He agreed; and I went on by assuring him, that the Ship was
made by Creatures like myself, who in all the Countries I had
travelled, as well as in my own, were the only governing,
rational Animals; and that upon my Arrival hither, I was as
much astonished to see the *Houyhnhnms* act like rational Beings,
as he or his Friends could be in finding some Marks of Reason
in a Creature he was pleased to call a *Yahoo*; to which I
owned my Resemblance in every Part, but could not account
for their degenerate and brutal Nature. I said farther, That if
good Fortune ever restored me to my native Country, to relate

my Travels hither, as I resolved to do; every Body would
believe that I *said the Thing which was not*; that I invented the
Story out of my own Head: And with all possible Respect to
Himself, his Family, and Friends, and under his Promise of
not being offended, our Countrymen would hardly think it
probable, that a *Houyhnhnm* should be the presiding Creature
of a Nation, and a *Yahoo* the Brute.

CHAPTER FOUR

THE HOUYHNHNMS NOTION OF TRUTH AND FALSHOOD. THE
AUTHOR'S DISCOURSE DISAPPROVED BY HIS MASTER. THE AUTHOR
GIVES A MORE PARTICULAR ACCOUNT OF HIMSELF, AND THE
ACCIDENTS OF HIS VOYAGE.

My Master heard me with great Appearances of Uneasiness
in his Countenance; because *Doubting* or *not believing*
are so little known in this Country, that the Inhabitants cannot
tell how to behave themselves under such Circumstances. And
I remember in frequent Discourses with my Master concerning
the Nature of Manhood, in other Parts of the World; having
Occasion to talk of *Lying*, and *false Representation*, it was with
much Difficulty that he comprehended what I meant; although
he had otherwise a most acute Judgment. For he argued thus:
That the Use of Speech was to make us understand one another,
and to receive Information of Facts; now if any one *said the
Thing which was not*, these Ends were defeated; because I
cannot properly be said to understand him; and I am so far
from receiving Information, that he leaves me worse than in
Ignorance; for I am led to believe a Thing *Black* when it is
White, and *Short* when it is *Long*. And these were all the
Notions he had concerning that Faculty of *Lying*, so perfectly
well understood, and so universally practised among human
Creatures.

To return from this Digression; when I asserted that the
Yahoos were the only governing Animals in my Country, which
my Master said was altogether past his Conception, he desired

to know, whether we had *Houyhnhnms* among us, and what was their Employment: I told him, we had great Numbers; that in Summer they grazed in the Fields, and in Winter were kept in Houses, with Hay and Oats, where *Yahoo* Servants were employed to rub their Skins smooth, comb their Manes, pick their Feet, serve them with Food, and make their Beds. I understand you well, said my Master; it is now very plain from all you have spoken, that whatever Share of Reason the *Yahoos* pretend to, the *Houyhnhnms* are your Masters; I heartily wish our *Yahoos* would be so tractable. I begged his Honour would please to excuse me from proceeding any farther, because I was very certain that the Account he expected from me would be highly displeasing. But he insisted in commanding me to let him know the best and the worst: I told him he should be obeyed. I owned, that the *Houyhnhnms* among us, whom we called *Horses*, were the most generous and comely Animal we had; that they excelled in Strength and Swiftness; and when they belonged to Persons of Quality, employed in Travelling, Racing, and drawing Chariots, they were treated with much Kindness and Care, till they fell into Diseases, or became foundered in the Feet; but then they were sold, and used to all kind of Drudgery till they died; after which their Skins were stripped and sold for what they were worth, and their Bodies left to be devoured by Dogs and Birds of Prey. But the common Race of Horses had not so good Fortune, being kept by Farmers and Carriers, and other mean People, who put them to greater Labour, and feed them worse. I described as well as I could, our Way of Riding; the Shape and Use of a Bridle, a Saddle, a Spur, and a Whip; of Harness and Wheels. I added, that we fastened Plates of a certain hard Substance called *Iron* at the Bottom of their Feet, to preserve their Hoofs from being broken by the Stony Ways on which we often travelled.

My Master after some Expressions of great Indignation, wondered how we dared to venture upon a *Houyhnhnm*'s Back; for he was sure, that the weakest Servant in his House would be able to shake off the strongest *Yahoo*; or by lying down, and rouling upon his Back, squeeze the Brute to Death. I answered, That our Horses were trained up from three or four Years old to the several Uses we intended them for; That if any of them proved intolerably vicious, they were employed for Carriages; that they were severely beaten while they were young for any mischievous Tricks: That they were indeed sensible of Rewards and Punishments; but his Honour would please to consider, that they had not the least Tincture of Reason any more than the *Yahoos* in this Country.

It put me to the Pains of many Circumlocutions to give my Master a right Idea of what I spoke; for their Language doth not abound in Variety of Words, because their Wants and Passions are fewer than among us. But it is impossible to express his noble Resentment at our savage Treatment of the *Houyhnhnm* Race. He said, if it were possible there could be any Country where *Yahoos* alone were endued with Reason, they certainly must be the governing Animal, because Reason will in Time always prevail against Brutal Strength. But, considering the Frame of our Bodies, and especially of mine, he thought no Creature of equal Bulk was so ill-contrived, for employing that Reason in the common Offices of Life; whereupon he desired to know whether those among whom I lived, resembled me or the *Yahoos* of his Country. I assured him, that I was as well shaped as most of my Age; but the younger and the Females were much more soft and tender, and the Skins of the latter generally as white as Milk. He said, I differed indeed from other *Yahoos*, being much more cleanly, and not altogether so deformed; but in point of real Advantage, he thought I differed for the worse. That my Nails were of no Use either to my fore or hinder Feet, he could not properly call them by that Name, for he never observed me to walk upon them; that they were too soft to bear the Ground; that I generally went with them uncovered, neither was the Covering I sometimes wore on them, of the same Shape, or so strong as that on my Feet behind. That I could not walk with any Security; for if either of my hinder Feet slipped, I must inevitably fall. He then began to find fault with other Parts of my Body; the Flatness of my Face, the Prominence of my Nose, my Eyes placed directly in Front, so that I could not look on either Side without turning my Head: That I was not able to feed my self, without lifting one of my fore Feet to my Mouth : And therefore Nature had placed those Joints to answer that Necessity. He knew not what could be the Use of those several Clefts and Divisions in my Feet behind ; that these were too soft to bear the Hardness and Sharpness of Stones without a Covering made from the Skin of some other Brute ; that my whole Body wanted a Fence against Heat and Cold, which I was forced to put on and off every Day with Tediousness and Trouble. And lastly, that he observed every Animal in this Country naturally to abhor the *Yahoos*, whom the Weaker avoided, and the Stronger drove from them. So that supposing us to have the Gift of Reason, he could not see how it were possible to cure that natural Antipathy which every Creature discovered against us ; nor consequently, how we could tame and render them serviceable. However, he would (as he said) debate the Matter no farther, because he was more desirous to know my own Story, the Country, where I was born, and the several Actions and Events of my Life before I came hither.

I assured him, how extreamly desirous I was that he should be satisfied in every Point ; but I doubted much, whether it would be possible for me to explain my self on several Subjects whereof his Honour could have no Conception, because I saw nothing in his Country to which I could resemble them. That however, I would do my best, and strive to express my self by Similitudes, humbly desiring his Assistance when I wanted proper Words ; which he was pleased to promise me.

I said, my Birth was of honest Parents, in an Island called *England*, which was remote from this Country, as many Days Journey as the strongest of his Honour's Servants could travel in the Annual Course of the Sun. That I was bred a Surgeon, whose Trade it is to cure Wounds and Hurts in the Body, got by Accident or Violence. That my Country was governed by a Female Man, whom we called a *Queen*. That I left it to get Riches, whereby I might maintain my self and Family when I should return. That in my last Voyage, I was Commander of the Ship and had about fifty *Yahoos* under me, many of which died at Sea, and I was forced to supply them by others picked out from several Nations. That our Ship was twice in Danger of being sunk ; the first Time by a great Storm, and the second, by striking against a Rock. Here my Master interposed, by asking me, How I could persuade Strangers out of different Countries to venture with me, after the Losses I had sustained, and the Hazards I had run. I said, they were Fellows of desperate Fortunes, forced to fly from the Places of their Birth, on Account of their Poverty or their Crimes. None of these durst return to their native Countries for fear of being hanged, or of starving in a Jail; and therefore were under a Necessity of seeking a Livelihood in other Places.

CHAPTER FIVE

THE AUTHOR'S GREAT LOVE OF HIS NATIVE COUNTRY. HIS MASTER'S OBSERVATIONS UPON HUMAN NATURE.

THE Reader may be disposed to wonder how I could prevail on my self to give a free Representation of my own Species, among a Race of Mortals who were already too apt to conceive the vilest Opinion of Human Kind, from that entire Congruity betwixt me and their *Yahoos*. But I must freely confess, that the many Virtues of those excellent *Quadrupeds* placed in opposite View to human Corruptions, had so far opened my Eyes, and enlarged my Understanding, that I began to view the Actions and Passions of a Man in a very different Light; and to think the Honour of my own kind not worth managing; which, besides, it was impossible for me to do before a Person of so acute a Judgment as my Master, who daily convinced me of a thousand Faults in my self, whereof I had not the least Perception before, and which with us would never be numbered even among human Infirmities. I had likewise learned from his Example an utter Detestation of all Falsehood or Disguise; and *Truth* appeared so amiable to me, that I determined upon sacrificing every thing to it.

Let me deal so candidly with the Reader, as to confess, that there was yet a much stronger Motive for the Freedom I took in my Representation of Things. I had not been a Year in this Country, before I contracted such a Love and Veneration for the Inhabitants, that I entered on a firm Resolution never to return to human Kind, but to pass the rest of my Life among these admirable *Houyhnhnms* in the Contemplation and Practice of every Virtue; where I could have no Example or Incitement to Vice. But it was decreed by Fortune, my perpetual Enemy, that so great a Felicity should not fall to my Share. However, it is now some Comfort to reflect, that in what I said of my Countrymen, I *extenuated* their Faults as much as I durst before so strict an Examiner; and upon every Article, gave as *favourable* a Turn as the Matter would bear. For, indeed, who is there alive that will not be swayed by his Byass and Partiality to the Place of his Birth?

When I had answered all his Questions, and his Curiosity seemed to be satisfied; he sent for me one Morning early, and commanding me to sit down at some Distance, (an Honour which he had never before conferred upon me) He said, he had been very seriously considering my whole Story, as far as it related both to my self and my Country: That, he looked upon us as a Sort of Animals to whose Share, by what Accident he could not conjecture, some small Pittance of *Reason* had fallen, whereof we made no other Use than by its Assistance to aggravate our *natural* Corruptions, and to acquire new ones which Nature had not given us. That, we disarmed ourselves of the few Abilities she had bestowed; had been very successful in multiplying our original Wants, and seemed to spend our whole Lives in vain Endeavours to supply them by our own Inventions. That, as to my self, it was manifest I had neither the Strength or Agility of a common *Yahoo*; that I walked infirmly on my hinder Feet; had found out a Contrivance to make my Claws of no Use or Defence, and to remove the Hair from my Chin, which was intended as a Shelter from the Sun and the Weather. Lastly, That I could neither run with Speed, nor climb Trees like my *Brethren* (as he called them) the *Yahoos* in this Country.

That, our Institutions of *Government* and *Law* were plainly owing to our gross Defects in *Reason*, and by consequence, in *Virtue*; because *Reason* alone is sufficient to govern a *Rational* Creature; which was therefore a Character we had no Pretence to challenge, even from the Account I had given of my own People ; although he manifestly perceived, that in order to favour them, I had concealed many Particulars, and often *said the Thing which was not*.

He was the more confirmed in this Opinion, because he observed, that as I agreed in every Feature of my Body with other *Yahoos*, except where it was to my real Disadvantage in point of Strength, Speed and Activity, the Shortness of my Claws, and some other Particulars where Nature had no Part ; so, from the Representation I had given him of our Lives, our Manners, and our Actions, he found as near a Resemblance in the Disposition of our Minds. He said, the *Yahoos* were known to hate one another more than they did any different Species of Animals ; and the Reason usually assigned, was, the Odiousness of their own Shapes, which all could see in the rest, but not in themselves. He had therefore begun to think it not unwise in us to *cover* our Bodies, and by that Invention, conceal many of our Deformities from each other, which would else be hardly supportable. But, he now found he had been mistaken ; and that the Dissentions of those Brutes in his Country were owing to the same Cause with ours, as I had described them. For, if (said he) you throw among five *Yahoos* as much Food as would be sufficient for fifty, they will, instead of eating peaceably, fall together by the Ears, each single one impatient to *have all to it self* ; and therefore a Servant was usually employed to stand by while they were feeding abroad, and those kept at home were tied at a Distance from each other. That, if a Cow died of Age or Accident, before a *Houyhnhnm* could secure it for his own *Yahoos*, those in the Neighbourhood would come in Herds to seize it, and then would ensue such a Battle as I had described, with terrible Wounds made by their Claws on both Sides, although they seldom were able to kill one another, for want of such convenient Instruments of Death as we have invented. At other Times the like Battles have been fought between the *Yahoos* of several Neighbourhoods without any visible Cause : Those of one District watching all Opportunities to surprise the next before they are prepared. But if they find their Project hath miscarried, they return home, and for want of Enemies, engage in what I call a *Civil War* among themselves.

That, in some Fields of his Country, there are certain
shining Stones of several Colours, whereof the *Yahoos* are
violently fond ; and when Part of these *Stones* are fixed in the
Earth, as it sometimes happeneth, they will dig with their
Claws for whole Days to get them out, and carry them away,
and hide them by Heaps in their Kennels ; but still looking
round with great Caution, for fear their Comrades should find
out their Treasure. My Master said, he could never discover
the Reason of this unnatural Appetite, or how these *Stones*
could be of any Use to a *Yahoo* ; but now he believed it might
proceed from the same Principle of *Avarice*, which I had
ascribed to Mankind. That he had once, by way of Experiment,
privately removed a Heap of these *Stones* from the Place where
one of his *Yahoos* had buried it : Whereupon, the sordid
Animal missing his Treasure, by his loud lamenting brought
the whole Herd to the Place, there miserably howled, then fell
to biting and tearing the rest ; began to pine away, would
neither eat nor sleep, nor work, till he ordered a Servant
privately to convey the *Stones* into the same Hole, and hide
them as before ; which when his *Yahoo* had found, he presently
recovered his Spirits and good Humour ; but took Care to
remove them to a better hiding Place ; and hath ever since
been a very serviceable Brute.

My Master farther assured me, which I also observed my
self ; That in the Fields where these *shining Stones* abound,
the fiercest and most frequent Battles are fought, occasioned
by perpetual Inroads of the neighbouring *Yahoos*.

He said, it was common when two *Yahoos* discovered such
a *Stone* in a Field, and were contending which of them should
be the Proprietor, a third would take the Advantage, and carry
it away from them both ; which my Master would needs
contend to have some Resemblance with our *Suits at Law* ;
wherein I thought it for our Credit not to undeceive him ;
since the Decision he mentioned was much more equitable
than many Decrees among us : Because the Plaintiff and
Defendant there lost nothing beside the *Stone* they contended
for ; whereas our *Courts of Equity*, would never have dismissed
the Cause while either of them had any thing left.

My Master continuing his Discourse, said, There was nothing

that rendered the *Yahoos* more odious, than their undistin-
guished Appetite to devour every thing that came in their Way,
whether Herbs, Roots, Berries, corrupted Flesh of Animals, or
all mingled together : And it was peculiar in their Temper,
that they were fonder of what they could get by Rapine or
Stealth at a greater Distance, than much better Food provided
for them at home. If their Prey held out, they would eat till
they were ready to burst, after which Nature had pointed out
to them a certain *Root* that gave them a general Evacuation.

I did indeed observe, that the *Yahoos* were the only Animals
in this Country subject to any Diseases ; which however, were
much fewer than Horses have among us, and contracted not
by any ill Treatment they meet with, but by the Nastiness and
Greediness of that sordid Brute.

My Master likewise mentioned another Quality, which his
Servants had discovered in several *Yahoos*, and to him was
wholly unacccountable. He said, a Fancy would sometimes
take a *Yahoo*, to retire into a Corner, to lie down and howl, and
groan, and spurn away all that came near him, although he
were young and fat, and wanted neither Food nor Water ; nor
did the Servants imagine what could possibly ail him. And the
only Remedy they found was to set him to hard Work, after
which he would infallibly come to himself. To this I was
silent out of Partiality to my own Kind ; yet here I could
plainly discover the true Seeds of *Spleen*, which only seizeth
on the *Lazy*, the *Luxurious*, and the *Rich* ; who, if they were
forced to undergo the *same Regimen*, I would undertake for the
Cure.

CHAPTER SIX

THE AUTHOR RELATETH SEVERAL PARTICULARS OF THE YAHOOS.
THE GREAT VIRTUES OF THE HOUYHNHNMS. THE EDUCATION AND
EXERCISE OF THEIR YOUTH. THEIR GENERAL ASSEMBLY.

As I ought to have understood human Nature much better than I supposed it possible for my Master to do, so it was easy to apply the Character he gave of the *Yahoos* to myself and my Countrymen; and I believed I could yet make farther Discoveries from my own Observation. I therefore often begged his Honour to let me go among the Herds of *Yahoos* in the Neighbourhood; to which he always very graciously consented, being perfectly convinced that the Hatred I bore those Brutes would never suffer me to be corrupted by them; and his Honour ordered one of his Servants, a strong Sorrel Nag, very honest and good-natured, to be my Guard; without whose Protection I durst not undertake such Adventures. For I have already told the Reader how much I was pestered by those odious Animals upon my first Arrival. I afterwards failed very narrowly three or four times of falling into their Clutches, when I happened to stray at any Distance without my Hanger. And I have Reason to believe, they had some Imagination that I was of their own Species, which I often assisted myself, by stripping up my Sleeves, and shewing my naked Arms and Breast in their Sight, when my Protector was with me: At which times they would approach as near as they durst, and imitate my Actions after the Manner of Monkeys, but ever with great Signs of Hatred; as a tame *Jack Daw* with Cap and Stockings, is always persecuted by the wild ones, when he happens to be got among them.

They are prodigiously nimble from their Infancy; however, I once caught a young Male of three Years old, and endeavoured by all Marks of Tenderness to make it quiet; but the little Imp fell a squalling, and scratching, and biting with such

Violence, that I was forced to let it go ; and it was high time, for a whole Troop of old ones came about us at the Noise ; but finding the Cub was safe, (for it ran away) and my Sorrel Nag being by, they durst not venture near us.

By what I could discover, the *Yahoos* appear to be the most unteachable of all Animals, their Capacities never reaching higher than to draw or carry Burthens. Yet I am of Opinion, this Defect ariseth chiefly from a perverse, restive Disposition. For they are cunning, malicious, treacherous and revengeful. They are strong and hardy, but of a cowardly Spirit, and by Consequence insolent, abject, and cruel.

The *Houyhnhnms* keep the *Yahoos* for present Use in Huts not far from the House ; but the rest are sent abroad to certain Fields, where they dig up Roots, eat several Kinds of Herbs, and search about for Carrion, or sometimes catch *Weasels* and *Luhimuhs* (a Sort of *wild Rat*) which they greedily devour. Nature hath taught them to dig deep Holes with their Nails on the Side of a rising Ground, wherein they lie by themselves ; only the Kennels of the Females are larger, sufficient to hold two or three Cubs.

They swim from their Infancy like Frogs, and are able to continue long under Water, where they often take Fish, which the Females carry home to their Young.

Having already lived three Years in this Country, the Reader I suppose will expect, that I should, like other Travellers, give him some Account of the Manners and Customs of its Inhabitants, which it was indeed my principal Study to learn.

Friendship and *Benevolence* are the two principal Virtues among the *Houyhnhnms* ; and these not confined to particular Objects, but universal to the whole Race. For, a Stranger from the remotest Part, is equally treated with the nearest Neighbour, and where-ever he goes, looks upon himself as at home. They preserve *Decency* and *Civility* in the highest Degrees, but are altogether ignorant of *Ceremony*. They have no Fondness for their Colts or Foles ; but the Care they take in educating them proceedeth entirely from the Dictates of *Reason*. And, I observed my Master to shew the same Affection to his Neighbour's Issue that he had for his own. They will have it that *Nature* teaches them to love the whole Species, and it is *Reason* only that maketh a Distinction of Persons, where there is a superior Degree of Virtue.

In educating the Youth of both Sexes, their Method is admirable, and highly deserveth our Imitation. These are not suffered to taste a Grain of *Oats*, except upon certain Days, till Eighteen Years old; nor *Milk*, but very rarely; and in Summer they graze two Hours in the Morning, and as many in the Evening, which their Parents likewise observe; but the Servants are not allowed above half that Time; and a great Part of the Grass is brought home, which they eat at the most convenient Hours, when they can be best spared from Work.

Temperance, *Industry*, *Exercise* and *Cleanliness*, are the Lessons equally enjoyed to the young ones of both Sexes: And my Master thought it monstrous in us to give the Females a different Kind of Education from the Males, except in some Articles of Domestick Management; whereby, as he truly observed, one Half of our Natives were good for nothing but bringing Children into the World: And to trust the Care of their Children to such useless Animals, he said was yet a greater Instance of Brutality.

But the *Houyhnhnms* train up their Youth to Strength, Speed, and Hardiness, by exercising them in running Races up and down steep Hills, or over hard stony Grounds; and when they are all in a Sweat, they are ordered to leap over Head and Ears into a Pond or River. Four times a Year the Youth of certain Districts meet to shew their Proficiency in Running, and Leaping, and other Feats of Strength or Agility; where the Victor is rewarded with a Song made in his or her Praise. On this Festival the Servants drive a Herd of *Yahoos* into the Field, laden with Hay, and Oats, and Milk for a Repast to the *Houyhnhnms*; after which, these Brutes are immediately driven back again, for fear of being noisome to the Assembly.

Every fourth Year, at the *Vernal Equinox*, there is a Representative Council of the whole Nation, which meets in a Plain about twenty Miles from our House, and continueth about five or six Days. Here they inquire into the State and Condition of the several Districts; whether they abound or be deficient in Hay or Oats, or Cows or *Yahoos*? And where-ever there is any Want (which is but seldom) it is immediately supplied by unanimous Consent and Contribution. Here likewise the Regulation of Children is settled: As for instance, if a *Houyhnhnm* hath two Males, he changeth one of them with another who hath two Females: And when a Child hath been lost by any Casualty, where the Mother is past Breeding, it is determined what Family in the District shall breed another to supply the Loss.

CHAPTER SEVEN

A GRAND DEBATE AT THE GENERAL ASSEMBLY OF THE HOUYHNHNMS. THE LEARNING OF THE HOUYHNHNMS. THEIR BUILDINGS. THEIR MANNER OF BURIALS. THE DEFECTIVENESS OF THEIR LANGUAGE.

ONE of these Grand Assemblies was held in my time, about three Months before my Departure, whither my Master went as the Representative of our District. In this Council was resumed their old Debate, and indeed, the only Debate that ever happened in their Country; whereof my Master after his Return gave me a very particular Account.

The Question to be debated, was, Whether the *Yahoos* should be exterminated from the Face of the Earth. One of the *Members* for the Affirmative offered several Arguments of great Strength and Weight; alledging, That, as the *Yahoos* were the most filthy, noisome, and deformed Animal which Nature ever produced, so they were the most restive and indocible, mischievous and malicious: They would privately suck the Teats of the *Houyhnhnms* Cows; kill and devour their Cats, trample down their Oats and Grass, if they were not continually watched; and commit a Thousand other Extravagancies. He took Notice of a general Tradition, that *Yahoos* had not been always in their Country: But, that many Ages ago, two of these Brutes appeared together upon a Mountain; whether produced by the Heat of the Sun upon corrupted Mud and Slime, or from the Ooze and Froth of the Sea, was never known. That these *Yahoos* engendered, and their Brood in a short time grew so numerous as to overrun and infest the whole Nation. That the *Houyhnhnms* to get rid of this Evil, made a general Hunting, and at last inclosed the whole Herd ; and destroying the Older, every *Houyhnhnm* kept two young Ones in a Kennel, and brought them to such a Degree of Tameness, as an Animal so savage by Nature can be capable of acquiring ; using them for Draught and Carriage. That, there seemed to be much Truth in this Tradition, and that those Creatures could not be *Ylnhni-amshy* (or *Aborigines* of the Land) because of the violent Hatred the *Houyhnhnms* as well as all other Animals, bore them ; which although their evil Disposition sufficiently deserved, could never have arrived at so high a Degree, if they had been *Aborigines*, or else they would have long since been rooted out. That, the Inhabitants taking a Fancy to use the Service of the *Yahoos*, had very imprudently neglected to cultivate the Breed of *Asses*, which were a comely Animal, easily kept, more tame and orderly, without any offensive Smell, strong enough for Labour, although they yield to the other in Agility of Body ; and if their Braying be no agreeable Sound, it is far preferable to the horrible Howlings of the *Yahoos*.

Several others declared their Sentiments to the same Purpose ; when my Master proposed an Expedient to the Assembly, whereof he had indeed borrowed the Hint from me. He approved of the Tradition, mentioned by the *Honourable Member*, who spoke before ; and affirmed, that the two *Yahoos* said to be the first seen among them, had been driven thither over the Sea ; that coming to Land, and being forsaken by their Companions, they retired to the Mountains, and degenerating by Degrees, became in Process of Time, much more savage than those of their own Species in the Country from whence these two Originals came. The Reason of his Assertion was, that he had now in his Possession, a certain wonderful *Yahoo*, (meaning myself) which most of them had heard of, and many of them had seen. He added, how I had endeavoured to persuade him, that in my own and other Countries the *Yahoos* acted as the governing, rational Animal, and held the *Houyhnhnms* in Servitude : That, he observed in me all the Qualities of a *Yahoo*, only a little more civilized by some Tincture of Reason ; which however was in a Degree as far inferior to the *Houyhnhnm* Race, as the *Yahoos* of their Country were to me.

This was all my Master thought fit to tell me at that Time, of what passed in the Grand Council. But he was pleased to conceal one Particular, which related personally to myself, whereof I soon felt the unhappy Effect, as the Reader will know in its proper Place, and from whence I date all the succeeding Misfortunes of my Life.

The *Houyhnhnms* have no Letters, and consequently, their Knowledge is all traditional. But there happening few Events of any Moment among a People so well united, naturally disposed to every Virtue, wholly governed by Reason, and cut off from all Commerce with other Nations; the historical Part is easily preserved without burthening their Memories. I have already observed, that they are subject to no Diseases, and therefore can have no Need of Physicians. However, they have excellent Medicines composed of Herbs, to cure accidental Bruises and Cuts in the Pastern or Frog of the Foot by sharp Stones, as well as other Maims and Hurts in the several Parts of the Body.

They calculate the Year by the Revolution of the Sun and the Moon, but use no Subdivisions into Weeks. They are well enough acquainted with the Motions of those two Luminaries, and understand the Nature of *Eclipses*; and this is the utmost Progress of their *Astronomy*.

Their Buildings, although very rude and simple, are not inconvenient, but well contrived to defend them from all Injuries of Cold and Heat. They have a Kind of Tree, which at Forty Years old loosens in the Root, and falls with the first Storm; it grows very strait, and being pointed like Stakes with a sharp Stone, (for the *Houyhnhnms* know not the Use of Iron) they stick them erect in the Ground about ten Inches asunder, and then weave in Oat-straw, or sometimes Wattles betwixt them. The Roof is made after the same Manner, and so are the Doors.

The *Houyhnhnms* use the hollow Part between the Pastern and the Hoof of their Fore-feet, as we do our Hands, and this with greater Dexterity, than I could at first imagine. I have seen a white Mare of our Family thread a Needle (which I lent her on Purpose) with that Joynt. They milk their Cows, reap their Oats, and do all the Work which requires Hands, in the same Manner. They have a Kind of hard Flints, which by grinding against other Stones, they form into Instruments, that serve instead of Wedges, Axes, and Hammers. With Tools made of these Flints, they likewise cut their Hay, and reap their Oats, which there groweth naturally in several Fields: The *Yahoos* draw home the Sheaves in Carriages, and the Servants tread them in certain covered Hutts, to get out the Grain, which is kept in Stores. They make a rude Kind of earthen and wooden Vessels, and bake the former in the Sun.

If they can avoid Casualties, they die only of old Age, and are buried in the obscurest Places that can be found, their Friends and Relations expressing neither Joy nor Grief at their Departure; nor does the dying Person discover the least Regret that he is leaving the World, any more than if he were upon returning home from a Visit to one of his Neighbours: I remember, my Master having once made an Appointment with a Friend and his Family to come to his House upon some Affair of Importance; on the Day fixed, the Mistress and her two Children came very late. Her Excuse for not coming sooner, was, that her Husband dying late in the Morning, she was a good while consulting her Servants about a convenient Place where his Body should be laid; and I observed she behaved herself at our House, as chearfully as the rest: She died about three Months after.

They live generally to Seventy or Seventy-five Years, very seldom to Fourscore: Some Weeks before their Death they feel a gradual Decay, but without Pain. During this time they are much visited by their Friends, because they cannot go abroad with their usual Ease and Satisfaction. However, about ten Days before their Death, which they seldom fail in computing, they return the Visits that have been made by those who are nearest in the Neighbourhood, being carried in a convenient Sledge drawn by *Yahoos*; which Vehicle they use, not only upon this Occasion, but when they grow old, upon long Journeys, or when they are lamed by any Accident. And therefore when the dying *Houyhnhnms* return those Visits, they take a solemn Leave of their Friends, as if they were going to some remote Part of the Country, where they designed to pass the rest of their Lives.

CHAPTER EIGHT

THE AUTHOR'S OECONOMY AND HAPPY LIFE AMONG THE HOUY-HNHNMS. HIS GREAT IMPROVEMENT IN VIRTUE, BY CONVERSING WITH THEM. THEIR CONVERSATIONS. THE AUTHOR HATH NOTICE GIVEN HIM BY HIS MASTER THAT HE MUST DEPART FROM THE COUNTRY. HE FALLS INTO A SWOON FOR GRIEF, BUT SUBMITS. HE CONTRIVES AND FINISHES A CANOO, BY THE HELP OF A FELLOW-SERVANT, AND PUTS TO SEA AT A VENTURE.

I HAD settled my little Oeconomy to my own Heart's Content. My Master had ordered a Room to be made for me after their Manner, about six Yards from the House ; the Sides and Floors of which I plaistered with Clay, and covered with Rush-mats of my own contriving ; I had beaten Hemp, which there grows wild, and made of it a Sort of Ticking : This I filled with the Feathers of several Birds I had taken with Springes made of *Yahoos* Hairs ; and were excellent Food. I had worked two Chairs with my Knife, the Sorrel Nag helping me in the grosser and more laborious Part. When my Cloaths were worn to Rags, I made my self others with the Skins of Rabbets, and of a certain beautiful Animal about the same Size, called *Nnuhnoh*, the Skin of which is covered with a fine Down. Of these I likewise made very tolerable Stockings. I soaled my Shoes with Wood which I cut from a Tree, and fitted to the upper Leather, and when this was worn out, I supplied it with the Skins of *Yahoos*, dried in the Sun. I often got Honey out of hollow Trees, which I mingled with Water, or eat it with my Bread.

I had the Favour of being admitted to several *Houyhnhnms*, who came to visit or dine with my Master ; where his Honour graciously suffered me to wait in the Room, and listen to their Discourse. Both he and his Company would often descend to

ask me Questions, and receive my Answers. I had also sometimes the Honour of attending my Master in his Visits to
others. I never presumed to speak, except in answer to a
Question; and then I did it with inward Regret, because it
was a Loss of so much Time for improving my self: But I was
infinitely delighted with the Station of an humble Auditor
in such Conversations, where nothing passed but what was
useful, expressed in the fewest and most significant Words:
Where (as I have already said) the greatest *Decency* was observed, without the least Degree of Ceremony; where no
Person spoke without being pleased himself, and pleasing his
Companions: Where there was no Interruption, Tediousness,
Heat, or Difference of Sentiments. Their Subjects are generally
on Friendship and Benevolence; on Order and Oeconomy;
sometimes upon the visible Operations of Nature, or ancient
Traditions; upon the Bounds and Limits of Virtue; upon the
unerring Rules of Reason; or upon some Determinations, to
be taken at the next great Assembly; and often upon the
various Excellencies of *Poetry*.

I freely confess, that all the little Knowledge I have of any
Value, was acquired by the Lectures I received from my Master,
and from hearing the Discourses of him and his Friends; to
which I should be prouder to listen, than to dictate to the
greatest and wisest Assembly in *Europe*. I admired the Strength,
Comeliness and Speed of the Inhabitants; and such a Con-
stellation of Virtues in such amiable Persons produced in me
the highest Veneration. At first, indeed, I did not feel that
natural Awe which the *Yahoos* and all other Animals bear
towards them; but it grew upon me by Degrees, much sooner
than I imagined, and was mingled with a respectful Love and
Gratitude, that they would condescend to distinguish me from
the rest of my Species.

When I thought of my Family, my Friends, my Countrymen,
or human Race in general, I considered them as they really
were, *Yahoos* in Shape and Disposition, perhaps a little more
civilized, and qualified with the Gift of Speech; but making
no other Use of Reason, than to improve and multiply those
Vices, whereof their Brethren in this Country had only the
Share that Nature allotted them. When I happened to behold

the Reflection of my own Form in a Lake or Fountain, I turned
away my Face in Horror and detestation of my self; and could
better endure the Sight of a common *Yahoo*, than of my own
Person. By conversing with the *Houyhnhnms*, and looking upon
them with Delight, I fell to imitate their Gait and Gesture,
which is now grown into a Habit; and my Friends often tell
me in a blunt Way, that *I trot like a Horse*; which, however,
I take for a great Compliment: Neither shall I disown, that
in speaking I am apt to fall into the Voice and manner of the
Houyhnhnms, and hear my self ridiculed on that Account
without the least Mortification.

In the Midst of this Happiness, when I looked upon my self
to be fully settled for Life, my Master sent for me one Morning
a little earlier than his usual Hour. I observed by his Countenance he was in some Perplexity, and at a Loss how to begin
what he had to speak. After a short Silence, he told me, he did
not know how I would take what he was going to say: That,
in the last general Assembly, when the Affair of the *Yahoos*
was entered upon, the Representatives had taken Offence at
his keeping a *Yahoo* (meaning my self) in his Family more like
a *Houyhnhnm* than a Brute Animal. That, he was known
frequently to converse with me, as if he could receive some
Advantage or Pleasure in my Company: That, such a Practice
was not agreeable to Reason or Nature, or a thing ever heard of
before among them. The Assembly did therefore *exhort* him,
either to employ me like the rest of my Species, or command
me to swim back to the Place from whence I came. That, the
first of these Expedients was utterly rejected by all the *Houyhnhnms*, who had ever seen me at his House or their own: For,
they alledged, That because I had some Rudiments of Reason,
added to the natural Pravity of those Animals, it was to be
feared, I might be able to seduce them into the woody and
mountainous Parts of the Country, and bring them in Troops
by Night to destroy the *Houyhnhnms* Cattle, as being naturally
of the ravenous Kind, and averse from Labour.

My Master added, That he was daily pressed by the *Houyhnhnms* of the Neighbourhood to have the Assembly's *Exhortation* executed, which he could not put off much longer. He
doubted, it would be impossible for me to swim to another

Country; and therefore wished I would contrive some Sort of Vehicle resembling those I had described to him, that might carry me on the Sea; in which Work I should have the Assistance of his own Servants, as well as those of his Neighbours. He concluded, that for his own Part he could have been content to keep me in his Service as long as I lived; because he found I had cured myself of some bad Habits and Dispositions, by endeavouring, as far as my inferior Nature was capable, to imitate the *Houyhnhnms*.

I was struck with the utmost Grief and Despair at my Master's Discourse; and being unable to support the Agonies I was under, I fell into a Swoon at his Feet: When I came to myself, he told me, that he concluded I had been dead. (For these People are subject to no such Imbecillities of Nature). I answered, in a faint Voice, that Death would have been too great an Happiness; that although I could not blame the Assembly's *Exhortation*, or the Urgency of his Friends; yet in my weak and corrupt Judgment, I thought it might consist with Reason to have been less rigorous. That, I could not swim a League, and probably the nearest Land to theirs might be distant above an Hundred: That, many Materials, necessary for making a small Vessel to carry me off, were wholly wanting in this Country, which however, I would attempt in Obedience and Gratitude to his Honour, although I concluded the thing to be impossible, and therefore looked on myself as already devoted to Destruction. That, the certain Prospect of an unnatural Death, was the least of my Evils: For, supposing I should escape with Life by some strange Adventure, how could I think with Temper, of passing my Days among *Yahoos*, and relapsing into my old Corruptions, for want of Examples to lead and keep me within the Paths of Virtue. That, I knew too well upon what solid Reasons all the Determinations of the wise *Houyhnhnms* were founded, not to be shaken by Arguments of mine, a miserable *Yahoo*; and therefore after presenting him with my humble Thanks for the Offer of his Servants Assistance in making a Vessel, and desiring a reasonable Time for so difficult a Work, I told him, I would endeavour to preserve a wretched Being; and, if ever I returned to *England*, was not without Hopes of being useful to my own Species, by celebrating the Praises of the renowned *Houyhnhnms*, and proposing their Virtues to the Imitation of Mankind.

My Master in a few Words made me a very gracious Reply, allowed me the Space of two *Months* to finish my Boat; and ordered the Sorrel Nag, my Fellow-Servant, (for so at this Distance I may presume to call him) to follow my Instructions, because I told my Master, that his Help would be sufficient, and I knew he had a Tenderness for me.

In his Company my first Business was to go to that Part of the Coast, where my rebellious Crew had ordered me to be set on Shore. I got upon a Height, and looking on every Side into the Sea, fancied I saw a small Island, towards the *North-East*: I took out my Pocket-glass, and could then clearly distinguish it about five Leagues off, as I computed; but it appeared to the Sorrel Nag to be only a blue Cloud: For, as he had no Conception of any Country beside his own, so he could not be as expert in distinguishing remote Objects at Sea, as we who so much converse in that Element.

After I had discovered this Island, I considered no farther; but resolved, it should, if possible, be the first Place of my Banishment, leaving the Consequence to Fortune.

I returned home, and consulting with the Sorrel Nag, we went into a Copse at some Distance, where I with my Knife, and he with a sharp Flint fastened very artificially, after their Manner, to a wooden Handle, cut down several Oak Wattles about the Thickness of a Walking-staff, and some larger Pieces. In six Weeks time, with the Help of the Sorrel Nag, who performed the Parts that required most Labour, I finished a Sort of *Indian* Canoo; but much larger, covering it with the Skins of *Yahoos*, well stitched together, with hempen Threads of my own making. My Sail was likewise composed of the Skins of the same Animal; but I made use of the youngest I could get; the older being too tough and thick; and I likewise provided myself with four Paddles. I laid in a Stock of boiled Flesh, of Rabbets and Fowls; and took with me two Vessels, one filled with Milk, and the other with Water.

I tried my Canoo in a large Pond near my Master's House, and then corrected in it what was amiss; stopping all the Chinks with *Yahoos* Tallow, till I found it stanch, and able to bear me, and my Freight. And when it was as compleat as I could possibly make it, I had it drawn on a Carriage very gently by *Yahoos*, to the Sea-side, under the Conduct of the Sorrel Nag, and another Servant.

When all was ready, and the Day came for my Departure, I took Leave of my Master and Lady, and the whole Family, my Eyes flowing with Tears, and my Heart quite sunk with Grief. But his Honour, out of Curiosity, and perhaps (if I may speak it without Vanity) partly out of Kindness, was determined to see me in my Canoo; and got several of his neighbouring Friends to accompany him. I was forced to wait above an Hour for the Tide, and then observing the Wind very fortunately bearing towards the Island, to which I intended to steer my Course, I took a second Leave of my Master: But as I was going to prostrate myself to kiss his Hoof, he did me the Honour to raise it gently to my Mouth. I paid my Respects to the rest of the *Houyhnhnms* in his Honour's Company; then getting into my Canoo, I pushed off from Shore.

CHAPTER NINE

THE AUTHOR'S DANGEROUS VOYAGE. HE ARRIVES AT NEW-HOLLAND, HOPING TO SETTLE THERE. IS WOUNDED WITH AN ARROW BY ONE OF THE NATIVES. IS SEIZED AND CARRIED BY FORCE INTO A PORTU-GUEZE SHIP. THE GREAT CIVILITIES OF THE CAPTAIN. THE AUTHOR ARRIVES AT ENGLAND.

I BEGAN this desperate Voyage on *February* 15, 1714/5, at 9 o'clock in the Morning. The Wind was very favourable; however, I made use at first only of my Paddles; but considering I should soon be weary, and that the Wind might probably chop about, I ventured to set up my little Sail; and thus, with the Help of the Tide, I went at the Rate of a League and a Half an Hour, as near as I could guess. My Master and his Friends continued on the Shoar, till I was almost out of Sight; and I often heard the Sorrel Nag (who always loved me) crying

out, *Hnuy illa nyha maiah Yahoo*, Take Care of thy self,
gentle *Yahoo*.

My Design was, if possible, to discover some small Island
uninhabited, yet sufficient by my Labour to furnish me with
Necessaries of Life, which I would have thought a greater
Happiness than to be first Minister in the politest Court of
Europe ; so horrible was the Idea I conceived of returning to
live in the Society and under the Government of *Yahoos*. For
in such a Solitude as I desired, I could at least enjoy my own
Thoughts, and reflect with Delight on the Virtues of those
inimitable *Houyhnhnms*, without any Opportunity of degenerating into the Vices and Corruptions of my own Species.

The Reader may remember what I related when my Crew
conspired against me, and confined me to my Cabbin. How I
continued there several Weeks, without knowing what Course
we took ; and when I was put ashore in the Longboat, how
the Sailors told me with Oaths, whether true or false, that they
knew not in what Part of the World we were. However, I
did then believe us to be about ten Degrees *Southward* of the
Cape of Good Hope, or about 45 Degrees *Southern* Latitude, as
I gathered from some general Words I overheard among them,
being I supposed to the *South-East* in their intended Voyage
to *Madagascar*. And although this were but little better than
Conjecture, yet I resolved to steer my Course *Eastward*, hoping
to reach the *South-West* Coast of *New-Holland*, and perhaps
some such Island as I desired, lying *Westward* of it. The Wind
was full West, and by six in the Evening I computed I had gone
Eastward at least eighteen Leagues ; when I spied a very small
Island about half a League off, which I soon reached. It was
nothing but a Rock with one Creek, naturally arched by the
Force of Tempests. Here I put in my Canoo, and climbing a
Part of the Rock, I could plainly discover Land to the *East*,
extending from *South* to *North*. I lay all Night in my Canoo ;
and repeating my Voyage early in the Morning, I arrived in
seven Hours to the *South-East* Point of *New-Holland*. This
confirmed me in the Opinion I have long entertained, that the
Maps and *Charts* place this Country at least three Degrees
more to the *East* than it really is ; which Thought I communicated many Years ago to my worthy Friend Mr. *Herman*

Moll, and gave him my Reasons for it, although he hath rather chosen to follow other Authors.

I saw no Inhabitants in the Place where I landed; and being unarmed, I was afraid of venturing far into the Country. I found some Shell-Fish on the Shore, and eat them raw, not daring to kindle a Fire, for fear of being discovered by the Natives. I continued three Days feeding on Oysters and Limpits, to save my own Provisions; and I fortunately found a Brook of excellent Water, which gave me great Relief.

On the fourth Day, venturing out early a little too far, I saw twenty or thirty Natives upon a Height, not above five hundred Yards from me. They were stark naked, Men, Women and Children round a Fire, as I could discover by the Smoke. One of them spied me, and gave Notice to the rest; five of them advanced towards me, leaving the Women and Children at the Fire. I made what haste I could to the Shore, and getting into my Canoo, shoved off: The Savages observing me retreat, ran after me; and before I could get far enough into the Sea, discharged an Arrow, which wounded me deeply on the Inside of my left Knee (I shall carry the Mark to my Grave.) I apprehended the Arrow might be poisoned; and paddling out of the Reach of their Darts (being a calm Day) I made a shift to suck the Wound, and dress it as well as I could.

I was at a Loss what to do, for I durst not return to the same Landing-place, but stood to the *North*, and was forced to paddle; for the Wind, although very gentle, was against me, blowing *North-West*. As I was looking about for a secure Landing-place, I saw a Sail to the *North North-East*, which appearing every Minute more visible, I was in some Doubt, whether I should wait for them or no; but at last my Detestation of the *Yahoo* Race prevailed; and turning my Canoo, I sailed and paddled together to the *South*, and got into the same Creek from whence I set out in the Morning; choosing rather to trust my self among these *Barbarians* than live with *European Yahoos*. I drew up my Canoo as close as I could to the Shore, and hid my self behind a Stone by the little Brook, which, as I have already said, was excellent Water.

The Ship came within half a League of this Creek, and sent out her Long-Boat with Vessels to take in fresh Water (for the

Place it seems was very well known) but I did not observe it until the Boat was almost on Shore; and it was too late to seek another Hiding-Place. The Seamen at their landing observed my Canoo, and rummaging it all over, easily conjectured that the Owner could not be far off. Four of them well armed searched every Cranny and Lurking-hole, till at last they found me flat on my Face behind the Stone. They gazed a while in Admiration at my strange uncouth Dress; my Coat made of Skins, my wooden-soaled Shoes, and my furred Stockings; from whence, however, they concluded I was not a Native of the Place, who all go naked. One of the Seamen in *Portugueze* bid me rise, and asked who I was. I understood that Language very well, and getting upon my Feet, said, I was a poor *Yahoo*, banished from the *Houyhnhnms*, and desired they would please to let me depart. They admired to hear me answer them in their own Tongue, and saw by my Complection I must be an *European*; but were at a Loss to know what I meant by *Yahoos* and *Houyhnhnms*, and at the same Time fell a laughing at my strange Tone in speaking, which resembled the Neighing of a Horse. I trembled all the while betwixt Fear and Hatred: I again desired Leave to depart, and was gently moving to my Canoo; but they laid hold on me, desiring to know what Country I was of? whence I came? with many other Questions. I told them, I was born in *England*, from whence I came about five Years ago, and then their Country and ours was at Peace. I therefore hoped they would not treat me as an Enemy, since I meant them no Harm, but was a poor *Yahoo*, seeking some desolate Place where to pass the Remainder of his unfortunate Life.

When they began to talk, I thought I never heard or saw any thing so unnatural; for it appeared to me as monstrous as if a Dog or Cow should speak in *England*, or a *Yahoo* in *Houyhnhnm-Land*. The honest *Portugueze* were equally amazed at my strange Dress, and the odd Manner of delivering my Words, which however they understood very well. They spoke to me with great Humanity, and said they were sure their Captain would carry me *gratis* to *Lisbon*, from whence I might return to my own Country; that two of the Seamen would go back to the Ship, to inform the Captain of what they had seen, and receive his Orders; in the mean Time, unless I would give my solemn Oath not to fly, they would secure me by Force. I thought it best to comply with their Proposal. They were very curious to know my Story, but I gave them very little Satisfaction; and they all conjectured, that my Misfortunes had impaired my Reason. In two Hours the Boat, which went loaden with Vessels of Water, returned with the Captain's Commands to fetch me on Board. I fell on my Knees to preserve my Liberty; but all was in vain, and the Men having tied me with Cords, heaved me into the Boat, from whence I was taken into the Ship, and from thence into the Captain's Cabbin.

His Name was *Pedro de Mendez*; he was a very courteous and generous Person; he entreated me to give some Account of my self, and desired to know what I would eat or drink; said, I should be used as well as himself, and spoke so many obliging Things, that I wondered to find such Civilities from a *Yahoo*. However, I remained silent and sullen; I was ready to faint at the very Smell of him and his Men. At last I desired something to eat out of my own Canoo; but he ordered me a Chicken and some excellent Wine, and then directed that I should be put to bed in a very clean Cabbin. I would not undress my self, but lay on the Bed-cloaths; and in half an Hour stole out, when I thought the Crew was at Dinner; and getting to the Side of the Ship, was going to leap into the Sea, and swim for my Life, rather than continue among *Yahoos*. But one of the Seamen prevented me, and having informed the Captain, I was chained to my Cabbin.

After Dinner *Don Pedro* came to me, and desired to know my Reason for so desperate an Attempt; assured me he only meant to do me all the Service he was able; and spoke so very movingly, that at last I descended to treat him like an Animal which had some little Portion of Reason. I gave him a very short Relation of my Voyage; of the Conspiracy against me by my own Men; of the Country where they set me on Shore, and of my five Years Residence there. All which he looked upon as if it were a Dream or a Vision; whereat I took great Offence: For I had quite forgot the Faculty of Lying, so peculiar to *Yahoos* in all Countries where they preside, and consequently the Disposition of suspecting Truth in others of their own Species. I asked him, Whether it were the Custom of his Country to *say the Thing that was not*? I assured him I had almost forgot what he meant by Falshood; and if I had lived a thousand Years in *Houyhnhnmland*, I should never have heard a Lie from the meanest Servant. That I was altogether indifferent whether he believed me or no; but however, in return for his Favours, I would give so much Allowance to the Corruption of his Nature, as to answer any Objection he would please to make; and he might easily discover the Truth.

The Captain, a wise Man, after many Endeavours to catch me tripping in some Part of my Story, at last began to have a better Opinion of my Veracity. But he added, that since I professed so inviolable an Attachment to Truth, I must give him my Word of Honour to bear him Company in this Voyage without attempting any thing against my Life; or else he would continue me a Prisoner till we arrived at *Lisbon*. I gave him the Promise he required; but at the same time protested that I would suffer the greatest Hardships rather than return to live among *Yahoos*.

Our Voyage passed without any considerable Accident. In Gratitude to the Captain I sometimes sate with him at his earnest Request, and strove to conceal my Antipathy against human Kind, although it often broke out; which he suffered to pass without Observation. But the greatest Part of the Day I confined myself to my Cabbin, to avoid seeing any of the Crew. The Captain had often intreated me to strip myself of my savage Dress, and offered to lend me the best Suit of Cloaths he had. This I would not be prevailed on to accept, abhorring to cover myself with any thing that had been on the Back of a *Yahoo*. I only desired he would lend me two clean Shirts, which having been washed since he wore them, I believed would not so much defile me. These I changed every second Day, and washed them myself.

We arrived at *Lisbon*, *Nov.* 5, 1715. At our landing, the Captain forced me to cover myself with his Cloak, to prevent the Rabble from crouding about me. I was conveyed to his own House; and at my earnest Request, he led me up to the highest Room backwards. I conjured him to conceal from all

Persons what I had told him of the *Houyhnhnms*; because the least Hint of such a Story would not only draw Numbers of People to see me, but probably put me in Danger of being imprisoned, or burnt by the *Inquisition*. The Captain persuaded me to accept a Suit of Cloaths newly made; but I would not suffer the Taylor to take my Measure; [however, *Don Pedro* being almost of my Size, they fitted me well enough. He accoutred me with other Necessaries all new, which I aired for Twenty-four Hours before I would use them.

The Captain had no Wife, nor above three Servants, none of which were suffered to attend at Meals; and his whole Deportment was so obliging, added to very good *human* Understanding, that I really began to tolerate his Company. He gained so far upon me, that I ventured to look out of the back Window. By Degrees I was brought into another Room, from whence I peeped into the Street, but drew my Head back in a Fright. In a Week's Time he seduced me down to the Door. I found my Terror gradually lessened, but my Hatred and Contempt seemed to increase. I was at last bold enough to walk the Street in his Company, but kept my Nose well stopped with Rue, or sometimes with Tobacco.

In ten Days, *Don Pedro*, to whom I had given some Account of my domestick Affairs, put it upon me as a Point of Honour and Conscience, that I ought to return to my native Country, and live at home with my Wife and Children. He told me, there was an *English* Ship in the Port just ready to sail, and he would furnish me with all things necessary. It would be tedious to repeat his Arguments, and my Contradictions. He said, it was altogether impossible to find such a solitary Island as I had desired to live in; but I might command in my own House, and pass my time in a Manner as recluse as I pleased.

I complied at last, finding I could not do better. I left *Lisbon* the 24th Day of *November*, in an *English* Merchant-man, but who was the Master I never inquired. *Don Pedro* accompanied me to the Ship, and lent me Twenty Pounds. He took kind Leave of me, and embraced me at parting; which I bore as well as I could. During this last Voyage I had no Commerce with the Master, or any of his Men; but pretending I was sick kept close in my Cabbin. On the Fifth of *December*, 1715, we cast Anchor in the *Downs* about Nine in the Morning, and at Three in the Afternoon I got safe to my House at *Redriff*.

The first Money I laid out was to buy two young Stone-Horses, which I keep in a good Stable, and next to them the Groom is my greatest Favourite; for I feel my Spirits revived by the Smell he contracts in the Stable. My Horses understand me tolerably well; I converse with them at least four Hours every Day. They are Strangers to Bridle or Saddle; they live in great Amity with me, and Friendship to each other.

FINIS